PRAISE FOR JESS

'I appreciate the recent uptick in books featuring sleuths of a seasoned age, particularly ones as prickly, opinionated and delightful as Vera Wong…Further adventures cannot arrive fast enough' ***New York Times***

'Packed with humour, heart and suspense, Sutanto proves once again that no crime – or nosy auntie – is too big to handle' ***Seattle Times***

'A mystery with warmth, humour and many descriptions of delicious teas and foods. Recommended for fans of Sutanto and of character-driven cozy mysteries' ***Library Journal***

'Charming, hilarious and heartfelt' **Emily Henry**

'If you ever need persuading to seize the day, you should read this gorgeous book of love and family and heartache and duty' **Laura Pearson**

'A comedy of errors, by turns macabre and romantic, hilarious and affectionate' ***Saga***

'Following the success of *Dial A for Aunties*, Sutanto is back with another charmer…. [She] excels at skewering with affection' ***Washington Post***

Select titles by Jesse Sutanto

DIAL A FOR AUNTIES

FOUR AUNTIES AND A WEDDING

VERA WONG'S UNSOLICITED ADVICE FOR MURDERERS

I'M NOT DONE WITH YOU YET

THE GOOD, THE BAD, AND THE AUNTIES

YOU WILL NEVER BE ME

VERA WONG'S GUIDE TO SNOOPING (ON A DEAD MAN)

NEXT TIME WILL BE OUR TURN

MS. MEBEL GOES BACK TO THE CHOPPING BLOCK

Ms. Mebel Goes Back to the Chopping Block

Jesse Sutanto

CORVUS

First published in paperback in Great Britain in 2026 by Corvus,
an imprint of Atlantic Books Ltd

10 9 8 7 6 5 4 3 2 1

A CIP catalogue record for this book is available from the British Library.

Paperback ISBN: 978 1 80546 606 2
E-book ISBN: 978 1 80546 607 9

Printed and bound by CPI Group (UK) Ltd, Croydon CR0 4YY

Corvus
An imprint of Atlantic Books Ltd
Ormond House
26–27 Boswell Street
London
WC1N 3JZ

www.atlantic-books.co.uk

Product safety EU representative: Authorised Rep Compliance Ltd., Ground Floor, 71 Lower Baggot Street, Dublin, D02 P593, Ireland. www.arccompliance.com

FSC www.fsc.org MIX Paper | Supporting responsible forestry FSC® C013604

To those who are looking for a second chance in life.
This is your sign. Do the thing.

Ms. Mebel Goes Back to the Chopping Block

Chapter 1

ALL HER LIFE, MEBEL TANADI HAS ALWAYS HAD A FEAR of—not so much death as much as situations that eventually lead to death. Like getting lost in a desert, for example. It'll hit her when she drinks a glass of water and sees a tiny bit remaining at the bottom of the glass. Her brain will go: *When you are wandering around a desert without any water, you will think back to this moment and wish you'd drunk every drop.* And Mebel will lift the glass once more and make sure she gets every single drop.

Or when she is swimming, treading water in the deep end of the pool, her brain might say: *Check for sharks.* And she'd look over her shoulder just in case a great white somehow found its way into the swimming pool in their backyard.

Sometimes, when Mebel cuts off a piece of steak a little too big, her brain says: *I wonder if your face will remain purple after you die from choking on that bite.* It would make for an interesting topic of conversation at the funeral anyway. And Mebel would cut the piece in half.

Long story short, Mebel's brain is a bit of an asshole.

Though not as big an asshole as, it must be said, her husband Henk. The thing about Henk is, Mebel fell in love with him when she found out his name was spelled H-e-n-k and not H-a-n-k. She's had an entire life of explaining to customs officers at airports that, no, that is not a misspelling in her passport, her parents really did mean to name her Mebel. Yes, they were aiming for Mabel. And "Henk" is so much more tragic than "Mebel" that she could not help falling for him. They were clearly created for each other. Except after forty years of peaceful marriage, Henk has just decided to drop a bomb right into their lives.

"You're leaving me for our chef, Wendy?" Mebel says now.

Henk has trouble meeting her eye. "Yes," he mumbles to a spot somewhere above Mebel's head. Maybe he's starting to lose his vision. Mebel makes a mental note to get an appointment with an ophthalmologist. Or maybe not, since he's just revealed that he is leaving her for their chef, Wendy.

"She's a baby," Mebel says. *And her name is spelled properly,* her brain says. She chooses not to say this out loud.

"She's twenty-four."

"Exactly. Her brain isn't even done developing!" Mebel is getting shrill and she knows it, but she can't help herself. "Once it's done developing, she might realize she doesn't even like you," she adds. It's petty, but Michelle Obama once said that when they go low, we go lower. Or something like that anyway. She's not one to argue with Michelle Obama.

Henk sighs. How can one short sigh convey so much? Though he doesn't say it, Mebel senses his frustration and exhaustion sinking into the marrow of her bones. Their entire marriage, she's sensed it, and she's tried so very hard to avoid triggering Henk's disappointment. She thought she'd done well; even at age sixty-three, Mebel is, dare she say it, fabulous. She was always, and always will be, a CHIP—a Chinese-Indonesian princess. When Mebel's son told her what a CHIP was, Mebel had been proud of being one.

"CHIPs are all the same, Ma," Sammy had said. "First of all, they're raised in some European-style mansion with a hyper-manicured Pomeranian. They get chauffeured around in Alphards, they get their bachelor's in economics from USC or UMich, and then come back to Indonesia to get married and become trophy wives."

Mebel has never understood why being a trophy wife is somehow looked down upon. She loves being a trophy wife. She makes such a fantastic trophy. She's even shaped like one, all slender curves and long thin legs, which she has maintained in the same exact shape for the last few decades. She takes pride in being a trophy, except now it seems that Henk has decided to swap her out for a new one, and the thought is unbearable.

"I understand why you might feel the need to go for petty jabs," Henk says in his reasonable tone. It's a tone that he has used on their Pomeranian, Riri, and their son, Sammy, up until the age of eight, and Mebel for as long as she can remember. "I will spare you the indignity of moving out," he adds magnanimously.

"Moving out?" Mebel echoes blankly. She hasn't even thought of that possibility. But as soon as Henk says it, she thinks: *I could do with a staycation for a few nights. Leave him in this big, empty house to think about what a mistake he's making. The*

St. Regis Jakarta has a magnificent spa where they massage your face with a South Korean serum made out of salmon sperm.

But before Mebel can WhatsApp her assistant to make a booking at the St. Regis, Henk says, "Yes, I will be moving out."

"You?" Mebel cries. "Where would you possibly stay?" Of course, as soon as the words are out of her mouth, she realizes the stupidity of her question. Henk is a real estate tycoon. The number of properties they own in the city is always growing, to the point that Mebel doesn't know how many of them they own. If Henk wants to move out, he doesn't have to worry about not having any options.

Henk shrugs. "One of the apartments in south Jakarta. I like that area."

They live in north Jakarta. It's only about twenty miles away from south Jakarta, but with Jakarta traffic, it's a journey that could take anywhere between twenty minutes and three hours. He might as well have told her he's moving to a different country.

"Since when?" she cries. She feels affronted by this. Years and years she's tried to get him to sample one of the many trendy restaurants that have sprouted in south Jakarta, and each time, she's been shot down with "It's too far away," and "Why bother? We have great restaurants here," and so on.

Henk doesn't answer, merely looks sheepish, and it begins to sink in with horrible clarity that the truth is: Since Wendy. Mebel is beginning to realize that from this point on, her life will be divided into two halves—one of them would be BW, Before Wendy, and the other would be AW, After Wendy. Kind of like BC and . . . uh, AD. *But wait*, a small voice pipes up in her atrociously messy mind, *why is it AD and not AC? Because,* replies a different small voice, *then it would be air-conditioning.* Mebel snorts.

Henk frowns. "This is not a joke, Mebel," he says.

"I know," she says, but she can't help releasing a tiny little demented giggle.

Henk shakes his head. "See, this is the problem. I can't have a proper conversation with you without you doing your . . . thing."

"My thing?"

"You know what I mean."

And now the mirth is gone, replaced by a searing hot rush of anger. "No!" Mebel snaps. "Actually, I don't know what you mean."

As though noticing the change in atmosphere, Henk deflates. "It's fine, forget about it. I'm sorry," he adds before Mebel can say anything. "I really am. I never thought—I didn't plan on this happening."

"Me neither," she says.

She can see the frustration crossing Henk's face. She's done it again, hasn't she? She's found herself in a terrible situation, and instead of reacting appropriately, she reacts with snippy remarks. Why can't she be honest with him, just for once? Show him her vulnerability, let go of the armor made up of humor and wit and acerbic comments? But, even as Mebel claws deep into the recesses of her heart, her ego embraces her tightly, refusing to let go. And so she stands there, unbending, as Henk takes a suitcase out of the walk-in closet. She can tell from the way he's moving that the suitcase is full of things. When did he pack that? He's never packed a single suitcase for as long as they've been married. Their helpers have always done that for them. She wonders for a horrifying moment if he did, in fact, ask their helpers to pack for him. Had Narti and Kus done that, knowing what they were packing for?

"Did Narti—" she starts to say.

"No," Henk sighs. "Of course not. I packed by myself."

Mebel releases her breath. She ignores the little glow of petty pleasure that comes at the realization that because Henk has packed his own suitcase, chances are he's forgotten a ton of things. His nighttime retainer, for one, without which he'll spend the entire night grinding his teeth. He doesn't even have pointy canines anymore; they've been ground flat like the rest of his teeth. Mebel has always hated Henk's teeth grinding. It sounds like someone rattling dice in a cup. *Hah, let's see how Wendy likes that.* But the thought of him sleeping next to Wendy is a punch to Mebel's heart. She thinks of Wendy, beautiful in her youth, her cheeks plump with natural collagen, and it makes her want to rip out her hair. She bets Wendy has none of her health issues—the stiff knees, the aching back, the dry eyes. Speaking of dry eyes . . . Mebel fishes a small bottle of eye drops from her pocket. These days, her eyes have become so dry that she has to make sure she always has eye drops on her all the time.

Halfway out of the bedroom, Henk says, "I've called Samuel. You shouldn't be on your own, especially now."

Horror sinks in with ruthless speed, and Mebel's entire body goes cold, as though someone's poured a jug of ice water into her veins. "You told Sammy?" she gasps, scandalized. The thought of her sweet baby boy learning about his father's indiscretion is, in fact, worse than the transgression itself. "How could you? He would be—"

"He's a thirty-four-year-old man with a wife and kids," Henk says flatly. "I don't think we need to be protecting him from the realities of life anymore."

"He's my baby!" Mebel says, and even she has to admit that, when put like that, she sounds like one of those overbearing moms who are obsessed with their useless sons. Except Sammy is far from useless, of course. And Mebel is anything but overbearing. You really can't be overbearing in full-body Chanel, it gets too warm.

Henk doesn't even bother with a response before striding out of the room, wheeling his enormous suitcase behind him. She hurries after him, dozens of questions crowding her mind. Dimly, she thinks: *I can't beg him to stay. That would be beyond pathetic. I'll tell him good riddance.* But when she opens her mouth, what comes out is: "Please stay, dear. Please." Damn it, so much for not begging.

"I wish you all the best, Mebel," Henk says, and starts going down their elegant curved staircase.

For a fleeting moment, Mebel hopes the wheel of his suitcase will snag on their rug and make him trip, but of course it doesn't. It's a Rimowa, after all. And so she stands breathing hard at the top of the stairs, watching her husband of forty years walk out of their north Jakarta mansion and into the unforgiving tropical heat. It's only when the front door clicks shut that it all sinks in. Mebel slides to the floor—gently, as her Chanel tweed skirt is somewhat snug, and if she split the seams, that would just be the icing on this cake of shit, wouldn't it? She senses tears filling her eyes, but before they can stream down her face, the snot arrives. She has never perfected the art of crying prettily. Her body has always produced snot far more efficiently than it does tears. Maybe that's why Henk left her. Maybe Wendy is one of those women who are able to cry prettily.

Girl, Mebel thinks, with another sob. *Wendy is barely a woman, she is a girl. Oh god, she's younger than Sammy. Ugh.*

Just as that revolting thought settles into her consciousness, the front door opens once more. Mebel's head whips up. Has Henk finally realized what a grand mistake he's made? Maybe this was all a big joke, one of those things that young people are always playing on one another and posting to the Instagram. She dabs at her wet cheeks, hoping she doesn't look too much of a mess.

"Mami?"

Mebel's shoulders sag. Not Henk coming back to beg for forgiveness, after all. Still, she reaches deep within her soul and finds a kernel of persistence to cling to. She mustn't let her sweet Sammy see her like this. She pulls herself up using the banisters for support, then straightens her skirt and tweed jacket.

"Mami?" Samuel calls out. "Are you there?"

"Ama," the high-pitched voice of Mebel's granddaughter Luciana shouts. "I wanna play makeup!"

"Shush, Luci," Samuel's wife, Hannah, says. "We're here to check on your ama, not play with her."

Mebel hurriedly dries her eyes and takes in a shuddery breath. She brushes down her outfit and primps her puffy hair. There, now she no longer looks like a woman whose husband of forty years has just left her. But when she comes down the stairs and sees her sweet Samuel, her Sammy baby, and his lovely family, the tears come rushing back, and she finds to her horror that she is crumpling like a piece of tissue. And when she opens her mouth to say, *Oh, Sammy, there's no need for you to come here,* what comes out instead is an elongated "Waaaah!"

Samuel wraps an arm around Mebel's shoulders. Luciana clings to her mother and stares at Mebel with wide eyes.

"What's wrong with Ama?" Luciana asks in a whisper loud enough to be heard all the way across the house.

"Shush," Hannah says again. She turns around to signal at their nannies—there are two of them, one for each of the twin toddlers, Freydis and Aelgifu. Apparently they're Viking names. Mebel has had to double-check to make sure that they've spelled Aelgifu correctly.

The nannies nod and take the toddlers, along with Luciana, away into the kitchen, leaving Mebel with her son and her daughter-in-law.

"Don't worry, Mami," Samuel is saying.

"Don't worry?" Mebel cries. "How can I not worry? Your father is leaving me for"—she lowers her voice into a scandalized whisper—"for someone younger than you!"

Samuel fidgets, and the crack in Mebel's heart deepens. "Oh, Mami. You'll be okay. He'll come to his senses. This is just a midlife crisis."

"He is almost seventy years old!" Mebel snaps. "He's much too old to be having one of those things. He had one of them already, when he was forty-five!"

"What happened then?" Hannah says.

"He had the old house knocked down and rebuilt into this." Even now, Mebel can't stop herself from gesturing at her palatial home with flourish. It really is a work of art, Italian marble everywhere, the walls gilded with gold, decorated with statues they'd flown in from Greece. "I thought, 'Well, as far as midlife crises go, this is a productive one.' But now"—she dissolves into another bout of tears—"I'm going to die here alone, in this big house."

"It's okay, Mami. You won't be alone," Samuel says. "Hannah and I will stay here with you. And the kids will be here as well. You'd like that, wouldn't you?"

Mebel startles, her gaze ping-ponging back and forth from Samuel to Hannah, who look at her with earnestness. "You'd do that? Truly? But aren't you kids all about privacy?"

"You have seven bedrooms in the house, Mami," Samuel says dryly. "I think there will be enough privacy for everyone."

Hannah, looking somewhat less confident, nods. She puts on a smile. "I bet that some days we won't even see each other."

Chapter 2

THEY WERE WRONG, OF COURSE.

Mebel may be a lot of things—glamorous, for one, blessed with good taste, for another—but it must be said that "unobtrusive" is not one of her positive attributes. She knows this about herself, and yet she cannot bring herself to stop. It's one of the things she's been brought up to be as a trophy wife, to always be at her husband's beck and call, not only to attend to all his needs but to predict them before he himself realizes it. Mebel had excelled at her job, and now to lose Henk means to lose not only her identity but the one thing that has occupied her brain for the last forty years. And she hasn't just lost Henk, but also her social circle, because she cannot bear the humiliation she would go through once their friends hear about Henk leaving her. And so for days after Henk leaves, Mebel steadfastly replies with noncommittal responses to all messages from their friends, all the while politely declining any dinner invitations.

How does one cope with the loss of not just one's marriage, but one's social life as well? It's simply impossible.

Which is why, at exactly six fifteen every morning, Mebel still gets up and makes a spinach, cucumber, ginger, turmeric, and carrot juice. (Well, she gets the helper to do it while she supervises.) Then, before the juice can turn brown—or browner than it already is—she putters up the curved staircase and knocks on Samuel and Hannah's bedroom door. The first morning she did this, Hannah opened the door and blinked blearily at her before thanking her for the juice. But now, three days after they have moved in with her, Mebel is comfortable enough to wait just one second after knocking before opening the door and letting herself in.

Hannah sits up in bed as Mebel walks in with the juices, and Mebel makes a good show of averting her eyes. "Mami, wha—"

"Don't worry!" Mebel trills. "I'm not looking! I'm just here to deliver your juice."

Samuel groans. "Mami, I told you, we don't need juice every morning."

"Nonsense," Mebel says. "Do you want a healthy colon or not?"

Samuel slaps his hands over his face. "Does the lock on the door not work? I could've sworn I locked it last night."

"Silly boy, I used my master key so you don't have to get out of bed. Now, drink your juice, there's a good boy. And you too, Hannah." But when she turns to give Hannah her brown juice, she's surprised to see a scowl on Hannah's normally sweet, placid face. Mebel blanches. When her mother-in-law was still alive, Mebel was always careful to school her face into a pleasant expression around her despite the many sharp jabs the woman doled out over everything from Mebel's makeup to the curtains that Mebel had chosen for the house. And now, here is Hannah openly frowning at Mebel, who's only here to serve her freshly squeezed juice, after all. Does she not realize how fortunate she is to have a mother-in-law like Mebel?

But as Mebel is about to say something, Hannah takes a deep breath and says, "Thank you, Mami." She takes the juice from Mebel and places it on the side table.

"You should drink it now, before it turns even browner," Mebel says helpfully.

Hannah's cheek twitches, then she gives a smile that doesn't reach her eyes and says, "I'll drink it later." With that, she lies back down on the bed and pulls the blanket up over her head.

For a second, Mebel stands there, unsure what to do. Times like these, Mebel feels like there are at least five different personalities inside her vying for control. Personality One, the caring mother, wants to nag Hannah and Sammy into drinking their juice now. Personality Two, the strident Chinese mother, wants to shout them out of bed; after all, it is seven in the morning, that's practically the afternoon already. Personality Three, the petulant child, wants to stride out of the bedroom and, if not slam the door behind her, then at the very least close it with a firm click to let Sammy know that she is displeased. Personality Four, the peacemaker, wants to make cheerful conversation to smooth over this awkward moment. Then there's Personality Five, who seems to have gained power these last few days. Five just wants to curl up into a tight ball and sob her eyes out, something that Mebel has been doing the last few nights as she lay alone in her super-king-size bed.

Mebel considers all five personalities, then adds one more to the mix. Personality Six, the doting grandmother. Her spirits lift, and with one last cheery "Okay, don't forget to drink your juice!" Mebel hurries out of the room. She crosses the hallway and lets herself into the bedroom where Freydis and Aelgifu are sleeping. One of the nannies is sleeping on a single bed next to their travel cots. She doesn't stir when Mebel lets herself in, but one of the twins does. Mebel thinks it might be Aelgifu, though she's isn't too sure. It's too dark in the room to tell which one is which. Not that she has better luck even under good lighting conditions. She still hasn't quite gotten the hang of telling the twins apart, which makes her wonder if she's a bad grandmother. Then again, it's hardly her fault if the twins insist on looking so much like each other, is it?

Aelgifu (or Freydis, who even cares at this point) lifts her little head and coos. The nanny remains sleeping. As Mebel walks toward the cot, Aelgifu pulls herself up and reaches for Mebel.

"Oh, my sweet darling," Mebel whispers, bending over and lifting the baby. Or rather, she tries to do so, but what actually ends up happening is Mebel's back twinges and she cries out, more in surprise than pain, and drops Aelgifu back into the cot. Aelgifu plops onto the soft padding, and there is a moment of shocked silence. Mebel says, "It's okay, don't—" But Aelgifu's little mouth opens wide, her eyes scrunch closed, and the next thing Mebel knows, the room is filled with a piercing wail.

The nanny bolts out of her bed, her eyes wild, her hair standing up in weird angles. She sees Mebel still bent over the travel cot and Aelgifu screaming, and hurries toward them. She lifts Aelgifu from the cot with the ease of someone in her early twenties who has no idea what back pain feels like and bounces her on her hip while walking away from Mebel. Meanwhile,

Freydis is awakened by the noise and she, too, starts to whimper. Mebel tries to straighten up, but her back catches once more, and so she hobbles to Freydis's cot, trying to make soothing shushing noises. They come out as gasps of pain, but she's hoping that at age one, Freydis wouldn't be able to tell the difference between the two.

The door swings open. "What's going on?" Hannah says. "Why are they awake?" Her gaze lands on Mebel, still crouched over the cot like an evil witch with a poisoned apple in her outstretched hand. Hannah's eyes narrow.

"I was just—" Mebel starts to say.

"I think she dropped Freydis," the nanny says.

"I did no such thing!" Mebel snaps. "And Freydis is right here." She looks down in time to read the name *Aelgifu* stitched onto the toddler's onesie. "Oh, right. This one's Aelgifu."

Hannah, her face cold as a stone, strides over to the cot and plucks Aelgifu from it.

"I really did not drop Freydis," Mebel says, and even she hears the guilty whine in her voice. Once again, she tries to straighten up, but her back isn't having it.

"Why are you in here?" Hannah says.

The acerbic tone in Hannah's voice fires Mebel up enough that she wills her back to straighten. She winces at the tension in her back; she's going to pay for this later, but right now, what she really needs to do is stand up for herself. "I wanted to see my grandbabies," she says in a voice as stiff as her back feels.

"It's not even seven o'clock in the morning," Hannah says, bouncing Aelgifu hard on her hip. "They're not supposed to be awake for another hour. You know how cranky they get when they don't have enough sleep."

"Actually, Aelgifu—sorry, Freydis—was already awake when I came in here. Which was why I was trying to lift her from the cot when I—"

"When you dropped her?" Hannah says.

"I wouldn't call it a drop . . ." Mebel's voice trails off guiltily. How in the world did she end up in this position, wringing her hands and standing like a guilty schoolkid in front of Hannah? She tries her best to channel her late mother-in-law, who had commanded fear out of all her daughters-in-law.

"What's going on?" Sammy says, appearing in the doorway while yawning. "Why are the twins up so early?"

"Ask your mother!" Hannah snaps. She calls out to the nanny to follow her, and they leave the room with the twins, who are both shrieking by now.

The silence they leave behind them is thick and heavy. Mebel stares at her only son. Sammy stares after the open door with confusion. Then he turns toward her. "What happened?"

"I came in to check on my grandchildren."

"Did you hear one of them crying or something?"

For a second, Mebel is tempted to lie and say yes. But then she thinks of Henk and the numerous lies he must have told her to cover up his affair, and the thought of lying, even if it is a small one, sickens her. "No. I just wanted to see them." At the last word, her voice wobbles, threatening to break.

Sammy sighs. "Mami, I understand this must be a hard time for you. That's why we're here. We want to help you through this. But you can't just barge into our bedrooms. We need"—he searches for the right word before finally settling on an English one—"boundaries."

"What is this 'boundaries'?" Mebel says suspiciously. She's

suspicious of English words. English words are like men—inconsistent, fussy, and make you look stupid when you pick the wrong one.

"It's like"—Sammy scratches his chin—"you know, like a wall that you can't cross."

"You mean like separate rooms? Don't we have that already?" With a huff, she strides out of the kids' bedroom and down the stairs.

Sammy hurries after her. "Kind of like separate rooms. But do you see how it defeats the purpose of sleeping in a separate room when you can just barge into our bedroom anytime you like?"

"I most certainly do not barge in anytime I like," Mebel says in a reasonable tone of voice as she walks into the kitchen. "I always wait until morning, in case you are making me more grandbabies."

Sammy closes his eyes. "You know what I mean. I don't think it's healthy for you to come into our room first thing in the morning."

"It's not first thing in the morning. I've had my breakfast," she says, gesturing at the used dishes on the kitchen island. "I've had time to make you freshly squeezed vegetable juice—"

"Please, please stop making us the vegetable juice," Sammy says.

"Nonsense, it's so good for your gut health. Everything starts in the gut, you know. There's a reason why it's called the body's second brain."

"Mami, just—stop!"

Growing up, Samuel has always been a sweet-natured boy, quiet and shy. He rarely ever raised his voice. And so, in this moment, when he does exactly that, it reaches deep into Mebel's brain and freezes every part of her. She stares at him, dumbfounded. Her little boy, who now has a wife and three children. Her little boy, who is all grown up and has a family of his own. And it sinks in then, with terrifying clarity. Sammy doesn't need her anymore. Even her grandchildren have no need for her. They all have nannies who know their routines much better than Mebel does. And the thought, terrifying in its coldness, seeps through her papery skin, spreading ice throughout her veins. If she is no longer needed as a wife or as a mother, then where does that leave her?

She thinks of her social circle. She and Henk belong to half a dozen clubs, each one more exclusive than the last, and so they have plenty of friends. But said friends are mutuals, and Mebel has no delusions about her inheriting any of them in the divorce. All the club memberships are under Henk's name, after all, with her trailing along as "the spouse."

"Mami? You okay?" Sammy is saying, and it sounds as though his voice is coming from so far away.

Mebel sees the future unraveling before her. Long days and even longer nights, the hours stretching like taffy until being conscious becomes an unbearable chore. Maybe she might pick up drinking, pretending that she has decided to become a whiskey connoisseur, sipping a glass each night, then two, then passing out drunk until late morning. She would waste away slowly, her skin puckering up like drying orange peel, the helpers whispering to one another about her slow demise as she gently decays in her lonesome.

I guess that's how you'll die, after all, her brain says. *Not quite as exciting as being eaten by a shark in the swimming pool, but I daresay it would be less messy, and you could at least have an open casket funeral.*

No. She mustn't let that happen. She can't. She clamps down on her spiraling thoughts. Without thinking, she says, "I won't go down without a fight."

Sammy regards her doubtfully. "Um . . . okay?"

"I mean it. I won't!" Mebel's chest rises impressively. "I am going to win your father back."

Instead of applauding her, Sammy merely stands there and stares.

"For the children's sake," Mebel adds, in a magnanimous voice. *Look at me,* she thinks. *Look how I'm setting aside my pride, my ego, and sacrificing everything for the sake of the kids.*

Sammy's eyes soften. "You don't have to do that for me, Mami. I'm a grown man. You can seek your own happiness now."

"Oh, I don't mean you," Mebel says with a flippant wave of her hand. "Like you said, you're a grown man. For the girls. Freydis, Aelgifu, and Luciana."

"I really don't think—"

"They can't grow up in a broken home."

"I'm not sure that having divorced grandparents counts as being from a broken home?" Sammy says.

"Don't be ridiculous, of course it does. And don't say the D-word around me, Sammy."

"I'm sorry, Mami," Sammy says quickly. "I should've known it would be triggering to you." The word "triggering" is said in English, and it catches Mebel off guard.

"What does that mean, 'triggering'? Like I've been shot?"

"It means it's a word that triggers a lot of emotions for you. A word that isn't just a simple word, but one that carries a lot of bad feelings and memories."

Mebel nods, filing the word away for later use. "Yes, I suppose you are right. The D-word is . . . triggering. But once I win your father back, it won't be, because we won't be getting one. In fact, what we'll do is celebrate—oh! We can renew our vows! Wouldn't that be wonderful? Nothing too fancy, we'll keep it intimate, just send out one thousand invitations, so with their plus-ones, it'll be two thousand guests max."

"I think you're getting a bit carried away, Mami. Why don't you ask Tante Meimei out for lunch?"

"Meimei?" Mebel cries. "That she-demon will tell the entirety of Jakarta that your father is leaving me!"

"Okay . . . or maybe any of your many, many friends? I'm sure some of them will be empathetic. I know you housewives are all about presenting the image of a perfect marriage to everyone, but I would bet money that many of them are hiding things that are much worse than what Papi has done."

Mebel ignores Sammy's patronizing tone of voice. "Aiya, this is not the time to think of socializing. This is the time to plan. I will have that designer Kris make me a gown, she's all the rage right now. Oh, I should call her now and let her know I'll need a gown from her; she's booked up for the next six months, you know." She looks around for her cell phone and spots it on the kitchen counter, but before she can take it, Sammy practically pounces on it. As Mebel watches, dumbfounded, he holds it behind his back. "What are you doing, son? Let me have my phone."

"No."

"Sammy!" she snaps.

"Mami," he begins, then he takes a deep breath, as though fortifying himself, "I cannot let you do this again. You're always doing this."

"Doing what?"

Sammy gestures at her. "This! You go on a wild tangent and get carried away without thinking of the consequences. I mean, you're about to have a gown made for a vow renewal—" He pauses, sighing with visible frustration. "Did you forget that you haven't won Papi back?"

"Oh, well, that'll happen."

"How?"

Mebel shrugs. Irritation mounts up inside her. "I'll figure it out. Now kindly give me back my phone and—"

"No, Mami. If you're going to win Papi back, you need an actual plan. You can't just sit back and do your trophy wife thing and trust that other people will take care of it for you."

He might as well have slapped her across the face. For a moment, Mebel blinks at her son, stupefied. Then the anger comes, a trickle at first, but it doesn't take long before it turns into a rush. "Do my 'trophy wife thing'?" she hisses. "Do you really think that lowly of me? Do you know how much I've done for you?"

"I didn't mean it that way," Sammy says. "I just meant, like, when it comes to the big, important things, you're used to letting Papi handle them. You always said the man is the head of the household and the wife's job is to follow along."

And, unfortunately, Mebel knows this is true. She has been fed on a steady diet of traditional gender roles, and she has turned around and fed Sammy the same thing.

"Mami," Sammy says gently, "I think you need to listen to what Papi wants. If he wants to have a divorce, then . . ." He raises his hands and shrugs. "Unless you have an idea of how to keep him around?" Sammy waits a moment for her to reply, and when she doesn't, he gives her a small, pitying smile, and says, "See? Papi has always been the ideas person in the house. He knows what he's doing. I think we need to trust him on this."

How dare her own son talk to her like this! Mebel has half a mind to smack him with one of her very expensive Le Creuset pans (which she has never once used, but she likes knowing that she could use them if she wanted to). The anger surges through her veins, pounding in her head, heating up her entire body until she feels like she might explode. The answer blurts out before her mind has time to catch up. "I'll go to cooking school!"

"What?"

The moment Mebel hears those words, she realizes she's right. That's exactly it. Her eyes light up with righteous flame. "Yes, that's it! That's what he wants, isn't it? A wife who can cook. That's the entire reason he's off with Wendy."

Sammy scratches the back of his head. "I don't know that that's the 'entire reason' . . ."

"Oh please, of course it is. Have you tasted her homemade pulled noodles? I dreamed about that dish for days. Honestly, she's so good I would turn into the lesbian for her."

"Please don't ever say that again."

"Another reason I know he's only with her for her food," Mebel continues, "is because she is flat-chested. Your father is a breast man."

"Oh god. No, Mami, enough. You have convinced me. Yes, Papi is only with Wendy because of her cooking prowess."

"Therefore, all I have to do is go to culinary school, learn how to cook, and voilà, I will win him back," Mebel says with a flourish. Despite herself, hope is dancing inside her, lighting a spark she has so desperately needed in the last few days. It's as though when Henk had left her, he'd taken all the light in the world with him, but now one of these precious lights has found its way back and is beckoning to her to follow it out of the darkness.

"It'll take a long time, Mami," Sammy says.

"You young people have no patience. All things that are worth having are things worth waiting for. And your father is definitely worth waiting for."

Sammy merely looks on with a sad expression. Mebel turns away. She can't allow herself to be talked down, not now when she's finally come up with an idea of her own. The thought strikes her: When was the last time she's had an idea that was fully hers, not Henk's or anyone else's? She's forgotten that feeling of being ready to fight for something she wants, and right now, all Mebel wants to do is fight—if not for Henk, then for the life she knows she deserves. The life to which she has devoted her entire being, spent all of her youth preparing herself for. The life of a trophy wife. And by god, Mebel is going to win that war.

Chapter 3

Mebel launches herself into her plan with newfound ferocity. The next few days are a flurry of research, which is no small task for someone who adopted to the use of smartphones in her fifties and still types with her index fingers "like T-rex," Luciana observed. Mebel ignores the less-than-flattering observation and continues squinting at her phone screen through her reading glasses. The amount of information to be found at her fingertips—or her index fingertips—is staggering.

Who knew that there were so many culinary schools around the world? There's the CIA, not the kind that trains spies, but rather the kind that trains people who feed the spies. The International Culinary Center, the International School of Culinary Arts, the Culinary School of America, and so on and so forth. To add to that, they are all over the globe, each one claiming to be the best at what it does. And, Mebel realizes, she needs to decide what kind of cuisine she wants to learn. Her first instinct is to gravitate toward Chinese cuisine. She and Henk are of Chinese descent, after all, and they mainly eat Chinese food at home, and on Sundays, they gather for dim sum, where they eat yet more Chinese food.

But then again, what's the point of learning how to cook Chinese food when one can so easily get it in Jakarta? She can get excellent Chinese food by ordering it through an app, and it'll be here in under thirty minutes. No, that won't win Henk back. He'll be like, "Great, now you're on par with half the wives in Jakarta."

Maybe Japanese food? But there's the same problem. Too many Japanese restaurants here. Mebel dismisses the idea of Korean food and Italian food for the same reason. Then, as she scans the never-ending list of culinary schools, it comes to her so clearly that she wonders why it took this long. French food.

Yes. What could be better than learning how to make soufflés and onion soup and—uh—whatever else they eat in France? Isn't France known as the most romantic country in the world? "I have such fond memories of Paris," Mebel says to Sammy and Hannah. She and Henk had been a handful of times, and each time was magical. Those trips to Paris were filled with multicourse meals at Michelin-starred restaurants and hours spent at the Hermès store at Saint-Honoré, letting her fingers trail across their silk scarves and luxuriating in the richness of the fabric. Once, she and Henk were in a cab. At the red light, a man broke their window, reached in, and grabbed her handbag. She would've prioritized her safety and let go of the bag if it hadn't been a quilted lambskin Chanel with vintage hardware, but as it was, she was not about to let this random man have it. Would he know to moisturize it every sixty days? Probably not.

Henk had hit him over the head again and again with a box of macarons they'd bought at Ladurée while the driver shouted, "Just give him the bag!" In the end, the light turned green and Henk shouted, "Drive!" and so they did, and Mebel had clutched her purse and Henk's arm, and they'd laughed hysterically and then popped a bottle of champagne back at their hotel room.

"Then we let off all that adrenaline by having the wildest, most passionate—"

Hannah clears her throat in what Mebel thinks is an unnecessarily aggressive way. "Right, well!" Hannah says, clapping her hands once. "Good memories from Paris, yes, point taken."

"I felt about twenty years younger there," Mebel says wistfully. "What a magical city."

"It does sound exciting," Hannah says. "And going to culinary school in Paris sounds like a dream. I would love to do something like that."

"Please don't," Sammy says. "At least not until the girls are older."

"Well, as you have pointed out yourself," Mebel says, "you are a grown man, and now there's nothing holding me back from realizing my lifelong dream."

"Mami, you literally thought of this dream a few days ago," Sammy says.

"Always such a pedant," Mebel mutters. "You must have gotten that from your father." She turns her attention back to her phone and taps on Paris, France, to get a list of schools there. There are so many of them, one would think there's one on every street corner. And their names sound so fabulous. Mebel taps on each link and looks for a sign-up sheet. She rejects the first three schools because their semesters have already begun and the next earliest course would be in four months' time, and who has that kind of patience?

Then, finally, she finds it. A school with vacancies that is starting—oh my—next Monday. In five days' time, in fact. Mebel can feel the large vein in her temple begin to pulse with excitement. The possibility suddenly feels so real. Oh my god, is she actually about to do this?

"Uh-oh," Hannah says to Sammy. "I think Mami's found one."

"What is it?"

"The Saint Honoré School of Culinary Arts," Mebel breathes. "Oh my god, it's a sign."

"Sorry, what's a sign?" Sammy says.

"Saint Honoré! Don't you get it?" Mebel says.

Sammy and Hannah both look blankly at her. Honestly, anyone would think she hadn't taken the time to educate her son.

"It's where the flagship Hermès store is?"

"So?" Sammy says while Hannah goes, "Ah. That's exciting, Mami. So you'll be within walking distance to the Hermès store?"

"Yes! I can just see it. Me giving out freshly baked culinary school treats to the Hermès store employees. Can you imagine? They'll be presenting all of their Birkins to me in no time."

"Tell me again, Mami," Sammy says, "are you doing this to win Papi back or to buy more Birkins?"

"Silly boy, why not kill two birds with one stone? And what a stone it is. I win not only your father back but also a Birkin." Mebel claps excitedly, then settles back down on the sofa. "Now, do not disturb me, I need to fill out this form. My goodness, term starts in less than a week."

"Is she really doing this?" Sammy says to Hannah.

Instead of answering him, Hannah turns to Mebel and

says, "You know, Birkins would make the most excellent souvenir."

Mebel laughs and shakes her head. She can already see it, her wearing a beautiful Hermès scarf around her head, her eyes shaded by her Dior sunglasses, a shiny new Birkin dangling on her arm, and a tray full of warm, richly indulgent pastries in her hands as she sashays down Rue du Faubourg Saint-Honoré. Mebel, a traditional, uptight Chinese-Indonesian housewife, has never sashayed a day in her life, but she feels strongly that this new version of her would adopt a French sashay as soon as she sets foot in the country. And when she comes back to Jakarta, she will bring that sashay home with her, present a Michelin-star-worthy meal to Henk, and he will fall to his knees and beg her to take him back. What a magnificent plan. Mebel can't wait to enact it.

GETTING EVERYTHING READY IS SURPRISINGLY NOT AS HARD as Mebel had expected. True, there are a million things to consider, such as which outfits she should take. Paris is the fashion capital of the world, after all, and Mebel would rather chew hot coals than turn up looking anything less than fashionable. But she has to take into account the weather. Most of her outfits have been curated for Jakarta—not quite tropical island weather since she spends 99 percent of her time in beautifully air-conditioned rooms, but they're still warm weather clothes, inappropriate for Parisian fall weather. Therefore, the first thing Mebel does after submitting her application is to jump in the car and speed—well, there is no speeding in Jakarta due to the bumper-to-bumper traffic on every road—to the nearest mall.

There, she pays homage to Gucci for a leather jacket, Louis Vuitton for two Monogram suitcases to add to her collection of Monogram LV suitcases, Tod's for sensible shoes, Ferragamo for less sensible shoes, Dior for a quilted handbag in lavender, Prada for a more casual handbag because leather is heavy (and at her age she secretly prefers nylon), YSL (she always says "YSL" because she can't pronounce "Yves Saint Laurent") for a wallet, Chopard for one of their Happy Sport watches to boost her spirit, and Burberry for a camel-colored trench coat. She also drops by Chanel, but can't find anything new that she doesn't already own, which is a shame. Something, she thinks, that she will rectify in Paris.

With all the shopping done, Mebel struts into the Singapore Airlines office on the fifth floor of the mall to buy her plane ticket. Sammy has been trying to get her to switch to buying plane tickets online, but Mebel doesn't believe in such things. If she were to purchase tickets online, she wouldn't be able to regale the salesperson with the entire story of her life and why she is going to Paris. The salesperson is staring at her with a dumbfounded expression, and when Mebel says, "And that is why I need a first-class one-way ticket to Paris, my dear," he jumps up and says, "Of course, ma'am, right away!"

After furiously typing into his computer for a few minutes, he glances at Mebel and says in a conspiratorial voice, "I've put in a note to say that you are a VIP on a very important trip. They will treat you like royalty."

See? Try getting that on Expedia.com.

On her way down to the lobby to be picked up, she decides at the last minute to buy a carry-on suitcase from Tumi because, let's face it, Monogram Louis Vuitton suitcases are pretty, but they're also a pain in the ass to drag around. By the time Mebel arrives back home, she is beaming from ear to ear. The first time she's smiled in days.

"You look happy," Sammy says, looking up from his laptop when she strides into the house.

"That's the name of my new watch," Mebel says, brandishing her wrist at him.

He glances at it, then does a double take. "Is that a Chopard?"

Mebel puts her hand up. "I know what you're about to say. I've always been a Franck Muller girl, I know, I know, and this is taking you by surprise. But hear me out: This is called the Happy Sport. Isn't that just the perfect name? And every time I move my arm, I can feel the diamonds and rubies swirling around in there, and it makes me happy."

"Mami," Sammy groans.

"Doesn't it make you feel happy too?" She shakes her wrist near his ear so he can hear the soft tap-tappings of the loose diamond and ruby pieces as they spin and rattle across the watch face.

"You can't be spending money like this."

"Why not?"

"Because you're getting a divorce? And you don't know how much you'll end up with. Or how little."

Mebel stares at him, her mind refusing to comprehend the words coming out of his mouth. "Well, in the event that I do end up getting divorced, which I won't because I'm winning your father back, but if I did, surely I would get half of everything?"

Sammy shrugs with a sigh. "I don't know, Mami. I hope you do, but surely you can also understand my caution. I don't know what Papi would do. He's got all the connections, all the lawyers. I just don't want you to be strapped for cash."

The concept of being strapped for cash is so foreign to Mebel that when she tries to think of it, her brain goes, *Nope, LOL!* She tries again, harder this time. "Do you mean I might need to shop at Tory Burch?" she says in a small voice.

"I mean you might not even be able to afford Tory Burch."

"Michael Kors?" she says in an even smaller voice.

"Not even Michael Kors." Before Mebel can answer, Sammy goes on, "And not even Coach or Kate Spade or . . . I don't know Mami, whatever else you think is 'affordable luxury.' No luxury items at all."

Tears rush into Mebel's eyes and she glares at her son. "My god," she gasps. "You are so cruel. How did I raise such a cruel son?"

Sammy rolls his eyes. "I'm just being realistic, Mami. If I could, I would obviously finance all of your shopping sprees, but I can't afford to just yet, okay? So in the meantime, can you please be more careful about your spending?"

It's probably the worst thing anyone has ever said to her, but somehow, Mebel manages to keep herself from breaking down. Mostly by moving her wrist a tad so she can feel the diamonds and rubies rattling in her watch, which soothes her. *My god,* she thinks, *whoever invented these Happy Sport watches knew what they were doing. These things are much better than Prozac.*

The acceptance letter comes in within two days, and that Sunday, Mebel stands at the front door of her mansion saying goodbye to her family. She's all packed and has four large suitcases and two carry-ons. Plus a hatbox, which contains her bouffant wig.

"I really don't think you should bring all this stuff with you to Paris, Mami," Sammy says, bouncing Aelgifu on one hip.

"My goodness, Sammy," Mebel says. "When did you turn into the counterweight to my joy?" She turns to Hannah, who's carrying Freydis. "Is he always like this?"

Hannah smiles. "He's just concerned, Mami. He wants you to be okay."

"I will be okay as soon as I finish this culinary degree and win your father back." Mebel crouches down so she is eye level with Luciana. "Lulu dear, you're going to look after my Dior sunglasses collection well, aren't you?"

"I told you not to give them to her," Sammy says. "She's five."

Luciana lowers the massive sunglasses and gives Mebel a conspiratorial look over them.

"I was four when I got my first pair," Mebel says, winking at Luciana, who smiles back at her.

"It's quite the collection," Hannah says.

"Feel free to wear them. But not the DiorClub. You don't have the cheekbones for it."

Hannah rolls her eyes but remains smiling. "Have fun in Paris, Mami."

"Oh, you know I will."

"Not too much fun though," Sammy mutters.

As Mebel steps into the waiting car, she overhears Hannah saying, "That city isn't going to know what hit it." Mebel doesn't bother with a retort. And, anyway, Hannah wasn't wrong about that.

Chapter 4

PARIS! THE CITY OF LOVE AND WONDER. MEBEL FEELS the magic as soon as she steps off the plane and onto the tarmac—well, not on the actual tarmac. Singapore Airlines would never allow their passengers to deplane onto the tarmac. But as soon as she steps off the airplane and onto the gangway, there it is, that sensation of infinite possibilities fizzing from the soles of her feet all the way up her legs. Few places have this effect on her. Los Angeles is one, New York is another. Tokyo. Dubai. Shanghai. Okay, so actually, a lot of places have this effect on Mebel. And Paris, thankfully, is one of them.

It is before dawn on a warm August morning, and Mebel gazes out the window as she makes her way toward customs. She can already tell it's going to be a bright, sunlit day, as though the city has ensured good weather for her arrival. She looks around with a smile, and it seems to her that everyone is in equally high spirits. When it's her turn to go through customs,

Mebel says, "Bonjour!" and the officer greets her warmly, welcoming her to France. And by the time she gets to baggage claim, her bags are all out and waiting for her, as though by magic. Sammy has arranged for a driver to pick her up right outside the baggage claim, and she watches gratefully as he lifts her backbreakingly heavy suitcases into the Benz, making a note to tip him generously.

Paris is just as gorgeous as Mebel remembers. Everything about the city is dripping with art and opulence. Even the balconies are beautiful, made out of wrought iron painstakingly curved into intricate designs. Whenever the car passes by a man urinating on the side of the street, which has happened three times in the last fifteen minutes, Mebel averts her eyes and focuses on yet another beautiful sight. That's life, isn't it? It's all about ignoring the less than sightly bits, like a man shaking off the last drops of pee on a sidewalk, and choosing to focus on the good, like, oh, those bright red flowers hanging off that windowsill. Life is what you make of it, Mebel thinks to herself. And she chooses to make it perfect.

The Saint Honoré School of Culinary Arts is located on Rue de la Ville-l'Évêque, just blocks away from the Hermès store. Mebel practices saying, "Ville-l'Évêque," under her breath several times until she's confident that she won't embarrass herself when she says it out loud. Against Sammy's advice, Mebel insisted on staying at the school's dorms.

"It won't be like the Four Seasons, Mami," Sammy said.

To which Mebel replied, "Well, of course not, but last holiday your father took me to that ghastly hotel in Zurich, do you remember?"

"You mean Sofitel?"

"Exactly."

"I really wouldn't call it ghast—"

"And I survived!" Mebel announced triumphantly. "I can survive a Parisian dorm."

And when the car arrives at their destination and she alights, daintily stepping out onto the sidewalk in her new Ferragamo shoes, Mebel knows she's going to do more than survive. She's going to thrive. In front of her is the most beautiful building she's ever seen. It's grandiose, the walls adorned with elaborate details, flowers, and medallions, all built lovingly out of stone. The enormous glass display at the front bears the words "The Saint Honoré School of Culinary Arts, est. 1901," and inside the display case is an array of perfectly baked breads and intricately designed pastries worthy of a museum. Pastries that Mebel has no doubt she will be whipping up in no time. Imagine the look on Henk's face when she presents him a—whatever one of these thingies is called.

Mebel turns when the driver, panting hard, lugs the last of her LV bags onto the sidewalk. "Ah, merci beaucoup!" She gives him a hundred-euro note, and he does a double take, then says, "Madame, would you like me to assist you with taking these bags inside?"

My goodness, Mebel thinks. *The French are so friendly!* "Yes, s'il vous plaît!" She pronounces it "silver plate" and chooses not to notice the way the driver winces at the way she has butchered his beautiful language. Though Mebel's first language is Indonesian, her second and arguably most universal language is cash, and she speaks it fluently, without any accent.

And so it is with much confidence that Mebel pushes open the brass doors of the Saint Honoré School of Culinary Arts and strides inside. The lobby is as impressive as the outside of the building, the reception table lined with dark green leather and people speaking in hushed voices and moving about with purpose. Mebel approaches the receptionist, her Ferragamo heels clacking across the marble floor and turning heads toward her. She reminds herself to do a little sashay. She is a trophy wife, after all, and what are trophies for but to be looked at and admired?

"Bonjour!" Mebel trills.

All noise in the lobby ceases as conversations pause mid-sentence. The receptionist glances up, gives Mebel a once-over, does a small approving sniff at Mebel's white-and-black double-sided Check'n'Dior virgin wool fitted jacket, and says, "Bienvenue à L'École des arts culinaires Saint Honoré. Puis-je vous aider?"

Mebel blinks. Clearly, the way she said "Bonjour" must have been so flawless that this young woman has falsely assumed that Mebel does, in fact, speak French. Something she needs to rectify immediately. "En Anglais, s'il vous plaît?" she says.

"Of course, Madame," the receptionist says without skipping a beat. "How may I help you?"

"Yes, thank you." It takes a beat for Mebel to switch from thinking in Indonesian and speaking in broken French to thinking in Indonesian and speaking in somewhat less-broken English. "I would like to check in. I have reservation here—"

"I'm afraid you are mistaken, this is not a hotel."

"Right, of course. No, that's not what I mean. I am checking in as student." When the receptionist doesn't respond, Mebel adds, "To the cooking school."

The receptionist visibly winces at the words "cooking school." "The culinary school," she corrects Mebel.

Mebel resists the urge to say, "Aiya, isn't it the same thing?" Instead, she nods and says, "Oui. The culinary school."

"Of course, madame. Can I please have your name?"

"Mebel Fransin Tanadi." Then she adds, "Mebel with an 'e' and Fransin with a—you know what? I write it down for you." She takes out her phone, types out her name onto her Notes app, and shows it to the receptionist. To her credit, the receptionist does not laugh out loud at the atrocious spelling.

After clacking away at her keyboard, the receptionist purses her lips. "Apologies, Madame, I am not seeing your name on the list."

"Did you spell correctly?" Mebel says, pushing the phone closer to the receptionist's face.

"Well, I spelled it incorrectly, the way you did."

Heat blooms in Mebel's cheeks. All her life, she's had to deal with customs officials and hospital receptionists and god knows what else who've had plenty to say about the spelling of her name. She is not about to take such abuse from this self-important young woman, especially not when she's busted out her Dior ensemble, for heaven's sake.

"I think maybe you try again, with correct spelling this time."

The receptionist's face hardens. "Madame, I have followed the spelling you gave me exactly, and there is no registration for anyone under the name of Mebel." She pronounces Mebel the way it's spelled, not "May-buhl," but "Meh-buhl," as though to highlight the misspelling to anyone who might be listening to their conversation, which at this point is everyone in the lobby.

Mebel's chest balloons, but before she can launch into a tirade (though a tirade based on what, Mebel herself hasn't quite decided), a smooth, rich voice says, "Excusez-moi, may I please interject?" Mebel looks up and finds herself staring into a pair of the most luxurious brown eyes she's ever seen. No, it would not be fair to call these eyes brown. They're more warm honey, golden, with flecks of earth. And the face that surrounds the eyes is devastatingly handsome. A straight nose, a strong jawline brushed with gray stubble, and salt-and-pepper hair that curls up at the ends. Quite possibly the most gorgeous man Mebel has ever laid eyes on in real life, and she's met George Clooney. Well, a George Clooney impersonator in Vegas, which is close enough.

The man nods at the receptionist and says, "I'll handle this, Simone." Simone flushes, and Mebel rolls her eyes.

How embarrassing, to be so easily charmed just because he's a good-looking older man. He turns his attention to Mebel, and Mebel flushes. Goodness, is that a hot flash rushing through her body? Is this menopause all over again? Before she can stop herself, her eyelids flutter open and close. *My lord*, she thinks. *I am literally batting my eyes at this man. Get a hold of yourself, woman!*

She catches Simone rolling her eyes, as though thinking: *How embarrassing, to be so easily charmed just because he's a good-looking older man. Touché, Simone*, Mebel thinks. She musters up whatever shred of dignity she has left and lifts her chin, meeting the man's eye. "Thank you," she says in her most regal voice. "Yes, if you can help find my registration, I appreciate it."

"Come, let's have a seat." With that, he—eek!—places his hand on the small of Mebel's back and leads her to one side of the lobby, where he gestures at the sofa for her to sit on.

Mebel can't quite remember the last time a stranger touched the small of her back. It's not something done in Asia, and it's doing very funny things to her loins, which she does not appreciate. Chinese-Indonesian grandmothers are not supposed to be aware of their loins. They're supposed to be above such things. Does she even still have loins, or have they shriveled up into a desiccated husk? *Now get your head straight, you harlot,* she scolds herself as she lowers herself onto the sofa primly.

"I am Alain Moreau. I am the director of the school," the man says in his velvety voice. "And you are Madame Mebel? It's a lovely name."

"Thank you." Mebel is sure that the tips of her ears are steaming by now. Somehow, in Alain's mouth, her name turns from a mere name into a love poem. Roses are red, violets are blue, and so are Mebel's balls right now. *My word,* she thinks, *where did that come from?* Vaguely, she recalls Sammy explaining the term "blue balls" to her decades ago, when he was a teen. She has never once thought of the concept of blue balls since, but apparently her perverted mind has tucked it safely away in the deepest folds of her brain to spit out at her at this moment. *Thank you for that, brain.*

Alain holds out his hand. It is massive, and Mebel stares at it, entranced, before putting her own hand in it. There is a momentary pause, then he lifts it to his lips and brushes her knuckles with the softest kiss, sending an electric spark straight through her—as she is now finding out—very much still present and active loins. He lowers her hand with a bashful smile and says,

"Sorry, I was holding out my hand to ask if I could take a look at the confirmation email you received from the school, but I couldn't help myself."

Somehow, Mebel manages to stop herself from bursting into flames with a furious mixture of embarrassment and delight. Somehow, when she does speak, her voice comes out even. "Of course," she says simply. She locates the email quickly and plops her phone on his palm before snatching her hand away so he won't notice how shaky it is. The spot where he's just kissed her is tingling.

Alain reads the acceptance email with a slight frown. "You are right, this is an official acceptance . . ."

Vindication, the favorite emotion of all Chinese mothers, flushes through Mebel, eradicating all traces of embarrassment. "Hah!" she says with a triumphant smile. "So it must be mistake on your system."

Alain is half nodding when he suddenly pauses and says, "Ah. I see the problem. Unfortunately, Madame Mebel, you seem to have been registered at our sister school."

"Sister school?"

"This is the flagship school. We have other branches all over the world. New York, Madrid, Geneva, Rome, and—"

Mebel scrambles to try to keep up. So far, none of these other options sound bad. She could see herself dressed in head-to-toe Balenciaga in Spain, or wearing five Chopards on each arm in Geneva, or dressed in Dolce & Gabbana in Rome, why not? "Which one did I get accepted into?"

Alain grimaces, as though he's sorry to deliver bad news. "England, I'm afraid."

"Oh, that's okay!" Mebel says with genuine happiness. "I love London. The West End theater, the afternoon teas, the—"

"It's not in London, I'm afraid."

"It's not? Where is it?"

"I believe the place is called Cowley."

"Cowley?" Mebel has never heard of such a name. "Where is that?"

"It's as good as in Oxford."

Mebel narrows her eyes. "As good as? Is it *in* Oxford?"

Alain makes a seesawing motion with his head and goes, "Eh. Thereabouts."

"I don't understand. Why your other branches are in big cities, but why the English one is in this cow place?"

"Cowley."

"Cowley, right. Why Cowley?"

"London is very expensive," Alain says simply.

Mebel takes a deep breath. As the wife of a real estate tycoon, she knows all about location.

"And we weren't sure if the English would be interested in signing up to a French culinary school in England when they can just hop on the Eurostar and take the course in Paris. The decision to open a branch in England was, as the English might call it, 'a bit of a lark.'"

"I see." And now she has fallen for the lark.

"But you'll like our Cowley campus, I'm sure. And Oxford itself is a gorgeous city. I'm opening a restaurant there next month because I love the place. I have no doubt you'll have a grand time there."

Mebel takes a deep breath. As much as she would like to

believe this handsome man, she also knows that she does not belong in a place called Cowley. "Okay. I'm sure you can fix this and enroll me here? In Paris? Since I am already here." She gives him her most winning smile and gestures at the mountain of Louis Vuitton suitcases blocking the hallway.

"I can most certainly do that."

"Oh, thank you—"

"But our current term is fully booked, with a very long waiting list. The earliest you can start here is in a year and half's time."

Mebel's face goes slack. Well, since she did have a forehead lift in South Korea a year ago, her face remains perky as ever, but on the inside, things are plummeting.

"Would you like me to put you on the waitlist?"

A light bulb goes on in her head. She is, after all, Indonesian. She knows how these things work. She dips into her black Cannage lambskin Dior bag and slips out a few hundred euros, which she hands to Alain subtly. "Maybe you can find place for me for this term? I am not going to be doing four-year degree, I just need to be here for one semester, just to learn enough to impress my husband."

Alain looks at her downturned hand, under which the bills are hidden, and clasps her hand with both of his. "Madame, please, I cannot do this." He pushes her hand gently before leaning back in his seat.

Aiya. Is there anything more infuriating than people who refuse to let a little bribery grease the wheels of life? When Mebel finally finds her voice, it comes out in a heartbroken whisper. "I must get culinary degree soon."

"May I ask why?" Alain says, and his voice is so kind and his face so earnest that Mebel finds herself wanting to be honest with him, this stranger she has just met.

"I need to win my husband back," she says simply.

Alain's eyes soften. "I see. And going to culinary school will do that?"

Mebel gives a firm nod, her lips pressed together into a thin line. "Yes."

"All right. Well, then let's do that—"

Mebel brightens.

"—in Cowley."

Mebel slumps in her seat. "Ah."

"I'm afraid it is our only option. Shall I book you a Eurostar ticket for London?"

"You say it's not in London."

"It isn't. You'll go from Paris to St. Pancras International in London, and from there, you will take the bus to Ox—"

"A bus?" Mebel gasps.

Alain pauses, his eyes lighting up with what she could've sworn is silent laughter. "Yes, Mebel, a bus. Have you ever been on one?"

Mebel thinks hard. "When I was six, my parents take me on double-decker bus to tour London."

"There you go. These are not so different. You'll take a bus to Oxford. I believe the bus from London to Oxford stops at Cowley. From there, you may take a local bus—"

"A local bus?" She can't keep the scandalized tone out of her voice.

"Or a cab. It will be a ten-minute ride from the bus station to where the school is." Alain glances over at Mebel's mountain of suitcases and says, "Or perhaps you might want to take a cab from St. Pancras International all the way to the school."

"Oh! Is that possible? Then, yes, that one. I choose that option."

"Wonderful. I will help you order a Eurostar ticket. In the meantime, let's get you a car to Gare du Nord station."

The next few minutes are a flurry as Alain makes several calls, and before Mebel knows it, a cab pulls up outside the school, and a beleaguered Frenchman steps out and flings her Louis Vuitton suitcases into the trunk and the remaining pieces into the back seat with savage abandon. Alain assures her that the school in Cowley has been notified to expect her arrival and that she now has a first-class Eurostar ticket to London, and soon, Mebel is bundled into the cab. She waves dazedly at Alain, and she is off, trundling down the beautiful Parisian streets once more, only this time, as she looks out the window, she is no longer filled with the excitement and fizz of being in Paris. Instead, she gazes out with a sense of loss and bewilderment and the words *What the hell is happening*? echoing through her mind.

Chapter 5

MEBEL HAS ALWAYS THOUGHT OF PARIS WITH TWO EXCLAMATION marks following it. It's never just Paris. It's Paris!! Land of beauty and romance and dreams. When she thinks of London, she takes away one of the exclamation marks. London! Not as magical as Paris, but exciting in its own way. As she said to Alain, she loves the West End theater and there is, of course, Harrods, Fortnum & Mason, Burberry, Vivienne Westwood, and all the other stuff that makes London *London!*

Unfortunately, Cowley is very much not London. As Mebel's black cab takes her down the wet London streets, she watches with increasing dread as the buildings around her dissolve from majestic architecture to more sedate buildings to factories and then, to her horror, to fields where sheep roam freely. Rain pours from the gloomy skies in a steady patter. For the next hour or so, Mebel gapes out the window and tries to hold back her tears as the sheep turn to cows, then to agriculture. She doesn't know what the massive fields of yellow flowers are; all she knows is that they are very much not farming beautiful shops from which she can source an overpriced calfskin handbag with golden hardware.

An excruciating half hour of farmland follows, and finally, they turn off the highway (or the motorway, as the driver calls it) and the houses appear. But these houses are what Mebel, as generous as she is trying to be, can only describe as "humble." Built out of red bricks, they are all uniform, small and cramped, with tiny windows. The car turns down one street, then another, and another, and Mebel half wonders if she's even still in England. How is it possible that this is the same country that boasts marvels like Big Ben and Buckingham Palace and Westminster Abbey? These buildings are nothing like the ones in London, and against the backdrop of the funeral gray English skies, the sight is almost too depressing to behold.

The cold air is wreaking havoc on Mebel's eyes, and she's just applied some eye drops when the car comes to a stop. Mebel stays there, unmoving, blinking away the eye drops. The driver gets out, yawns, and stretches outside, as though oblivious to the rain steadily drizzling around him. He opens the door for Mebel and she starts.

"Here we are, luv," he says.

"What?"

"The Saint Honor Cooking School, yeh?"

"Saint Honoré School of Culinary Arts," Mebel says, pronouncing it the way the French do.

"Right, that's the one. Out we get then, luv."

Mebel has no choice but to step out gingerly, curving her body to protect her precious Dior handbag, even though she knows it is futile against the rain. She looks up at the building in front of her, half hoping that it would be half as gorgeous as the one in Paris. But there's no such luck. The Saint Honoré School of Culinary Arts, Cowley, is a humble affair, located in what looks like a converted block of old English houses. She turns back to the driver, about to ask him if there's been a mistake, but her words catch in her throat as he flings her beloved suitcases out of the cab and onto the curb.

"Cheers," he says, and with that, he ducks back into the cab and drives away.

Mebel looks around her at the relatively empty street. There's no one to help her with her bags, and the rain, though not heavy, is unrelenting. It is now that Mebel realizes that in addition to being damp and miserable, she is also freezing. It is barely September. What in the name of autumn is going on? Teeth chattering, she grabs the nearest Louis Vuitton suitcase and drags it down the driveway and into the building.

This reception hall is a far cry from the one in Paris. No one talks in hushed voices and no one is walking around like they're on their way to some important meeting, namely because there is only one person present—a short middle-aged woman with mousy brown hair shorn into an unforgiving bob is dozing off behind the reception desk.

"Excuse me?" Mebel says, and the woman jerks up with a snort.

"Oh, hello!" she says, grabbing a pair of glasses from the desk and shoving them onto her face. "Are you"—she checks her notes—"Mebel Tan—Tana—"

"Tanadi," Mebel says. "Yes."

"Ah yes, of course. We've been expecting you."

Despite the gloom that has settled over Mebel in the past few hours, the words "We've been expecting you" bring about a wave of relief so intense that she almost breaks down then and there.

"You have?" she says in a wobbly voice.

"Yes, Mr. Moreau called ahead to let us know you'd be arriving today. I'm Agatha, I'm the—well, I do everything around here. I'm the building manager, the school registrar, what have you. You need anything, you come to me."

Mebel thinks of the numerous people the Paris branch had on staff. There had been at least six that she could see in the reception hall alone, and probably more bustling about behind the scenes. And in this one, all they have is . . . Agatha. Agatha smiles at her. Mebel thinks of Simone, the cool French receptionist. Well, to be fair, Mebel would much rather deal with Agatha than Simone. Having come to this conclusion, she smiles back at Agatha, whose smile widens in response. For a moment, the two women grin with manic nervousness at each other, then Agatha stands.

"Well! We've got your room all ready for you." She spots Mebel's suitcase and says, "Oh good, you've got just the one bag. Our rooms aren't very big, I'm not even sure if it can fit that suitcase, but we'll—"

Grimacing, Mebel says, "I have more bags."

"Oh? Where are they?"

"Outside."

Agatha has not struck Mebel as the athletic type. There is a softness about her and she wears shoes that can only be described as orthopedic, and yet as soon as she hears the word "outside," she bursts into a sprint that would put Usain Bolt to shame. Before Mebel's brain can even catch up with what's going on, Agatha is out of the building, shouting, "You can't just leave fancy bags like these outside, not in Cowley!"

Mebel hurries outside, the Dior handbag bouncing off her arm, the goldware jangling as she jogs after Agatha. To her horror, Agatha is shouting, "Get back here, you villains!"

Sure enough, Mebel spots two youths sprinting away, each one carrying one of her Monogram Louis Vuitton suitcases on his back. "No!" Mebel cries. But even she knows that it's too late, that there is no point in trying to run after them. The boys are too fast and too far away for her and Agatha to catch up to. And anyway, these Ferragamos were made for the runway, not actual running.

And so Mebel stands at the end of the driveway and watches helplessly as two of her Louis Vuitton suitcases disappear down the street and round the corner. The sight is so surreal that Mebel can't quite grasp the magnitude of it. What did she have in those two suitcases? God, please let neither be the one that has all her handbags. She doesn't know what she would do without her bags. What if—oh no—what if they were the ones that contained her underwear? Mebel glances at Agatha. As friendly and warm as Agatha has been so far, Mebel doubts that she'd be comfortable sharing her underpants with Mebel.

"Oh dear," Agatha says, trudging back toward Mebel. She is breathing hard, her hair plastered in a sweaty mess to her forehead. "I'll help you file a police report about this, but I'm afraid that'll probably be the last time we see those boys and those beautiful suitcases of yours. The coppers here are hopeless. Have you got any valuables in there?"

"Both the suitcases and the insides of the suitcases very

valuable, yes," Mebel says. She must be in shock. If this had happened to her while she was traveling with Henk, she would be in absolute pieces. But somehow, something is keeping Mebel together in this moment, and she doesn't quite know what it is. Maybe it has to do with the fact that, compared to losing a husband and a forty-year marriage, losing two suitcases full of stuff isn't quite as horrible? Or maybe she's in denial. Whatever the case, something allows Mebel to merely shrug. She grabs hold of the one remaining LV suitcase, the two carry-on bags, and the hatbox and says, "Well, at least now I know all my things can fit inside my dorm room, ya?"

As it turns out, Mebel is wrong about that. She suspects that she might have been too optimistic about the size of her room as Agatha leads her up a flight of the narrowest staircase she has ever gone up. The staircase is so narrow, in fact, that both of Mebel's shoulders brush against the walls as she walks up backward, dragging her heavy suitcase and cursing whoever designed this godforsaken building. When she finally reaches the second floor, Agatha leads her down a stuffy hallway, speaking in a hushed voice as she walks.

"These are all accommodations for our esteemed students, like yourself," Agatha says.

Mebel is confused by how closely spaced the doors are to each other. They pass by six doors before Agatha stops at number 9 and says, "Here you are." She unlocks the door and pushes it open. "Ta-da!"

Do not cry, Mebel tells herself for what seems like the hundredth time that day.

It is a challenge not to. In front of Mebel is the smallest, dingiest room she has ever seen in real life. It reminds Mebel of a prison cell, except without a personal toilet in the corner. Instead, there is, inexplicably, a sink in one corner of the room. Why is there a random sink inside this bedroom? Why is the window so tiny? Why is the bed so narrow? Why is she here instead of being home in her luxurious mansion, ordering air-fried truffle fries from Wendy?

Mebel steps gingerly inside, pushing her suitcase in front of her. There is just about enough space for the remaining suitcases to fit inside the room, but once she's pulled them all in from the hallway, she finds that there's no way she can lay them down and open them up. Agatha stands in the doorway, smiling in a way that can only be described as "silently shrill."

"Right!" she says, her hands clasped in front of her bosom. "Well, I'll let you settle in then, shall I? It's rather late, so get some rest. Classes start bright and early tomorrow. Cheerio!" With that, she backs out and closes the door gently behind her.

Mebel's phone buzzes then, and she pounces on it. Maybe it's Henk? Maybe he's finally realized what a huge mistake he's made and he's begging her to come back? But it turns out to be Meimei, one of her friends from the country club.

The message reads:

> Mebel, where have you been? You've missed our monthly luncheon. The theme was "citrus," just awful. Look at these photos. We all had to wear citrus-themed outfits, and that shameless Natalia wore a see-through yellow top with lemon-printed bra underneath. Just look at that! You can see the bra! If you'd been there, she would never have dared to wear something like that. How are you?

> Where are you? I saw Henk at the club yesterday, but when I asked him where you were, he said you were away. Are you traveling?

Heart pounding, Mebel types out a reply. It takes her a long while to do it, as she keeps deleting and rewriting her message. She's dying to know if her friends have heard by now about Henk leaving her, and the problem is, they would never come out and ask her straight up about it. They'd hint and beat around the bush and ask questions skirting it, like Meimei has just done.

She finally settles on:

> Oh my goodness, I can't believe she wore that thing! I would've loved to see that in person. I've been really busy traveling and can't wait to catch up soon!

She adds a few laughing emojis to really hammer home that she's totally fine, then she turns the phone off and places it face down on the table.

Then, finally, what little strength Mebel has leaks out of her, and she slumps down onto the single bed. It creaks, and the mattress sags so much that Mebel almost falls backward. She cries out as her feet leave the floor. There is a moment of struggle as Mebel kicks and flails like an upturned turtle, then she finally manages to heave herself back up. The tears that had threatened to fall ever since Alain Moreau said the word "Cowley" are unleashed. Covering her face with her hands, Mebel begins to cry. She has never felt so far away from home, so alone, and so frightened. What is this awful damp space? She'd comforted herself on the Eurostar by looking on Google Maps and telling herself that Cowley seems to be part of Oxfordshire, which she'd mistakenly thought meant that it's as good as being in Oxford, and how bad can Oxford be, given that it's where the most prestigious university in the world is? But here she is now in Cowley, and it is most definitely not as good as being in Oxford. It's like saying that Bintan is as good as being in Singapore, or Staten Island is as good as being in Manhattan, or—or—oh, what's the point of it all?

For a while, the only sounds in the room are Mebel's sniffles. They don't last long. They never do. Mebel doesn't have the kind of attention span that a good, prolonged crying session requires. After a few minutes, her tears dry up, and though she tries her best to will more to come, she starts to feel silly, so she dabs at her face and pushes herself off the bed. What she needs to do right now, she thinks, is to come up with a plan of attack. Right. Taking a deep breath, Mebel makes a mental list.

1. Make the best of my situation.

She looks around her. What she needs is an attitude adjustment. Yes. She needs to look on the bright side of things.

Downside: The room is small and miserable.

Upside: The room does not have rats or mold.

Downside: The bed feels like it's older than she is.

Upside: The bed does not have a random naked man in it.

Hmm, maybe that upside isn't really much of an upside. Well, no use moping about. One of the skills that Mebel has honed as a trophy wife is maintaining an upbeat attitude during the worst situations. Like that one time Henk was fined for being "tax efficient," i.e., evading taxes. They'd been in Santorini when his accountant called with the bad news, and Henk had been so grumpy it almost ruined their entire trip, but Mebel managed to cheer him up by surprising him with a new yacht.

Mebel tilts her head to one side, deep in thought. Unfortunately, this does not seem like a situation that would be helped by the purchase of a shiny yacht. Maybe she should consider staying in a hotel instead, as Sammy had suggested. But is that making the best of the situation or is that running away? It feels a lot like running away, and Mebel is not the type to run away from a problem, more the type that would run straight into it. Just like how she's decided to tackle Henk leaving her by grabbing life by the neck and squeezing until it admits that it's made a mistake.

With that thought in mind, she grabs hold of the nearest LV suitcase, and in a burst of strength that her knees will no doubt regret later, she flings it onto the bed. Opening it, Mebel releases a sigh of relief. This is the bag that contains her clothes. Well, thank goodness she won't have to ask Agatha for clean underwear, after all. She removes a few choice outfits, closes the suitcase, and opens the other one, which contains her makeup. That means the suitcases containing her handbags and her shoes are now gone. Once again, Mebel fights the tears back. She's going to make it through this ordeal. Even so, her brain can't help filing through all the handbags she has now lost. The Gucci Jackie 1961 shoulder bag in cuir leather that she'd bought in Seoul. The Garden Party 49 voyage bag that she'd bought in

Singapore. The Fendi baguette chain bag Henk had bought her as a souvenir from New York.

Okay, stop this right now, she tells herself. *It's neither productive nor helpful. And don't even start thinking about the shoes. Oh, the shoes!*

Mebel forces herself to unpack as much as she can and put the clothes into the small wooden cupboard, then she undresses, shivering as the cold, damp English air touches her bare skin. Wrapping herself in a robe, she creeps out of her room and into the—*oh my*—shared bathroom, where she takes a long scalding shower. As she lathers her hair, Mebel closes her eyes and tells herself her new mantra: *Everything will be better in the morning. Every bad, no-good, awful day has its bright side, which is that things can only look up from here.*

Chapter 6

THE THING ABOUT TROPHY WIVES IS THEY ARE OFTEN misjudged. They are often dismissed as airheaded gold diggers, but the truth is so much more complex than that. Mebel would never be caught digging for anything, for one thing. For another, as a trophy wife, Mebel has had to get very good at many things. She could write a whole guidebook on how to be a good trophy wife.

1. A good trophy wife knows that while her husband is the head of the family, the wife is the rock on which he stands. Mebel has always strived hard to be Henk's rock. She is always there for Henk to lean on—or trip over—and hasn't he always said he appreciates her consistency? Her dependability?

2. A good trophy wife must be able to fit into any environment she is thrown into. Mebel has lost count of the

number of uncomfortable, boring events she's had to attend because of Henk. The private banks that they bank with, for example, are always holding what they call "financial forecasts," which take place over multi-course dinners at fancy hotels. There, Mebel has to make small talk with stuffy businessmen, and in order to not embarrass Henk, she's had to brush up on her knowledge of world politics and economics. Because she prides herself as a first-class trophy wife, she would never allow herself to be one of the many wives there who are so obviously bored, their attention riveted to their phones as their husbands prattle on about emerging markets.

3. Last but not least, a good trophy wife mustn't ever forget that she is, first and foremost, a trophy. This means she must have qualities that would make her husband want to show her off. Mebel has a facial at La Prairie once every two weeks, salmon sperm injections once a month, and every six months, she flies to Seoul to get Botox, Ultherapy, and Pico laser done. She is such a good customer that her aesthetician gave her a tote bag that reads: "The most expensive thing I'm wearing today is my face." She does Pilates three times a week, Bikram yoga once a week, and goes on a three-mile run twice a week. She keeps her wardrobe religiously updated so she will never embarrass Henk by wearing last season's Prada.

Which is why, when Mebel turns up at the first class of the day, everyone stops and stares at her. She pauses at the door, a polite smile frozen on her face, and looks around at the surprisingly large kitchen that Agatha has ushered her into.

Given the humbleness of the building (and Cowley in general), Mebel hadn't been expecting much, but the kitchen where the classes are to take place is actually an impressive space. A space that is currently filled with a dozen very confused-looking cooks.

The one wearing the tallest chef's hat finally says, "Er, mornin'."

"Good morning," Mebel says with a pleasant smile. "Is this the CULS 110 class, Culinary Fundamentals?"

"Er, yes. Yes, it is. Sorry, are you a teacher here?" he says.

"Oh! No, of course not. I am student. My name is Mebel."

"Right." The chef looks down at his list, and his eyebrows rise. "Mebel Tanadi?"

"Yes."

"Okay. Right, yes, I have your name here. I'm Chef Clarke."

Mebel gives him a warm smile, still painfully aware of the fact that everyone is staring at her. But that's just one of the many qualities that trophy wives have had to get good at—accepting that in every room, you will be the one they stare at. "Nice to meet you, Chef Clarke."

"Er, yes. Uh, sorry, Mebel, did Agatha not give you your chef's uniform when you checked in?"

"She give me, yes."

"Right." Chef Clarke looks up at the ceiling for a second, then looks back at her. "Then, why are you not wearing it?" He gestures at everyone else, who is clearly wearing their chef's uniforms.

"Oh!" Mebel laughs. "Well, is not to be rude, but I think my chef's uniform is better, no? I order custom-made from Hermès. The trim is in their signature orange. Isn't it beautiful?" She lifts her arms and does a little twirl so they can better admire her outfit.

"Very nice," Chef Clarke mumbles, "but this is really—I don't think—the purpose of uniforms is so everyone is, well, uniform."

"Not a problem," Mebel says cheerily. "I will order for everyone else too. And yours will have extra-tall hat."

"I—uh—I don't think that will be necessary." Chef Clarke dabs at his forehead as the class breaks into excited whispers.

"Okay, no tall hat. Same hat as everyone."

"I meant—uh—never mind. Please go to your station. We have wasted quite enough time this morning, and we have a lot to get through." He gestures at an empty worktable.

Mebel slides behind the workstation and smiles at her classmates, all of whom are staring at her. Everyone else in the room looks significantly younger than her. She supposes it's to be expected, but she would be lying if she said she wasn't slightly intimidated by that. What generation are these people? Are they of the dreaded millennial generation? No, they look even younger than Sammy, which means they must be—*oh my*—of the Z type. She has heard that the Z generation is so scary that even millennials avoid them at all costs. And now, here she is in a roomful of them.

The girl next to Mebel leans in and says, "I think your uniform ate."

Mebel blinks. "I'm sorry? What is it eating?"

"No, I mean, like, it ate. You know, it's cool."

"Ah." Mebel considers this. "It does eat. Thank you."

The girl smiles at her. "I'm Gemma."

"Mebel."

Chef Clarke clears his throat. "Right, can everyone please pay attention? In front of you is your toolkit. You may now open it."

Mebel looks down, and sure enough, there is a big black bag on the worktop in front of her. She unlatches it and is surprised to find how heavy the bag is. It's shaped like a massive scroll, and when Mebel unrolls it, she finds a highly impressive selection of knives strapped onto the inside of the bag. It makes her think of a bag that a serial killer might find handy.

"This is your chef's toolkit," Chef Clarke says. "You must turn up to class with it every day. Inside, you will find the classic nine-inch chef's knife—this is the knife you will be using most of the time. Yes, that's the one. It will behoove you to get used to this knife as soon as possible. Think of it as a natural extension of your arm."

Mebel takes the nine-inch knife out from its clasp and studies it, feeling the weight of it in her hand. She can't remember the last time she cooked anything, and therefore she can't remember the last time she held a knife.

As though reading her mind, Chef Clarke says, "Now, can everyone share, what was the last thing you cooked?"

Gemma, the nice girl next to Mebel, raises her hand and says, "A beef Wellington."

"A classic," Chef Clarke says, nodding with appreciation.

"Shepherd's pie," a boy with a pimply chin says.

"Roast chicken," someone else calls out.

Chef Clarke nods at all of them before looking expectantly

at Mebel. She stares back. She's painfully aware that they all probably expect some impressive answer from her, given she is older than anyone else here by miles and therefore must have a lot more experience in the kitchen. For a second, Mebel considers lying and telling them that the last thing she cooked was some elaborate Michelin-star-worthy dish that required fourteen different ingredients. But she quickly rejects the idea—one of her many rules to be a successful trophy wife is to not tell stories that she cannot back up. So she lifts her chin, and meeting him in the eye, she says, "A Nespresso."

Several students laugh at this.

Chef Clarke looks like he's considering early retirement. "A Nespresso."

"A Ristretto, I think it was."

"Right . . ." Chef Clarke clears his throat once more and wrenches his attention back to the toolkit. "Uh, next we have your six-inch boning knife, and if anyone so much as snickers at that, I will have you removed from the class." He gives the class a wry smile, and moves on to the next knife.

By the time Chef Clarke is done going through the list of tools that they've been given, Mebel's head is spinning. Who knew there were so many of the damn things? And she's supposed to lug this unsightly, heavy thing around with her every day? Unthinkable. And why are these bags so ugly? Would it kill them to reach out to Louis Vuitton and get a collaboration going? Just think of the possibilities!

But even as her mind wanders to different tool-bag designs, Chef Clarke is already droning on about how this class will teach them fundamental cooking theories and techniques.

"Over the course of this semester, we are going to develop your knife skills," he says, "classical vegetable cuts, boning of different carcasses, and so on."

Mebel grimaces. As a meat eater, she does not enjoy thinking of them as "carcasses." But no one else seems to be disturbed by the chef's choice of words, so Mebel wisely decides to keep her thoughts to herself.

"You will learn how to make various stocks and sauces. How many of you have planned an elaborate dinner party—"

Mebel's hand shoots up. Finally, a question she can answer.

"—and lost track of time and find that your soup has boiled over, and your chicken is overcooked and dry, and you've burned the croutons?"

Mebel puts her hand down.

"Mebel, you've never had that problem?" Chef Clarke says.

"No," Mebel says with all the sincerity in the world. "Is quite simple. All you have to do is hire enough cooks to make the dinner."

Chef Clarke utters a long-suffering sigh. "Right. Well, in this class, you won't be able to hire cooks. You will learn how to multitask and keep track of time so you don't end up with a disaster on your hands. We will go through station organization, and you will learn ratios and formulas and know them like the back of your hand by the time we are done with the course."

To Mebel's surprise, she's enjoying Chef Clarke's introduction. Everything he's saying, apart from the boning of carcasses, sounds like things that she will be good at. She is nothing if not a great hostess, and what is hosting but multitasking while wearing an uncomfortable shiny dress and putting out various fires with a winning smile on your face?

When Chef Clarke is finally done with his talk, he then begins a slideshow on food safety. Mebel takes out her notebook and jots down as many notes as she can, which is a challenge because the cold, damp English air has stiffened her fingers, but she persists, nevertheless. She marvels at the numerous guidelines there are surrounding the preparation and storage of food. Back home, she only told the helpers that they are to wash their hands before they begin cooking, and that was that. But now she's learning that even the way she washes her hands is wrong. Who knew there were so many steps to washing one's hands? Then she watches in horror as Chef Clarke heaves a fire extinguisher and tells them that they will have to get comfortable with using one. The only heavy thing Mebel has deigned acceptable to carry is her Monogram Louis Vuitton suitcase, and she is certainly not about to change that. By the time Chef Clarke goes over the difference between "cleaning" and "sanitizing," Mebel's brain has completely shut down.

They're clearly just making things up now, because what could possibly be the difference between cleaning and sanitizing? Mebel tries to pay attention to Chef Clarke, but the thing about being a trophy wife is Mebel has never had to do cleaning or sanitizing for a single day in her life. Back home in Jakarta, the house is kept spotless, and Mebel has never once thought: *I wonder what brand of cleaning solution I should buy for the sink*. The irony is she often watches cleaning videos when she mindlessly scrolls on social media. In theory, Mebel knows that the best way to clean your kitchen sink is by pouring salt on a half lemon and using it as a scrub. She also knows that you should pour baking soda and vinegar down your sink once in a while. Maybe. But her sink never seems to require those things, and also, Chef Clarke has been talking about the art of cleaning a kitchen sink for over ten minutes now, and not once has he mentioned lemons or baking soda. This whole thing is nowhere near as relaxing as a TikTok.

The class goes on for two more interminable hours, during which Mebel fidgets endlessly in her seat and half listens to the lecture. Then finally, thank god, they break for lunch. The students file out, some of them chatting with one another, down the hallway and to the dining hall. Mebel has to admit that she is pleasantly surprised by the vastness of the building. From the outside, it is a humble affair that can't possibly be compared to the flagship school in Paris, but on the inside, it's turning out to be much larger than she expected. The dining hall is large, easily fitting over fifty people, with large windows on either side that let in a generous amount of sunlight. There are rows of long tables where students from other courses are seated, and the food is served buffet style.

And this is where Mebel stops and appreciates, for the first time since her arrival, the fact that she is in a culinary school. There are tureen after tureen of international dishes, each one looking more delectable than the last. The first few tureens have obviously come from the Meat Identification and Preparation class. They contain roast chicken and cuts of minute steak, all of them meticulously butchered by the students and cooked to perfection. As Mebel walks on, she comes to the results of the Seafood Identification and Fabrication class. The tureens are filled with freshly shucked oysters and beautifully filleted seared fish. The baked goods section is even more impressive. The school offers a wide range of baking classes, from basic ones that go over foundational methods of creaming, blending, foaming, and so on, to advanced classes that go into food science and methods that are so complicated they require a basic grasp of molecular chemistry. There is a wide selection of freshly baked breads as well as pastries that range from humble café fare to pristinely decorated little cakes that look like they belong at Harrods.

Mebel helps herself to a small piece of chicken and some roasted vegetables, then makes her way to the tables. And here, she pauses. It has been decades since she last found herself in a school cafeteria, and the last time she was in one, she was in a very different position. It was at USC, where she had long established herself as the queen bee of the Chinese-Indo society, and wherever she turned up, people would bend over backward to ensure there was a spot at the table for her.

But here, at the Saint Honoré School of Culinary Arts, Mebel is not only a new student but also—ugh—the oldest student in the school. She scans the room and adjusts the thought to: *Not only the oldest student here, but the oldest by at least two decades.* It is official; she is at least one, if not two, whole generations older than the toddlers in here. If Mebel didn't know any better, she would mistake the chest tightness she's currently experiencing as social anxiety. But, no, that's not possible, because trophy wives do not have social anxiety; they have Gucci.

Taking a deep breath, Mebel keeps her chin up and plunges into the crowd with her tray of food. She passes by a long table that is half-empty and ignores the instinctive reaction to perch at the very end of that table and eat quietly while training her eyes on nothing but her food. It would be comforting, yes, but she did not become the president of the Chinese-Indo Club at USC by seeking comfort. And she is not about to allow herself to backslide like this, not when she's just arrived at a whole new school. What is this place but a chance for her to establish dominance?

And so she finds the loudest table filled with the most gregarious students and slides her tray right in the center of it. She smiles. These kids are not going to know what hit them.

Chapter 7

IN HINDSIGHT, PERHAPS ONE COULD SAY THAT OVERCONfidence has been Mebel's downfall throughout her life. Take Henk, for example. She should never have let herself become comfortable. Yes, she kept herself in excellent shape even after childbirth and menopause, but she let other things slide. Things like physical intimacy and making sure that Henk knows she thinks he's the most attractive male organism in the known world. (He isn't, of course. George Clooney is still alive and breathing, after all. But Mebel has always thought it's in everyone's best interest if Henk thought himself more attractive than George Clooney. And anyway, George wouldn't have minded, she's sure of that.) But it's been years since Henk had turned to her, like the wicked queen in *Snow White* turning to the mirror, and asked, *Sweetheart, do you still find me attractive*? If he did, she would've answered without any doubt: *Of course, Henk. You are just as handsome as the day we first met*. But he hadn't asked, and so she hadn't thought to answer, thinking that maybe they'd come to a stage in their marriage where they no longer needed to affirm each other like that anymore. She'd been too confident to see that he, in fact, still needed that affirmation. He was simply getting it from someone else. See? Overconfidence.

She should have known that sliding into a seat at a busy dining table and hoping it would all work out is yet another example of her overconfidence. Thankfully, since Mebel is in England, after all, the polite English people on either side of her scoot away to give her some room. The conversation at the table dies down, and all eyes turn to Mebel, who treats them to her most charming smile.

"Hello," she says. "I am Ms. Tanadi."

There is a long silence, then one of the students—a boy who to Mebel looks like he can't possibly be older than fifteen years of age—raises his hand.

"Yes?" Mebel says.

"Sorry, ma'am," he says, "but which course do you teach?"

"Oh!" Mebel laughs. "No, I am not teacher here. I am student, just like you."

There is another long silence, this one accompanied by confused back-and-forth stares.

"Are you a first-year student, then?" a girl says.

"Yes," Mebel says cheerfully.

They look more relaxed at this, which gives Mebel a false sense of security. *There,* she thinks, *I'm fitting right in.*

"What's your name?" the girl says.

"I tell you already. Ms. Tanadi."

"No, like, what's your first name?"

Slightly taken aback by the question, Mebel says, "Mebel. But you call me Ms. Tanadi."

But then the teenage-looking boy says, "Thing is, Mebel, we're all third years here. We're taking advanced classes."

Mebel's mind has short-circuited at being called by her first name by this young chit of a boy. *Aiya*, she thinks, *he's barely out of diapers, and look at him, sitting there and calling me by my first name. What European nonsense is this?*

At her silence, he continues talking. "I think the first years are sitting over there. You'd be quite lost at this table, Mebel. You should sit with your peers."

"My peers?" Mebel mutters, blinking. She turns to look at where he's pointing. It's the table two rows down, at which even younger-looking kids are sitting. She recognizes some of the students from her class. She didn't pay too much attention to them back in the classroom, but here in the cafeteria, they look even more youthful. She could've sworn their faces still have yet to lose the fat of babyhood. Mebel utters a quick prayer of thanks for the filler injections she's had done in Seoul six months ago. Thank god her own face has been beautifully rejuvenated, her cheeks plumped up; otherwise, she would be roiling with envy at the sight of all that collagen just being flaunted at her.

"Yes." The boy is still talking in an obnoxious voice as he looks down his nose at her. *Collagen*, Mebel thinks, *is wasted on youths.* "I think you should go on and join them, Mebel."

"And I think you should respect your elders!" Mebel snaps.

The boy's mouth drops open.

"I can be your mother," Mebel says. "And you sitting there

and calling me by my first name? Give me your mother telephone number. I am going to call her and tell her she needs to discipline you better."

"I—uh—" He looks around at his seat mates, who are exchanging glances with one another, but none of them comes to his aid.

"Now, you all can call me Ms. Tanadi and we continue eating." With that, Mebel picks up her fork and knife and begins to eat her chicken daintily. Really, what she would very much like to do is stab the piece of chicken to drive her point home, but she's been a trophy wife for way too long to let go of her table manners.

The rest of the lunch resumes in silence. Mere minutes later, everyone at the table seems to have finished their food. Glances are exchanged, mouths are wiped, and one by one, they stand, retrieve their trays, and leave the table. Soon, Mebel is left all alone. She's not delusional enough to fail to realize that she's just been excluded, and the pain of this hits her unexpectedly hard. When was the last time Mebel had been rejected in a social setting?

Well, the last time would be Henk choosing to walk out on their marriage. But other than that, she really can't think of another occasion where she was the one being excluded as opposed to being the one who was excluding someone. To be fair, though, Mebel has always prided herself on being inclusive. Whenever she plans functions, she makes sure to invite those who would normally have been left out. Because Mebel may be a queen bee, but she is not a cruel one. And so the fact that she is now being left out stings. She's surprised by how humiliated she feels, how exposed, sitting all alone at this long table, painfully aware of the curious stares from the other students around her. Perhaps she shouldn't have threatened to call the boy's mother? But, no, she thinks. If Sammy were being rude to an elder, she would expect them to inform her about it so she could discipline him and tell him how he's disappointing his ancestors.

Mebel has lost her appetite now. She stands, avoiding everyone's eyes, and returns her tray to the collection table, then she walks out of the cafeteria, feeling everyone's gaze crawling across her back like curious ants. To her credit, she manages to keep from bursting into a run. Outside, she locates the bathroom and locks herself in one of the stalls. She rests her face in her palms and counts her breaths. One, two . . . it's okay. Three, four . . . these are just teething problems. Five, six . . . hasn't she always managed to fit in? It's one of her many gifts, the ability to integrate into most social situations and establish herself as an asset to the group instead of a liability.

After a few minutes of silent pep talk, Mebel finds enough strength to walk out of the stall. She splashes some cold water on her face and pats it dry before fluffing up her hair. Then she reaches into her handbag and pulls out her Chanel lipstick. She's wearing number fifty-six today, because the bright red color gives her courage.

"You can do this," she murmurs to herself as she stares into the mirror. "This is nothing. It's just a silly class. A silly, silly class."

But it isn't just a silly class, is it? the hateful voice in her head says. *It's a class that's supposed to win Henk back. So the stakes are very high. They're not just you getting a good grade. The stakes are . . . well, you losing your marriage.*

"I know," Mebel says to the voice.

And also your access to money, which would mean you losing everything you hold dear.

"I know!" Mebel hisses to the voice.

The houses, the apartments, the incessant traveling in business class, the—

"Please shut up," Mebel moans, and just at that moment, the door opens and Gemma, the pretty blond girl that Mebel was standing next to in class, walks in.

"Sorry!" Gemma says, freezing in the doorway. She's wide-eyed like a tiny furry animal that's just heard the caw of an eagle. "Uh, I'll go."

Oh, great, Mebel thinks. *She thinks I told her to shut up.* "No," Mebel says hurriedly. "I not talking to you. I talking to myself."

This does not have the desired effect of soothing Gemma. Now she looks genuinely worried. "Um . . . okay, well, I'll give you the space you need to, uh, converse with yourself." And with that, she leaves the bathroom.

"Tsk." Mebel scowls at her reflection. All in all, not a wonderful start to the day. She really needs to get things under control. "Deep breaths, Mebel," she mutters to herself. She takes a deep inhale. *Look on the bright side,* she tells herself, *at least the bathrooms in here are kept obsessively clean.* As they should be, in a culinary school. She takes a couple more deep breaths, then brushes down her Hermès uniform and corrects her posture before leaving the sanctuary of the bathroom.

The next class of the day is what's technically known as the "lab work." Chef Clarke explains that the first half of the day is devoted to lectures, and the second half will be spent doing actual, practical work.

"Welcome to Culinary Fundamentals," he says to the class when everyone is present. "This is your introduction to the basics of cooking theory and technique. Knife skills, basic concepts, techniques for basic protein and starch and vegetables and all that fun stuff. I'm not going to stand here talking though. I've done enough of that today. I want you to take out your chef's knife. The nine-inch one, yes, that one."

Finally, Mebel thinks. She's had just about enough of Chef Clarke droning on about safety, and she is raring to get to work. She slides the knife out of its holder and grips it firmly. This is her time to shine.

Well, in actuality, the only knife Mebel has held in the past few years was a butter knife at breakfast and a steak knife at dinner, but how hard can chopping vegetables be, anyway?

Chef Clarke points to a large bowl next to him, which is full of potatoes. "You will be chopping these babies. When you come up here to collect the potatoes, you also need to collect one of these boards." He picks up a square board on which are differently shaped pieces of wood. The borders of the board have been marked with measurements, like a ruler. "This is your chopping guide. Memorize it. Today, we are going to be working on the cube, chop, and dice. That's these three cubes here. Your potatoes need to be cut to these precise measurements." He points at three different wooden cubes on the board. "Understand?"

There is a chorus of "Yes, Chef."

"Right, please come up and collect your board and your potatoes. Twenty potatoes a person."

Mebel struts from behind her workstation to the front of the classroom. To her irritation, the other students ahead of her aren't falling over themselves to let her go to the front of the line. In Chinese culture, young people are taught to always give way to their elders, and it would be unthinkable for someone her age to stand in line behind these twenty-something-year-olds. *Still,* she reminds herself, *you are no longer in Asia, and as they say, when in Rome, wear Versace.* And so she waits patiently and graciously (which for Mebel means not glaring at the other students and telling them that their ancestors are disappointed in them) until her turn comes.

"Here you are, Mebel," Chef Clarke says.

Mebel tries not to wince at the use of her first name. Chef Clarke looks like he's in his fifties, which must mean he's in his forties, and really, he should be calling her Big Sister at the very least. *When in Rome,* she reminds herself. God, how she wishes she were in Rome.

Twenty potatoes make for a surprisingly heavy load. Mebel grunts as she lifts her bowl and nearly topples over. The bowl thumps back on the countertop. Heads turn, and once again, she is the subject of everyone's stare.

Come on, Mebel thinks. *Do not let me down now.* She does Pilates, for heaven's sake. But Pilates is different from, well, what can only be described as menial labor. The words "menial labor" very nearly send Mebel over the edge. How far she has fallen!

Chef Clarke peers over the counter, down at her feet, then says, "Er, Mebel, are you wearing high heels?"

Mebel smiles primly. "These are Louboutins."

"Right. Well, in the kitchen, we wear comfortable footwear. Sneakers. Shoes that allow you to be on your feet for six consecutive hours."

"Six consecutive hours?" Mebel cries.

"At a minimum. Some places will require you to be on your feet for eight, ten hours. You may end up taking double shifts, which—"

Mebel laughs. "Oh, no. I won't take double shift. I won't even take one shift."

Chef Clarke looks blankly at her.

"I am not going to work in restaurant."

"Right. Then can I ask why you are here?"

"To win back my husband. I learn to cook white people food for him, and he will see that he make mistake."

"White people food," Chef Clarke murmurs, as though in a daze.

"Yes, authentic white people food, taught to me by you. A white person."

"Er, right. Yes, well, that is me." He laughs weakly and tugs at his collar. "Uh . . . well. Might I suggest that even though you don't have plans of working in a restaurant, you should still consider changing your footwear?"

Mebel looks forlornly at her feet. "I will consider."

"Good." He looks over her shoulder at the student behind her, then looks back at her again. "Is there anything else I can help you with, Mebel?"

"Can you carry my potatoes back to my table?"

Chef Clarke frowns. "I'm afraid not. This is part of being a chef. You need to be able to carry heavy loads back and forth from the freezer to the worktop."

Mebel's mouth drops open, aghast. "Why you are so disrespectful?" she cries. "First of all, I tell you already, I don't want to be chef. I am going to be home cook for my husband, so he don't leave me for our private chef."

"Er—" Chef Clarke's eyes roam wildly around the room, as though hoping for someone to come to his rescue. No one does.

"Second of all, I am lady. I am wearing Louboutins. Do you think that when Christian Louboutin design these shoes, he think, 'Ah, the lady wearing this will be carrying twenty potatoes'? Of course not. I thought you English man are taught to treat women like ladies. Where is the English manners now?"

Chef Clarke's mouth opens and closes. He looks like a fish drowning on land.

"I'll help," Gemma says.

Before Mebel or Chef Clarke can say anything, Gemma picks up the bowl of potatoes and marches to the back of the classroom. She puts the bowl down on Mebel's workstation and proceeds to the front once more to collect her own bowl of potatoes.

Mebel utters an audible *hmph,* narrows her eyes at Chef Clarke to let him know that he's far from being off the hook, and returns to her workstation. When Gemma returns to her spot next to Mebel, Mebel reaches out and catches her attention. "Thank you," Mebel says.

Gemma smiles. "No problem." She turns her attention back to her worktop, signaling that the conversation is over.

With a small sigh, Mebel picks up her measuring board. There are nine pieces of wood stuck to it, all of them in different shapes. Each shape has been labeled, and Mebel's eyes swim as she scans them. These names are ridiculous: Brunoise. Chiffonade. Julienne. Why don't they give these cuts more sensible names, like "Thinly sliced" and "Very thinly sliced"? How is one supposed to remember any of these?

Well, never mind that, she doesn't have to worry about brunoise and so on today. She's supposed to be doing the . . . what was it again? Ah. Mebel locates the three cubes on the board. The chop, cube, and dice. Again, she glowers at the board. Why didn't they just name them the "small cube," the "medium cube," and "the large cube"?

With the potatoes distributed among the students, Chef Clarke asks for their attention once more and demonstrates how to first do the "cube."

"After peeling the potatoes, you want to slice them like so—we are looking for one-centimeter cubes today, and you really want every side to be as even as possible. Notice how I'm holding the chef's knife." He holds up his knife before bringing it back down. "Tip of the knife, then down, like this. Use the measurements on your board to guide you. Understand?"

The class says, "Yes, Chef."

Mebel begins to peel a potato, which starts out as a peaceful task but quickly turns into a boring chore. By the fifth potato, Mebel's wrist and left hand are killing her. Every few seconds, she has to put the potato down and clench her hand into a fist, open it, clench, rotate the wrist, and so on in an effort to get feeling back into her hand. She gives up after the sixth potato and decides to start chopping first. Maybe the difference in hand movements will ease the throbbing ache.

I'm pretty good at this, Mebel thinks as she makes quick work of her first potato. These are good cubes, and Mebel is pleased with her efforts. But when Chef Clarke gets to her table, he frowns down at her handiwork.

"I cube the potato," Mebel says with pride.

Chef Clarke picks out one of the cubes and puts it next to the wooden cube on the measuring board. Mebel's smile slips. Before, she'd thought her cubes were decent. But when compared side by side to the wooden cube, her cube looks pathetic. It's wonky, for one, the angles all haphazard instead of right angles. And for another, it doesn't even look like a cube. More like a trapezoid with four different lengths. And it's almost twice as big as the wooden cube. *My goodness*, she thinks. *How could I have been so off?*

The answer is obvious, of course. She's off because she's never had to do anything that requires hand-eye coordination and the kind of motor skills needed to handle a chef's knife to chop a root vegetable up into precise shapes. Her fine motor skills have been devoted to things like applying makeup meticulously (in fact, Mebel thinks, put her in a painting class, and she'll probably knock their socks off) or penning handwritten thank-you cards to send to her guests after one of her dinner parties (once more, if only this were a painting class, she would be painting circles around everyone).

"These are not adequate, I'm afraid," Chef Clarke says, and even though he is a soft-spoken man, Mebel knows that every pair of ears in the class is pricked, everyone secretly listening in as they pretend to be hyperfocused on their potatoes. "These are so badly cut that I won't be using them in the dish we are making. These can go into the mashed potato bowl."

The mashed potato bowl? None of these four words, used in isolation, can be accused of being a slur, but put together in this context, somehow they have become the most offensive thing Mebel has ever had spoken to her. Tears prick the backs of her eyes, and she can't trust herself to speak. She merely nods and keeps her eyes on her knife and reminds herself that if she were to stab Chef Clarke with it, she would only have herself to blame for getting her custom-made Hermès uniform bloody.

"This way, Mebel," Chef Clarke is saying, and Mebel struggles to pay attention to the way he holds the knife and how he slices into the potato. "Understand?" he says.

She nods again, trying to swallow the lump of humiliation in her throat. She breathes a sigh of relief when Chef Clarke leaves her station and goes to the next one. The rest of the time, she struggles to follow his instruction, but really, her mind is alternating between going from: *I'm too pretty to be chopping potatoes into cubes* to *Waaah, I want to go home!*

She gives it her best shot over the course of the next few potatoes, but by her fifth potato, her arms are hurting so badly that there is no longer any point in attempting to be precise. She can barely keep her hand from shaking as she holds the knife. Her brain packs up its bags and leaves the building, and her chops become haphazard, more hack and slash than an intentional slice. In fact, Mebel is so exhausted that she doesn't feel the knife slicing into her index finger. The first thing to register in her mind is the sound the blade makes being different to the sound it's been making as it bites into the potato. She looks down and sees a pale white line appear along the side of her finger, then as she watches, the line turns from white to red, and now all of a sudden blood is flowing, not spurting—thank god—but a definite drip. It dribbles down her fingertip and splashes onto the (badly chopped) potatoes.

For a moment, Mebel doesn't move. She still has yet to feel any pain. In fact, the one who notices is Gemma, who goes, "Oh my god. Chef? Chef! We need help!"

Chef Clarke appears at Mebel's side, and a towel is wrapped around her finger, and as Chef Clarke squeezes down, the pain finally makes its entrance. And, boy, what an entrance it is, explosive and flamboyant, demanding all of Mebel's attention into laser-sharp focus. She gasps out loud, her senses screaming back into focus. "Is my finger gone?" she cries.

Chef Clarke gives her a flat expression. "No, Mebel. It's not a very deep cut. I've had much worse." He holds up his left hand, which is marked with not just knife scars but also burn scars. "But let's get you to the doctor in case you need stitches."

"Stitches?" Mebel gasps. "But I'm wearing Cartier," she says weakly.

Instead of being understanding, Chef Clarke gives her a stern look and says, "You really should have taken all those rings off. We went over this in the food sanitation lecture. Right, come on. And put pressure on that cut."

And, in a daze, her right hand clamped around her left, Mebel totters after him. Everyone watches her leave. Mebel has always believed in the power of a good exit, which requires (a) everyone's attention, and (b) memorable parting words. And so as she steps out of the kitchen, she pauses, turns around, and says, "Maybe don't put my potatoes in the mashed potato bowl. There is blood on them." With that, she turns and leaves the school.

Chapter 8

CHEF CLARKE TAKES MEBEL TO THE TEMPLE COWLEY Health Centre, where she is ushered to the Minor Injuries Unit and asked to sit down and wait for the next available doctor on duty. Mebel does so. Chef Clarke walks up and down the hallway, talking on his phone. She is sure he's talking about her, probably trying to get her kicked out of the school for disrupting his class. She can't blame him. Fifteen minutes pass by. People come and go. A boy with a badly scalded arm is seen to. A woman with an alarmingly huge, swollen insect bite is seen to. Nurses bustle past, barely sparing her a glance. Another fifteen minutes crawl by. Mebel's finger throbs with irritating persistence. She can't even use her phone because she's too scared to unwrap her right hand from her left in case blood starts gushing out and she dies of a hemorrhage here.

After what seems like an hour, Mebel is finally seen to, but her relief is short-lived as the attending doctor tries to unwrap the towel. The blood has dried around her finger and the towel is now stuck to it, and when the doctor gives the barest hint of a tug, the pain is so sharp and so alarming that Mebel gives a most unladylike squawk. She snatches her hand back.

"I think maybe we leave towel there?" she pleads.

"I'm sorry, Mebel, but we do need to take it off so I can see if you need stitches or not. And we really should sanitize the wound."

There's that cursed word again: "sanitize." Mebel is so sick of it. Prior to today, she has never had to so much as think about sanitation, and now all of a sudden, she can't seem to escape the concept of it.

"I'm going to lubricate the towel with some warm saline solution," the doctor says, gently pulling Mebel's hand back. She places a kidney-shaped bowl under Mebel's hand and takes out a bottle of saline solution.

Mebel holds her breath, her toes curling in anticipation of the pain as the doctor begins pouring the solution over the towel. It stings, but it isn't as bad as she'd feared, and soon enough, the towel is thankfully off. The doctor continues to squirt saline solution all over Mebel's finger, turning her hand this way and that and studying the wound. As the dried blood is washed away, the wound starts oozing once more.

Dear god, Mebel prays, please do not let me need stitches. My hands were built for Chopard watches and Cartier rings, not for knife scars.

"I think we can get away with gluing the wound shut," the doctor says.

"Oh, thank god."

"It will scar though," the doctor says.

Mebel's shoulders sag. So much for maintaining beautiful, pristine hands. She watches glumly as the doctor—ugh—sanitizes the wound and then applies a layer of medical glue over it. Once the glue dries, the doctor covers up the wound with some gauze, tells Mebel not to get it wet, and finally, finally she is released. She comes out of the room to find Chef Clarke still talking on the phone. He spots her and ends the call, then hurries over to her.

"All right then?" he says.

She holds up her bandaged finger.

"Stitches?"

Mebel shakes her head. "They use glue. Very high tech."

"Oh, good! That's really good news. Right, it's way past dinner time—"

Mebel brightens up. The mention of dinner serves as a reminder of how hungry she is. She didn't have much to eat for lunch, and she is now starving. She could really use a good meal and good company. Though perhaps expecting good company from Chef Clarke is asking for too much, but at least he'd be somewhat better to talk to than an empty chair.

But then he says, "I have to run. My family is waiting for me." He gives a quick pat on Mebel's shoulder and says, "I'm glad you're okay, Mebel. I'll see you in class tomorrow."

With that, he turns and walks away, his steps just shy of breaking into a jog, as though he can't bear another second in this medical center with her. To be fair, he probably can't. He's already gone above and beyond his duty to accompany her here, and Mebel should be grateful that he took the time and effort to do that. But right now, watching Chef Clarke leave, Mebel feels the acute pain of loneliness stabbing into her heart. It's worse than the pain of slicing into her own finger. Well, actually, it's less bad than the pain of trying to take the towel off the wound, so there's that, at least.

Mebel makes her way out of the building and looks around her. She has no idea where she is. She sighs. Chef Clarke could've at least dropped her off at the school building on his way home, she thinks petulantly. But, no, she mustn't think that way. She's trained herself over the years to never expect more than what others can give her. With a deep breath, Mebel slips her phone out of her handbag and orders an Uber back to the school. The driver doesn't bother with much chitchat, which is just as well. Mebel can't remember the last time she has felt so forlorn, so spent. Oh, right, that would be the day before, when she found out that she was in the wrong school and had to leave Paris for Cowley.

By the time Mebel arrives back at the school, she is so dejected and glum that she half wonders if she should skip dinner altogether and just go to bed. But her stomach gives a loud growl at this. Just as she pulls open the front door, it swings open, very nearly hitting her in the face. Five people spill out, laughing and chattering, and she recognizes them as students from her class. One of them, a boy she believes is named Adam, spots her and says, "All right, Mebel? How's your finger?"

"Oh!" Mebel says, caught off guard by the fact that he's talking to her. "It's okay. They glue it shut." She holds up her bandaged finger.

"All right, good to know you didn't need stitches," Adam says. "Have a good 'un." He turns his attention back to the others, as though Mebel has immediately ceased to exist. She watches as the group walks down the street, talking good-naturedly. She hears snatches of conversation, enough to know that they're headed into town for dinner.

Silence descends as their voices fade into the night air, and a cold weight settles over Mebel. It's nearly impossible for her to keep her head high, and she walks into the school building drooping like a wilted flower. The dining hall is only a third full of students, and everyone is sitting with someone and caught up in what seems to her like very interesting, very animated conversations. Mebel takes one look at the scene and walks back out into the hallway. She's lost her appetite for dinner. What she needs right now is a hot shower, preferably hot enough to scald every memory of this cursed day away.

But it seems that the day isn't done with torturing her yet. In the shower, Mebel learns that keeping her injury dry is a lot tougher than it seems. For one thing, she can't use both hands to lather her shampoo. For another, water keeps spraying onto her left hand. In the end, Mebel has to shower while holding her whole arm straight up as though she is saluting some demented army general. Back inside her room, Mebel finally finds some comfort. Dressed in her cozy pajamas and fuzzy socks, she flops onto the bed. And only then does she acknowledge her utter exhaustion. She can't remember the last time her body has hurt so much. Every part of her aches. Her feet are begging for a foot rub, her calves feel like they've run a marathon, her back is stiff, and every movement makes it twinge, and her neck refuses to bend at all. And her hands! Her poor, stiff hands! God, she is miserable. She is not cut out to be a cook. What had she been thinking, leaving her life of luxury behind and coming all the way to this awful place?

She picks up her phone to call Sammy so she can cry to

him, but a quick calculation tells her that it's three in the morning in Jakarta. He probably won't be too empathetic if she was to call right now. She can't call her friends either, because of the time zone, yes, but also because she can't bear the humiliation of having to tell them what happened with Henk. There is no one in the world who she can count on right now.

This is it, she thinks. *I have hit rock bottom, and well, the thing with rock bottom is, the only direction you can go after this is up, right?*

Sure, except under the rock is actually molten soil, also known as lava, her ever-so-helpful mind chirps. *So, actually, you can still fall deeper. You'd just be incinerated.*

Thank you, Mebel thinks to herself. *That is exactly what I wanted to hear right now.*

Her mind goes quiet. Mebel sniffs. There, at least she will have peace, if only for a little bit. And with that lonely, depressing thought, Mebel closes her eyes and drifts off into a deep sleep.

Chapter 9

THE FIRST WEEK OF CULINARY SCHOOL ENDS UP BEING the longest and toughest week of Mebel's life. The classes get no better after that first day. The second day is spent making vegetable stock, which requires yet more chopping. Mebel, still traumatized by her accident and reminded of the pain and shock every time she looks down at her bandaged finger, chops the carrots so slowly that she misses the call to pour the vegetables into the pan and has to stay back an extra hour after everyone else is dismissed to finish cooking her stock. The third day is spent learning about nutrition. Chef Clarke drones on and on about basic nutrients and nutritional principles, as well as current applications of such principles. Things only slightly look up when they are asked to do nutritional analyses of recipes, because if there's one thing that calculating discounts and VATs in luxury stores has taught Mebel, it is basic math. But then they move on from calculations into chemistry, and Mebel is once again lost.

The last straw comes at the end of the week, when they are presented with a surprise test. No one else seems surprised, and when at Mebel's affronted expression, Chef Clarke says, "It is in your student handbook, Mebel. Page thirteen, second paragraph. It says: 'Expect a test at the end of each week to review the week's lessons.'"

The most irritating thing about Chef Clarke is his fancy British accent, which makes everything he says sound reasonable even when it's not. Obviously it is extremely unreasonable to expect anyone to read the student handbook. The thing is at least fifty pages long, with font so small that Mebel had to squint every time she tried to read it, until she gave up because the amount of Botox she will need to erase the squint lines is simply not worth the effort.

To make the long story short, Mebel does not do well on the test. In fact, she does so badly that Chef Clarke asks her to stay back after classes end for the day.

Mebel watches the other students file out of the kitchen and feels, ironically, the fleeting sensation of youth once again. Except this time, she doesn't enjoy the emotion because she doesn't feel like a carefree twenty-one-year-old. She feels more like a five-year-old kid who just got caught drawing on the wall. *You are a sixty-three-year-old woman*, she hisses silently at herself. *Chef Clarke is in his fifties. You are his elder and you must demand the respect that you deserve.*

But when she stands before Chef Clarke and sees the disappointment in his face, all of Mebel's indignant spirit leaves her body.

"Mebel," he says, "please, take a seat."

She does so, folding her hands on her lap. Her fingers press down on her knuckles. Is she going to be expelled? Can one be expelled from culinary school?

"I notice you are struggling in the class," Chef Clarke says.

Aiya, he is so direct! Aren't the British supposed to be known for being subtle?

"I think maybe is not really called 'struggling,'" Mebel says.

"Oh? What would you call it then?"

Mebel purses her lips. "I think maybe I call it 'getting used to.'"

"Getting used to," Chef Clarke says dryly.

"Yes. There is a lot of things I have to get used to here, you know."

"Such as?"

"Well, Chef, maybe you don't know this, but back home, all this . . . cooking? Is usually done by helper. Is menial labor, you know. No offense, Chef."

"None taken," Chef Clarke says. "I understand what you are saying, but the fact remains that you are here now. You are not back home in Indonesia, where you leave all of the cooking to your helpers."

"Why you don't use helper here?"

Chef Clarke blinks at her, looking very confused. "I'm not quite following."

"Well, things like chopping vegetable, that's not good use of school hours. We don't come here to learn to chop vegetables, we come here to learn to cook impressive dish. So I think maybe if you hire helper to chop the vegetables, then that get rid of the problem."

Chef Clarke massages his temple with one finger. "No,

Mebel. We won't be hiring helpers to chop things up for you, because we want you to learn knife skills. It's an essential part of being a chef."

"But I'm not here to become chef."

"Yes, you have made that perfectly clear." He leans forward, clasping his hands on the table. "Listen, I think you may be at the wrong place. I understand you want to learn how to cook for your husband. In that case, may I suggest going on YouTube or Instagram or whatever other social media platform and doing a search for hashtag-cooking? I think what you want is online recipes, not culinary school."

Mebel leans back in her chair, feeling as though she's just been punched in the gut. "Am I expelled?" she says finally.

Chef Clarke's face softens. "No. We don't expel students unless there has been a serious breach of conduct. But I am having this talk with you because I think your time could be more productively spent by just watching cooking shows. You don't have what it takes to be a chef, Mebel."

Mebel nods glumly. Anyone can see she doesn't have what it takes to be a chef, even her.

"Think about it?" Chef Clarke says. He doesn't wait for a reply before standing up. "Have a good weekend."

They leave the kitchen, and Mebel trudges back up to her room. For a while, she lies down on her bed and stares up at the ceiling. This is such an unfamiliar feeling. To be asked to reconsider her placement in the school because she's so bad at it? It's truly baffling.

The thing is, Mebel has always been good at everything she's tried her hand at. At school, she passed her classes with minimal effort. She graduated from USC with no honors, but she had perfectly decent grades. Her parents had enrolled her in tennis and golf lessons as a child because they knew that she would one day become a trophy wife, and she rewarded them by being good at both sports, but not so good that it would make any man she was with feel threatened. They didn't bother with things like cooking or sewing, because what self-respecting trophy wife would have to do those? Mebel had gone through sixty-three years of life applying herself steadfastly to the roles she'd been given—the filial Chinese-Indo daughter, then the pleasing Chinese-Indo trophy wife, and finally, a doting Chinese-Indo mother. And now, she finds herself untethered, lost in a body of water that's suddenly decided to go wild.

Chef Clarke is right. There is no place here for someone like her. What is she even doing here? Learning how to cook French food to impress Henk? It sounded like a fun idea back in Jakarta, but now, in Cowley, England? It sounds ridiculous. She is ridiculous. She needs to give this all up and take the next flight home to Jakarta. But first, a shower.

As Mebel gets up from the creaky single bed, she catches her reflection in the mirror. She pauses, staring at herself. She has not, ever since she got married to Henk those forty years ago, gone a single day without looking her best. Every morning, even when she had no plans of going out, Mebel would apply her makeup. Her war paint, as she thinks of it. She's always been so proud of keeping herself looking pristine for Henk. But this week has worn her down to her bones, and now she finds herself gazing at a naked face, and what a sight it is! She looks, for once, like her age. Haggard and forlorn and defeated, the corners of her mouth turned down, her cheeks slack, her eyes dull. She barely even recognizes herself.

"Well, this just won't do," she mutters in Indonesian. If she's going to leave, she's going to do so looking fabulous.

With that, Mebel hops into the shower, then goes back into her room and applies a snail slime sheet mask on her face. When the mask is done, she rubs the remnants of the slime into her skin and revels in how plump it's made her skin feel. She smiles into the mirror, then swipes on a layer of tinted lip balm. There. Just those simple steps have refreshed her beautifully. She sits there for a while, tilting her face to one side, studying her reflection. She recalls how she'd always been the queen bee, both at school and afterward, among their friends at the country club. But maybe she's only ever been the queen bee because she was so good at the things she had to be good at to gain popularity, whether it be schoolwork or golf or tennis. People are attracted to competence. And how difficult can cooking be, really? Mebel's mouth sets into a thin line. She will leave this place tomorrow, but before that, she is going to master just one skill.

Before Mebel can talk herself out of doing this, she walks out of her room still dressed in her pajamas with a fluffy robe on top of them and marches all the way down into the kitchen. Not wanting to draw unwanted attention, she turns just one of the lights on. This late at night, the ground floor is deserted, as everyone has either gone out to party in town or retired to their bedrooms upstairs, and Mebel revels in the peaceful silence. She goes into the pantry and locates the potatoes. She loads up her bowl with as many potatoes as it can hold, then carries them to her workstation. There, she rolls up her sleeves, sharpens her knives, and begins to work.

Peeling is just as boring a task as ever, but this time, Mebel knows to expect the ache, so it doesn't catch her off guard like it did on that first day. Plus, she has righteous indignation fueling her, and there is no emotion quite as powerful as pettiness. She finishes peeling them in no time, then she moves on to the chopping. Her first few attempts come out wonky, but instead of getting frustrated, Mebel takes her phone out and opens up YouTube. Chef Clarke suggested it in a somewhat patronizing way, and now she is going to take his advice to heart and utilize the app, though perhaps not quite in the way he was thinking. He wanted her to use social media to find fun little recipes to cook for Henk. She's going to use it to find videos on how to correctly cube a fucking potato, damn it.

The next thirty minutes are spent hyperfocusing to get the potatoes into uniformly sized cubes. At first, Mebel obsesses over each cube, painstakingly pushing it up against the measuring board to make sure all its sides are the appropriate length. It's a mind-meltingly boring, arduous task, and several times, Mebel is tempted to throw her knife down in the most dramatic fashion and call it a day. But somehow, she keeps going, fueled by an inner flame that she hasn't felt in decades. In fact, she can't quite remember the last time she'd applied herself so wholly to a singular task, and she's surprised to find that part of her is kind of enjoying itself.

It isn't long before she's managing consistent cubes. She goes to a state that's somewhere between conscious and subconscious, a beautiful flow where she is able to watch herself wield the knife, nowhere near expertly, but somewhere close to comfortably, at least. And before she knows it, there is a small mountain of cubes next to her. Mebel steps back and marvels at her work.

She picks up one piece and measures it, then another, and another, and they're all the correct size. Joy flows throughout her body, effervescent, and she does a quick hop and goes, "Woo!"

There is a gasp from the doorway. Mebel's heart stops. She swings round, all of her senses screaming—oh my god, she is definitely going to get kicked out now, for sure. But it isn't Chef Clarke at the door; it's Gemma.

"Sorry," Gemma says, and is about to close the door when Mebel calls out to her.

"Wait!"

Gemma hesitates. Why does she look so guilty? Then again, Mebel probably looks guilty as hell too. For a moment, the two of them stare at each other, each woman trying her hardest to not look like she's up to no good.

Finally, Mebel decides that instead of asking Gemma what she's doing in the kitchen, she should offer up a piece of information as a show of goodwill. So she says, "I'm practicing my knife skills." She holds up a cubed potato.

"Oh!" Gemma's shoulders lower ever so slightly. She looks a little less like a hamster who's just sensed an eagle overhead and more like a hamster who thinks there might be an eagle overhead but isn't too sure about it.

"I don't know if it's allowed, technically," Mebel says with a shrug. She gives Gemma a cunning glance. "And why you are here?"

Gemma grimaces. "Um, I was kind of hoping to get in a bit of practice too."

"I don't remember you have trouble cubing potatoes," Mebel says.

"No, I don't have trouble with that. I just wanted to—uh . . ."

As Gemma's voice trails away, Mebel notices the large bag she's carrying. "What is that?"

Gemma shies away, as though to hide the bag from Mebel, but then she pauses, taking a breath, and says, "Oh god, I feel so stupid, this is the first time I'm doing this, truly, I—"

"As long as not someone's severed head inside, I think you are fine," Mebel says.

Gemma's mouth closes abruptly. Then she laughs out loud. "Thank you for that. No, it isn't someone's severed head, though I feel like it would almost be less mortifying if it was." With a sigh, she unzips the bag and shows Mebel the contents. "It's ingredients to cook with, plus this." She takes out a foldable tripod and camera ring light with an embarrassed smile.

"Ooh. Are you one of them—wait, I hear this from my friend who recently find out her grandson goes to this horrible pornographic website—I think it's called Only Vans? You know, I always wonder why the name, but then I realize it makes sense, because only shady people own vans. So—"

"No, oh my god, Mebel!" Gemma cries. "No, this isn't for OnlyFans." She pauses. "How would this even work with OnlyFans?"

Mebel gives her a cynical sideways glance. "I don't know what you young people are up to these days. Maybe you are about to cook naked in front of the camera. There are all sorts of fetish and I don't judge."

"Oh god. Please stop talking." Gemma looks so genuinely horrified that Mebel feels sorry for the poor kid. "No, I only take videos of my hands. *Not* in a sexual way," she adds when

Mebel is about to say something. "I do cooking videos. They're shot top-down and they only show my hands doing the cooking."

"Oh! Well, like that is okay. Why are you so acting so sus about it?"

Gemma stares at her. "So 'sus'? Mebel, I beg you, please stop trying to use Gen Z slang."

"My granddaughter says it all the time. Is it my fault if I am on fleek?"

"Oh god," Gemma mutters, but Mebel catches the hint of a smile. "Okay, the reason I am acting 'sus' is because I'm pretty sure the school wouldn't be happy about me using their premises to shoot my own personal videos. Same reason why you're being sus about chopping potatoes."

Mebel looks down at her small mountain of cubed potatoes. "You have a point. So you are going to shoot a video now? I watch, okay?"

Gemma chews on her lower lip. "I don't know, I don't do well with an audience."

"Have you ever had audience?"

"No."

"Then how you can know if you do well with an audience or not?"

In the ensuing silence, Gemma's teeth grind audibly. "Okay, I suppose you have a point. You can watch. Quietly."

Mebel makes a zipping motion along her mouth. With another sigh, Gemma heads for her worktable and begins unloading the ingredients onto the kitchen counter.

"What are you making?"

"A Scotch egg, but with a twist."

Mebel has no idea what an untwisted Scotch egg is to begin

with, so she simply smiles and says, "Oh yes, wonderful idea." She watches as Gemma sets up the tripod and carefully positions her phone. When she turns the ring light on, a dramatic spotlight appears, aimed straight down at the ingredients on the countertop. "Oh my," Mebel says appreciatively. Who knew that there's so much that goes on behind the scenes of a simple cooking video?

Cooking has never been a thing that Mebel fully appreciated. For her, food was something to be enjoyed in the consumption of it, not the creation. Food was something that was prepared behind the scenes and appeared at the table every mealtime. She can count on one hand the number of cooking shows she has watched in her lifetime, and she's never once spared a thought for the amount of prep work that has to be done behind the scenes. And she is thoroughly gobsmacked by how involved Gemma's "Scotch egg with a twist" turns out to be.

First, there's the eggs themselves. Gemma boils four of them in water with a splash of vinegar for six minutes exactly before transferring them to an ice bath. Then there's the meat mixture. Gemma chops up chives and parsley and garlic with such ease that Mebel is both surprised and humbled. So this is what proper knife skills look like. The parsley in particular looks like green dust by the time Gemma is through with it. She opens up a bunch of fat sausages and squeezes out the meat into a mixing bowl, then pours the chopped up herbs and garlic into it. Mebel admires the deftness with which Gemma folds the mixture together.

"You are very skilled," Mebel says. "What you are adding to the meat now?"

"English mustard. It adds a bit of a zing to it." Now that

Gemma is actually cooking, she's lost all traces of her earlier anxiety. In fact, after a while, she begins to narrate what she's doing to Mebel. "Traditional Scotch eggs are crusted with breadcrumbs and then fried, but I wanted to do something different, so I'm wrapping mine in puff pastry and then baking it." She presents her puff pastry with pride to Mebel. "I made this earlier today. Have you ever made puff pastry?"

Mebel shakes her head. To her, the sheet of pastry looks like any other pastry dough.

"It's one of the toughest things to master. Layers of dough alternating with butter. You have to make sure the temperature is just right so the butter doesn't melt into the dough, so you've got to work fast. Took me years to get it right."

"Why anyone would bother making puff pastry?" Mebel says. "I've never eat a single puff pastry in my life."

Gemma stares at her. "So, you've never eaten a croissant?"

"What that has to do with puff pastry?"

"Mebel," Gemma groans. "Good grief, why are you at culinary school?"

"Because my husband decide to leave me for our twenty-four-year-old chef," Mebel says dryly.

Gemma is now back to gaping at her. "Wait, seriously?"

"Oh yes. It is a bit of shock."

"Jesus, that's horrible. I'm so sorry, Mebel."

"Yes, she make best five-spice roast pork belly. The skin is so crispy and fragrant."

"I mean, like, it must've been horrible to lose your husband like that?" Gemma says.

"Oh, right. Yes, that too. That is why I'm here, you know.

To learn how to cook and win him back. They say that the way to man's heart is—"

"Through his stomach, yeah I know that one."

"I have always thought the way to man's heart is through his penis, but where has that one got me? So here I am, I try the route of the stomach."

"God, I never want to hear you say the P-word ever again," Gemma mutters.

Mebel waves her off. "Don't be such prude, Gemma. And also, you are not allowed to call me Mebel. I am at least forty years older. Is so disrespectful. You call me Auntie Mebel."

"No can do, Mebs," Gemma says cheerfully. "In here, we're schoolmates. We're equals."

Mebel is torn. Gemma is right, in a way. At the Saint Honoré School of Culinary Arts, both she and Gemma are first-year students. But still, a large part of Mebel can't let go of the fact that she's Gemma's elder and should be treated with the deference she deserves. But then again, she's no longer in Asia, where elders are treated with reverence. As her brain clacks away at this convoluted thought, she watches Gemma roll out the puff pastry. Gemma wraps the soft-boiled egg with a layer of sausage meat, then wraps that up in the puff pastry before sliding it into the oven. It's impossible to take her eyes off Gemma's hands as she works. They move so deftly it's almost like watching a ballet. And it is then that Mebel realizes Gemma is right. Here in the school, they're classmates. Equals. Just because Mebel is older doesn't necessarily mean she knows better. In fact, Gemma can cook circles around her. She needs to accept that youth doesn't mean a lack of wisdom.

"Okay," she says finally.

Gemma glances up from the second egg she's wrapping. "Okay what?"

"Okay, you call me by my first name."

"Cool."

That's it? Mebel wants to say. Here she has come to the choice only after having a mental wrestling showdown with herself, and there's Gemma just calmly cutting out a puff pastry leaf to use as decoration. Mebel sighs. Try as she might, she will never understand these youngsters.

Chapter 10

How curious it is to find how much your whole life experience can change after just one night. In the morning, Mebel wakes up tired but strangely cheerful. She bounces out of bed and smiles at her reflection. She goes through her morning routine while humming under her breath, tightening the knot of her apron with a determined tug. When she arrives at the kitchen, she notes with satisfaction that for once, she is the first to arrive, and she doesn't waste any time before prepping her workstation, wiping everything down and sharpening her knives.

Chef Clarke walks in a few minutes later, as Mebel is sharpening her ten-inch, and his eyebrows raise with obvious surprise when he spots her.

"Good morning, Chef," she says.

"Er, morning, Mebel." He hesitates, then continues. "Did you have a think about our last conversation?"

"I did, and I just—" Mebel stops herself. She's starting to realize how many times she says the word "just," and it sounds silly in her ears. "I want to show you something."

"Oh?" Chef Clarke watches as Mebel strides to the industrial-sized refrigerator and takes out a big metal bowl.

She marches to him and presents the bowl solemnly. She can't quite remember the last time she's felt this proud of herself. Maybe when she was a child, presenting her scrawled childish drawing to her parents? Her heart is thumping somewhere in the vicinity of her throat as Chef Clarke looks dubiously at the contents of the bowl.

"What's this then?" he says at last, raising his eyebrows at her.

"I cubed some potatoes last night," she says.

Still holding her gaze, Chef Clarke reaches into the bowl and picks up a piece of potato. He studies it closely, turning it this way and that. Mebel doesn't dare to draw a single breath, in case doing so somehow makes the potato change proportions.

"It's perfect cube," she says helpfully. "They are all. I measured them."

"How many potatoes did you use?"

"I lose the count. Twenty?"

"I see. We were supposed to julienne them today. To make potato pancakes."

It feels as though the tips of Mebel's ears have caught on fire. "I—ah—"

"Well, never mind. There are always more potatoes." He replaces the cubed potato back in the bowl and turns away.

Mebel is about to say something when the door opens once more, and several of her classmates stream into the kitchen, chatting with one another. They barely spare her a glance. Normally, Mebel would not move out of their way because she is the elder and they're supposed to move out of her way, but then she recalls Gemma's words, and as the youths walk in her direction, Mebel forces a smile and nod and steps out of their way. They don't notice, of course, but it feels to Mebel as though she has jumped over a very strange hurdle. She catches Chef Clarke watching her, and when their eyes meet, he gives her the barest hint of a nod. She walks back to her table with a little smile, feeling far more accomplished this morning than the day of her graduation from USC.

When Gemma arrives, looking tired and out of sorts, Mebel waves at her.

Gemma's entire face lights up. "Mebs, babe!" she calls out.

Heads lift, their classmates watching from the corners of their eyes with bemused expressions as Gemma hurries to Mebel's side, loudly saying, "And how are you today?"

Mebel isn't quite sure how she feels about "Mebs babe." Part of her wants to admonish Gemma, but when she opens her mouth, what comes out is, "I'm fine, thank you, Gemma." Because, in a very strange way, "Mebs babe" feels kind of badass. Someone named Mebel would only wear Chanel tweed, but someone called Mebs babe would rock a leather jacket (but only one from Gucci, because she has standards).

"My video came out fantastic. Thank you for your help," Gemma chirps. She turns to the guy in front of them, who isn't even trying to hide the fact that he's listening in, and says, "Adam, Mebs here is helping me with my cooking videos."

Adam glances at Mebel, and she sees that he's blushing,

probably because the beautiful Gemma is speaking to him. "Uh, cool," he says in a way that makes it clear he's trying very hard to seem cool.

Mebel is saved from having to come up with a socially acceptable answer by Chef Clarke clapping once for their attention. Everyone ceases their chattering and turns to face him.

"We have come to a very fun part of the class," Chef Clarke says.

Ooh! Mebel thinks. She could do with a little bit of fun. Maybe they'll make fresh pasta. That's always been something Mebel fancied she might like to do. She likes the idea of rolling out the dough under her palms and scattering flour over it before cutting it into creative shapes.

Chef Clarke reaches down and lifts up a huge foam box. He drops it onto the kitchen counter with an ominous thump.

Uh-oh, Mebel's brain goes. *That does not look like it contains ingredients to make fresh pasta.*

And indeed it does not. Chef Clarke opens it with a flourish and takes out a wriggling lobster. "Today, we are going to learn how to properly kill and cook lobster, as well as other seafood."

Mebel's hand flies to her mouth.

"Yes, Mebel? Did you have a question?" Chef Clarke says.

Every pair of eyes turns to Mebel. With some effort, Mebel tears her horrified gaze from the lobster, which is now frantically flapping its tail. "Uh . . . no. I love . . . lobster."

Chef Clarke nods. He places the lobster on a chopping block and picks out his knife. "For this, you are going to use your chef's knife. Hold it like so, and here is the most humane way to kill it—"

Mebel shuts her eyes, but she hears the crack of the lobster's shell as Chef Clarke pushes his knife clean through its head. Oh *god,* she thinks. *I'm going to be sick.*

Then, from nowhere, another voice appears in her head. *No you won't,* it says, quite calmly. *You won't be sick because you are here with a clear purpose: to win Henk back. So pick up your chef's knife, damn it, and swing it right into that lobster's head.*

In a daze, Mebel watches as Chef Clarke dismantles the rest of the lobster, and all too soon, it is time for them to go up to the awful foam box and claim a lobster to murder. Twice, Mebel's legs buckle under her and she almost falls over, but somehow, she manages to make it to the chef's table. When she gets there, she finds that she can't bear to look Chef Clarke in the eye, but then she glances down into the box—and that was a horrible mistake to make. It looks like a scene straight out of a nightmare, a box filled with crawling, flapping lobsters, their shells an ugly shade of bruised brown. Mebel can practically hear their mounting anxiety. The poor things probably heard their friend getting knifed outside the box. Chef Clarke is watching her with an expression that can only be described as "dubious amusement" and so, averting her gaze, Mebel reaches down into the box and grabs the nearest lobster. She flinches as her fingers close around its body, almost dropping it, but she manages not to.

"Ah, you picked the biggest one," Chef Clarke says. "Good job."

Mebel looks down in horror, but it is now too late to change her mind. She lifts the monstrous thing out of the box and, holding it as far away from her as possible, staggers back to her workstation, where she drops it onto her chopping board. The lobster, its claws tied up, scrabbles on the board, its tail flapping madly. *Oh god, this is a nightmare.*

"You all right, Mebs?" Gemma says.

Mebel doesn't trust herself to answer without retching, so she just shrugs in reply.

"It's all right," Gemma says. "It's very straightforward, really. Watch me."

And Mebel watches as Gemma expertly dismantles her lobster. "How you are so good at that?"

"I'm a food influencer," Gemma says simply. "Your lobster's getting away."

Mebel pounces on her lobster right before it flaps off the countertop. "Aduh," she moans, "I don't know how I do this. I am more comfortable eating lobster, not cooking it."

"Yes, we know that. Don't think too hard about it."

By now, a couple other students have wandered over, watching Mebel with amused looks on their faces. Mebel vaguely recognizes them as Adam and a brunette girl with striking golden eyes named Bella.

"You can do this, Gran," Adam says.

"Adam!" Bella snaps. "You can't call her that."

Adam shrugs, looking sheepish.

Mebel is torn between having Adam call her by an honorific and that honorific being "Gran." She meets Gemma's eye, and Gemma glares at her meaningfully, which makes Mebel go, "Ah, yes, you can call me Mebel."

"Cool," Adam says with another shrug. "Go on then, Mebel."

"It helps if you wrap a towel around the lobster so you can grip it tight," Bella says.

Mebel does so, and is grateful for the tip because it does help to make this whole business feel less grisly.

"Lay it down on the board," Gemma says, "yes, just like

that. Place your knife here, in the center of the head, there you go. And now chop down."

Mebel shuts her eyes, thinks better of chopping down with her eyes shut, and forces them back open. Then, before she can chicken out, she plunges the tip of her knife. Her knife blade crunches into the lobster head, slicing it in half neatly. The lobster stops moving.

Adam and Bella clap politely.

"Great job, Mebs! C'mere and gimme a hip bump!" Gemma says, sticking her hip up.

Mebel blinks at Gemma, then she lifts the (now very dead) lobster and bumps it to Gemma's hip.

"All right, not the best hip bump, but we'll work on it," Gemma says with a wink.

"Good job, Mebel," Adam says, before he and Bella return to their respective workstations.

Mebel goes back to working on her lobster. Now that she's managed to get past the worst part, something seems to have come over her. Adrenaline rushes through her, and as she gazes down at the lobster, Mebel is overcome by a sensation. She can do anything. She can do everything. She is a glorious warrior. It takes her no time at all to take apart the lobster just as Chef Clarke has shown them, and what surprises Mebel the most is the sense of peace that comes over her as she works. It's something novel, something that comes from putting her hands to work. Something about it eases her mind, allowing the usual cacophony of noises in it to come to a resting place where there is, for once, blessed silence.

After the lobster, they move on to mussels, and again, Mebel doesn't allow herself time to get squeamish. She doesn't let herself think of how disgusting it is to have to scrape away the "beard" of the mussels, and how dangerous it is to shuck oysters, and how much of a scallop has to be thrown away. She hyperfocuses on each task, and her hands move like—well, not like an oiled machine, but like an old machine that has suddenly realized that it has more to do in life than lie still.

At the end of the session, they all arrange their seafood on a large plate and then stand at attention with their hands behind their backs as Chef Clarke comes to their workstations and examines their handiwork. He's satisfied with a few and less so with others, telling them in his clipped British accent that they've "nicked the scallop meat here" or "left a bit of digestive tract there." When he finally arrives at Mebel's table, she squares her shoulders and looks somewhere an inch to the left of Chef Clarke's ear because she can't bear to meet his eye. She braces herself for the inevitable reprimand, and maybe this time, Chef Clarke won't bother with a private talk, maybe he'll just tell her in front of the whole class that she doesn't belong here.

"Ah," he says, and there is a note of pleasant surprise in his voice that makes Mebel's ears prick up. He lifts the lobster head, which has been sliced in half, and studies it closely. "This is quite neatly done."

Quite neatly done, Mebel thinks. *That sounds like a good thing, right?*

He moves on to her scallop. "You've cleaned it well while preserving its shape." He prods at the mussels and the oysters, and then says, "That is sufficient." He moves on to the next table.

As Mebel stares after him in shock, she catches sight of Gemma, who is grinning at her and giving her a thumbs-up. Joy sparkles through Mebel's body like champagne. She grins and nods at Gemma. Adam turns around and mutters, "Yo, good job, Mebs."

"Thank you," Mebel says. *And you know what?* she thinks to the stuffy voice in her head. *I kind of like being called Mebs.*

Maybe.

THE NEXT CLASS, THEY LEARN HOW TO BUTCHER A CHICKEN, and though everything inside Mebel rebels against her picking up the slimy chicken carcass, once again, she manages to bull-doze through it. At the end of the day, Mebel is tired but also strangely energized. Who would've known how empowering culinary school would be? She feels so empowered, in fact, that she decides that tonight she is not going to eat dinner at the school's cafeteria. No, tonight, Mebel Tanadi is going to dress up and go into town for dinner.

Except that, hours later, when Mebel finally arrives at the heart of Cowley, all dressed in Ferragamo, she realizes that there isn't a single restaurant in Cowley that is worthy of her fabulous outfit. The downtown street, very creatively called "Cowley Road," is full of what one might generously call "take-out places" or, if one weren't feeling generous, "dives." Mebel walks past a Chinese take-out place in which she's pretty sure two patrons are having a fist fight, then a culturally confused place that serves both "authentic Japanese ramen" and "authentic pad Thai," then a Tesco, followed by a convenience store, before she loses hope of finding a Michelin-starred restaurant.

Two men spill out of a nearby pub, talking in low voices, and when they spot Mebel, something in their leers makes her pause. She wraps her coat around her tightly.

"Didja see that fancy bint?" one of the men says loudly.

"Heya, luv, where are you headed?" his friend, who sports a large beard, calls out.

Back in Jakarta, Mebel was chauffeured everywhere, from home straight to fancy restaurants, and so running into two spirited strangers who are now talking to her is a newfound experience that she doesn't quite understand, but is nevertheless filling her with both fear and also, bafflingly, excitement. She wonders if this would be an appropriate time to put her keys in between her fingers before throwing her meanest punch, but just as she's about to rummage for her keys in her purse, Beard goes, "Ow!"

He clutches at his eye and bends over, his huge shoulders rounding.

"You all right?" his friend says.

"No, I'm fucking not, something flew into my eye—ah, it hurts like a motherf—"

Mebel steps carefully toward him and taps him daintily on the arm.

"What?" he snaps.

"I have the eye drops," Mebel says, holding out a small bottle.

Beard glares at her with one eye for a moment, then snatches the bottle from her. He raises his head and squirts way more drops than are needed. Then he blinks furiously and releases a long sigh of relief. "Thanks," he mutters, handing the bottle back to Mebel.

"You walk around with eye drops in your purse?" his friend asks, something close to awe in his voice.

"Of course," Mebel says smartly. "Always be well prepare." She puts away the drops, then says, "Maybe you gentlemen can be so kind and direct me to nicest restaurant in town?"

The men blink slowly at her. Their breath fogs up in the cold night air and smells like stale alcohol. It is beginning to dawn on Mebel that perhaps these two might not be the best food connoisseurs around, and that maybe she wouldn't trust their judgment when it comes to fine dining. Or anything else in life, for that matter.

"'Ow about the Goat and Eagle?" Bearded Man says.

Mebel wrinkles her nose. "So, they serve goat meat? I like goat meat. Not sure about eagle, but I will give it a try. I am a bit surprise that they serve the eagle meat here."

"No, they don't serve actual eagle meat, good grief. The Goat and Eagle is a pub down the road," Mr. Beard says. "I go there when I'm feeling posh. They serve a good kidney pie."

"I like the King's Arms, m'self," his friend says. Mebel mentally calls him Ears, on account of the way his stick out. "Get yourself a nice plate of bangers and mash, and wash it all down with a pint of cider."

"That sound good," Mebel says.

"They do a mean spotted dick at the King's Arms every Thursday."

Mebel frowns. "I don't know if I like spotted dick, is sounding quite unhygienic."

Ears shrugs. "Don't knock it until you've tried it. Tell you what, why don't you come with us, and—"

Whatever else he was about to suggest is interrupted by a group of youths coming out of the pub. They're laughing and carousing with one another, not looking where they're going, and one of them crashes into Mr. Beard, who swings around and grabs the offending person by the collar of his shirt. The easygoing laughter dies a quick death.

"Watch where you're going, mate," Beard says.

Mebel reflects on how funny it is that in every part of the world, the words "mate" and "buddy" and "pal" are often used in situations where it's clear that neither party thinks of the other as a friend. She surmises, not unwisely, that now would be an appropriate time for her to make her exit, because there is nothing worse than a guest who doesn't know when to leave. But as she's inching away, the guy whose shirt collar is currently being squeezed in the massive hands of Mr. Beard squeaks, "Mebel?"

"Oh!" Mebel finally looks, really looks, at him. It's a boy she recognizes as Bruce from her class. And behind him are Gemma, Bella, and Adam. "Oh, hello," she says.

"Mebel!" Gemma says. "How nice to see you here!"

"Um, Mebel?" Bruce says. "Could you ask your friend to let go of me?"

Mebel looks at Beard. "Can you stop choking my classmate?"

Beard looks back and forth from Mebel to Bruce. "This little shrimp is your classmate? What class are you taking?"

"I am student at the Saint Honoré School of Culinary Arts," Mebel says with an amount of pride that surprises even her.

"Sounds posh," Beard says.

"Does, don't it?" Ears says. "You learning them posh French dishes then?"

Mebel thinks for a second. "Well, so far I have learn how to cube a potato and how to butcher shellfish, like lobster and oyster," Mebel says primly. "Not yet posh French dishes, but I'm sure they come soon. And when they do, then maybe you two can come and try them. You can be my trial customer, because I am learning how to make nice French food to win my husband back, you know."

"Sounds good," Beard says, and lets go of Bruce.

Bruce stumbles back, holding his collar, looking back and forth between Mebel and Beard with wide eyes.

"I don't like the look of that one," Beard says to Mebel, gesturing at Bruce.

"Hey," Bruce whines.

"I know what you mean," Mebel says, "but actually he is not so bad."

"Here's my number," Beard says, handing Mebel a business card. "You let me know when you cook them soupe à l'oignon." The French words roll out of his mouth with shocking grace and smoothness. "That's my favorite, that is. See you later then."

"Goodbye," Mebel says. She tucks the business card safely into her purse, then turns to Bruce and the others, who, with the exception of Gemma, are staring at her with wide, somewhat scared eyes.

"How do you know those guys?" Gemma says. "They looked like really . . . well, very interesting."

"Townies," Bruce says.

"Townies?" Mebel says. "What is that mean?"

"In Oxford, the population is divided into two groups," Bruce explains. "The students and the townsfolk, also known as 'townies.' Townies are generally a tough crowd."

"We are not townies?" Mebel says.

Bruce groans. "No, Mebel, we're students. We're literally enrolled in a school."

"Yes, but we are not in Oxford University student, are we?"

Mebel says. "The requirement to get into Saint Honoré School of Culinary Arts very different from the ones to get into Oxford University."

"Marginally," Bruce says with confidence. "I bet it's not that different, honestly."

"All they ask from me was name and credit card details," Mebel says flatly.

"All right, maybe the requirements are slightly different. I'm just saying, we are definitely not townies."

Mebel gives a vague shrug. It's not that she doesn't see the difference between the students and the "townies," but this is the exact sort of thing that would've bothered Henk. He had always been about labels. He would've also insisted that he's a student and not a townie, and Mebel, as the dutiful trophy wife, would've followed suit accordingly. But now that Henk isn't here, Mebel is realizing that maybe she doesn't actually give a damn about such things. So what if some people see her as a student or a townie? She is a student and she does live in this town; therefore, she is both.

"Bruce has had too much to drink," Bella mutters to Mebel. "He gets like this when he's drunk. Lecturing everyone, telling us that he knows way more than we do."

"Sound like fun," Mebel says. She is beginning to think that perhaps she should've let Beard and Ears give him a good beating, after all.

"Anyway, that was so cool, what you did back there," Gemma says, and her admiration sends a fierce wave of pride coursing through Mebel. When was the last time someone had been proud of her? Or rather, not proud of her but of something she did. Because plenty of people have been proud of who Mebel is;

Henk used to be proud of how beautiful and polished she was, her parents used to be proud of how well behaved she was, and her friends were proud of being friends with an affluent person like her. But Mebel can't, for the life of her, think of an instance when someone has been proud of something she's done.

"Let us take you out to dinner tomorrow night to thank you for tonight, Mebel," Gemma says.

"What?" Bruce whines. "But tomorrow we're going to that posh new place in town. The French one that just opened, remember? My dad booked us a table there."

"I'm sure we can fit one more in," Bella says.

Mebel is about to tell them it's okay when it hits her that a fancy new French restaurant is exactly what she needs to nourish her soul. It has been two weeks since she arrived in Cowley, England, and she is in dire need of a fine dining experience; otherwise, she is wont to go berserk. So she stands there smiling her best *I will make a fantastic dinner guest* smile.

"She did save your life," Adam points out.

"Oh, fine." Bruce looks Mebel up and down. "Dress nicely, Mebs."

"Bruce, she is in head-to-toe Ferragamo," Gemma whispers. She winks at Mebel.

Bruce has the decency to look abashed at this. "All right, well, tomorrow evening then."

"See you in class tomorrow," Mebel says, and traipses away with a huge grin on her face.

Chapter 11

IT IS TO MEBEL'S UTTER SURPRISE AND DELIGHT THAT THE following evening, the youths, as she refers to them in her head, take her not to Cowley Road but to the actual city of Oxford. How funny, Mebel thinks as she walks down High Street, that she's been in Oxfordshire for two weeks, but it is only now that she's left Cowley and come into Oxford proper. And despite Cowley's vicinity to Oxford, it is like entering a different universe altogether.

While Cowley is full of squat, humble houses that look like they were built in haste in the seventies, Oxford itself is a city straight out of a fairy tale. The university, made up of several different colleges, looks like a collection of little castles, each one with its own distinct architecture. Mebel drinks in the gorgeous sights around her hungrily, she's been so starved of beauty down in Cowley. There's All Souls College, which has the most intricate wrought iron gates she has ever seen, painted in gold. There's the Radcliffe Camera, a round building that is part of the Bodleian Library and built in a Baroque style. As they walk past the Sheldonian Theatre, Mebel can hear the beautiful sound of orchestral music spilling from the building. Everywhere Mebel turns, Oxford is ready to remind her that it is a city of culture, of art and philosophy and music and brilliance. How is it possible that this place is only a ten-minute car ride from where Mebel has been staying this whole time?

"You all right, Mebs?" Gemma says.

Mebel nods, still speechless. They're now walking past a small bridge that arches between two buildings. Though it is small, it's somehow the most beautiful bridge that Mebel has ever seen.

"That's the Bridge of Sighs," Gemma says, following Mebel's gaze. "Lovely, isn't it?"

"Why is called the Bridge of Sighs?"

"Not sure," Gemma says, "but I like it. I like to think it's because Oxford students are probably so stressed that they sigh all the time."

Mebel smiles, her mind going back to her college days at USC. She had been under a lot of pressure back then with her studies, but at the same time, it had been pleasant in its own way. A strong purpose in mind, goals with clear guidelines—study hard, get decent grades, and get your degree. And, beyond that, the long-term goal of any self-respecting CHIP—get a good husband with a stable paycheck. Mebel sighs. Things had been so straightforward back then.

"Mebs," Bruce says, catching up with her. "When we get to Le Provençal, maybe you might want to stay behind us."

Gemma glares at him. "And why would she need to do that?"

Bruce ignores Gemma, keeping his eyes on Mebel. "It's just

that they might wonder if you're actually with us because—you know." He gestures to himself, then to Mebel.

"Because I am so better dressed than you?" Mebel says innocently.

Bella and Adam, walking a step behind them, giggle. Bruce rolls his eyes.

"I hope I am not rude," Mebel continues, "but you pair that newsboy cap with that tweed jacket, is somewhat . . . old-fashioned?"

Red splotches bloom on Bruce's cheeks while the others hide their laughter behind their hands. "It's English fashion," Bruce cries. "You can't talk, you're wearing—" He gestures wildly at Mebel.

Mebel looks down at her outfit. For tonight's exciting dinner, she has chosen to wear a black embroidered wool Chanel dress with gold detailing. She has paired it with a Macrocannage cropped jacket from Dior and finished the look with a pair of the iconic J'Adior slingback pumps in transparent, embroidered mesh. Now she is beginning to wonder if the shoes are a touch over the top.

"Bruce," Gemma says to Bruce, "what are you talking about? Mebs looks like a total baddie."

"Yeah," Adam says. He waves his hands over Mebel. "I love your look, Mebs. I would describe it as elegant, with a hint of hussy."

Mebel can't decide whether to be horrified or delighted by Adam's description, but since it makes Bruce look like he is questioning his existence, she decides she likes it.

Le Provençal is the newest French restaurant on Saint Giles'. On the outside, it is understated, its facade clean and simple, the words "Le Provençal" hanging on a swinging sign above the door in a straightforward black font. But its doors are open, patrons crowded outside, chatting with one another while waiting and hoping for a table. Mebel scans the crowd; there are at least thirty people out here, all of them dressed in tasteful dinner attire. Despite herself, she is impressed by Bruce for being able to secure a reservation here.

"Come on," Bruce says to the group. "I'll let the hostess know we're all here." He jogs up the stone steps into the restaurant, and the rest of them follow.

Mebel catches a few stares as she slips through the crowd and hugs her jacket tightly around herself, feeling self-conscious. It's an older crowd than undergrads, thank god, but they are still massively younger than her, and she is really beginning to question the wisdom of her shoes. They are so coquettish, clearly meant for a woman below thirty, maybe forty at a push.

"Come on, Mebs!" Gemma calls out, and Mebel hurries toward her, feeling grateful that Gemma has thought to wait for her.

Inside, the restaurant is gorgeous. The walls are painted a soft dusty blue and are lined with wainscotting, with black-and-white pictures of iconic French stars hung here and there. The lighting is warm and comfortable, and soft piano music plays in the background. Everyone in here, from the guests to the servers, looks like they have just stepped out of a movie set. Mebel spots black Prada dresses and red-soled Louboutins. The men are wearing Pateks and the women are adorned with Franck Muller. *Well, well,* she thinks. *Toto, we are not in Cowley anymore.*

She turns around to see that Bruce is in an animated

conversation at the reception desk, with Bella and Adam looking confused and worried next to him. Sharing a look with Gemma, Mebel goes up to Bruce.

"What's wrong?" she says.

Bruce holds up a hand in front of Mebel's face and continues berating the hostess. "—last Tuesday. I spoke to—well, my assistant spoke to—well, I don't know who exactly she spoke to, but there's got to be a reservation, it's under Bruce MacLeod."

The hostess, a red-haired woman who looks somewhere in her late twenties, gives Bruce an apologetic half smile and says, "I'm really sorry, Mr. MacLeod, but I don't see a reservation under that name here."

"But that's impossible. Look, I'm calling my assistant right now, and she'll sort this out."

"All right." She waits with hands folded patiently, and when Mebel catches her eye, she gives Mebel a tight-lipped smile and says, "Yes, madam, do you have a reservation with us tonight? It's reservation only, I'm afraid. We are fully booked."

"I'm with him," Mebel says.

"Oh, right. Of course." If the hostess thinks it strange that Mebel is with this group of youths, she doesn't show it. She merely goes back to watching Bruce with her long-suffering smile.

"Ceci," Bruce says, "didn't you say you made the booking at Le Provençal? They can't locate my—what? Ceci, what the fuck? Well, why didn't you tell me? Ceci—" There is a pause. Bruce glances at them with a furtive gaze and then lowers the phone with an expression that clearly says: *Shit, now what do I say to preserve the last of my dignity?* Clearing his throat, he turns to the hostess and says, "Ah, it turns out there was a miscommunication and my sister—my assistant—didn't actually make the booking?"

"On a scale of one to ten, how surprised are you to find out that his 'assistant' is his little sister?" Gemma whispers to Mebel.

Mebel laughs. "Is very enterprising of his little sister." She taps Bruce on the shoulder. "We shall go somewhere else?"

"No," Bruce snaps. "I will get us a table here."

"I am telling you, sir, there is no table here tonight," the hostess says. She is no longer wearing the put-upon smile. Now she's full-on frowning.

"Come on, Brucey," Bella says. "Let's just go somewhere else."

Bruce looks like he's torn between throwing a hissy fit and throwing a tantrum. "No, I—"

Mebel sighs, mentally tuning Bruce out. His behavior is nothing new to her. As a member of numerous private clubs—including a country club, a yacht club, and a business club—Mebel has seen more than her fair share of privileged grown men losing their shit because something didn't go their way. Henk has been guilty of many such an occasion himself, and the more these occasions occur, the faster Mebel has had to learn to shut down her senses and spare herself the mortification of watching these meltdowns. How tiresome to come all the way to Oxford, England, only to find that the problem is a universal one.

"Well," she says to the group in general, ignoring Bruce's tirade, "I think I get going now." If there's one thing Mebel is good at doing, it's making a timely exit. She turns to leave, and promptly bumps into a solid chest. "Whoops, excuse me."

"That's quite all right," a man's rich, velvety voice says. It is a voice that Mebel recognizes at once.

"Alain!" His name is out of her mouth before she even fully registers his presence. Delight courses through her body at the familiar sight of him, and before thinking twice, Mebel envelops him in a tight hug.

"Mebel," Alain says, kissing both her cheeks.

"How come you are here?" she cries.

"Well, it is customary when one opens a restaurant to be present on the opening weekend," Alain says, his eyes dancing with amusement as he gazes down at her.

Is Mebel imagining it, or is his gaze moving back and forth from her eyes to her lips? "This is your restaurant?"

"Oui. What do you think?" Alain says, turning his body slightly and letting Mebel take in the surroundings.

She gives him an appreciative nod. "Very nice. I like the style. Is classic. Without time." Her mind goes: *Are we talking about the restaurant or about the man?* Blushing, Mebel shushes her traitorous thoughts.

"Ah, wait until you try the food," Alain says.

Bruce, whose presence Mebel has blissfully forgotten for the last few minutes, pops his head over Mebel's shoulder and says, "She won't be trying the food. There was a mess-up with our reservation, and they haven't got a table for us."

Alain frowns. To his credit, he only pauses for a beat as he takes in Mebel's unlikely dinner friends. "Your dinner companions?" he says to her, gesturing at the motley group. Mebel nods, and Alain says, "Give me a moment." He walks to the hostess and speaks to her in rapid French. Though Mebel doesn't speak French, she has a rough idea of what he must be saying to the hostess, and the knowledge of it fills her with pleasure. And when the hostess says, "Of course, right away, sir," and turns to Mebel and says, "Follow me please, madame, your table is waiting," Mebel almost squeals with excitement.

Had Mebel been in her twenties, or even her thirties, she might have turned to Bruce and made some snide remark about him telling her to wait outside earlier this evening. But, no, Mebel is a grown woman, and she won't stoop to such pettiness. She suffices with giving him a smug smile before gesturing for the rest of the group to follow her.

The restaurant is much bigger than the outside led her to think and reminds her of a classic French ballroom, with its crystal chandelier and gilded paneling. They are seated in a corner of the room next to a large picture window overlooking Saint Giles'. As soon as Mebel sits, a server comes over and hands them each a leather-bound menu. Mebel takes out her reading glasses and studies her menu closely for a few minutes. When she glances up, she finds everyone else staring at her over their menus.

"Yes?" she says. "Why you are all staring? I have something on my face?"

"Mebs," Gemma says carefully, putting her hand on Mebel's arm. "Please tell me you did not just casually reveal that you've got an inside line to *the* Alain Moreau?"

"What is this inside line?" Mebel says.

"Like you've got a hookup with him," Bella says.

Mebel looks blankly at her.

"She means that you're tight with him," Adam says helpfully. "You know, like the two of you are . . . buddies? Or maybe lovers?"

Mebel's eyebrows disappear into her hairline. "Lovers?" she cries. "Pah, such rubbish! No, of course not. I am married woman! Alain and I are friends." Though as she says the word "friends," Mebel realizes that she hasn't ever had male friends. Oh, she has plenty of connections who happen to be men—people she knows from the country club, her friends' husbands, Henk's business partners, and so on. But none that she could call an actual friend. In a circle as traditional as Chinese-Indo society, that would be highly inappropriate.

"Is he single?" Gemma says.

"How I know? Or care," Mebel adds, though funnily enough, she can feel her cheeks warming up even as she says it. *Stop that, you hussy,* she tells herself.

"Girl," Gemma cries. "He is hot as sin and he's wealthy? Why wouldn't you be interested?"

"I am married," Mebel says simply.

Gemma rolls her eyes. "Your husband doesn't sound like all that."

"Rude," Adam says.

Gemma shrugs. "I'm just saying!"

Just as well, their server comes back with a bottle of chilled Chardonnay. He pours a splash into Mebel's glass and presents it to her.

"I think maybe has mistake. We did not order this," Mebel says.

"Monsieur Moreau has requested the best bottle we have for your table, madame," the server says. "Is it to your liking?"

Somewhat dazzled, Mebel raises the glass to her lips, feeling the weight of her classmates' stares on her. The wine is refreshing and crisp, the kind of thing Henk would have easily paid upward of five hundred dollars for. "Is very good," she manages to the server.

"Very well," he says, and pours them all a generous portion. "Monsieur Moreau has also requested that the chef prepare a special meal for you and your guests tonight. It will be a four-course meal, and of course, if there is anything you'd like to add from the menu, it would be our pleasure to serve."

"Oh!" Mebel looks down at the menu, flustered, then says, "Four course is a lot. I don't think I can eat more than that, so I won't order anything else." She hands the menu to the server, and the others follow suit. Bruce looks like he's torn between appreciation and having a conniption fit, and Mebel would be lying if she said she wasn't enjoying his annoyance.

When the server leaves, Gemma leans forward and says in a low voice, "Okay, Mebs, it's official: this Alain dude has the hots for you."

Mebel laughs, shaking her head, but Bella leans forward and says, "Oh yeah, totally. He's trying so hard to impress you."

Bruce rolls his eyes. Mebel takes another sip of wine. It really is very good wine. "Is he . . . what you kids might call 'flexing'?"

Gemma, Bella, and Adam burst out laughing. "Yes, Mebs," Adam says. "He is totally flexing."

"Showing his rizz," Bella adds.

Mebel's eyebrows knot together. "Why would he show me his risoles?"

"What?" Bella says. "No, Mebs, 'rizz' is short for charisma."

"Ah." Mebel takes another sip of wine to keep from having to explain that her treacherous mind had jumped to "risoles," which is a phallic-shaped Indonesian dish, the thought of which had both excited and scandalized her for a moment.

All thoughts of risoles are wiped away from Mebel's mind

as the meal begins. They open with a starter of truffled Comté gougères—choux pastries filled with deeply rich Comté cheese custard flavored with white truffle oil. The cheese puffs are so delicious that Mebel's eyes flutter closed as she bites into one.

"Are you liking the amuse-bouche?" Alain says.

Mebel's eyes fly open and she hurriedly swallows, flustered at having been caught with what is probably an orgasmic expression on her face. Dabbing at the corners of her lips, Mebel nods. "Is delicious."

"We bought the truffle oil from a farm in the Cotswolds, only about a one-hour drive from Oxford," Alain says. "Have you ever been?"

Mebel, a true city dweller, never bothered to venture outside London when she did visit England. She's heard of the Cotswolds, of course, but never even considered going there. Painfully aware of Adam, Bruce, and Bella's eyes on her, she shakes her head.

"Oh, Mebs," Gemma says, "you've never been to the Cotswolds?"

Mebel shrugs. "England has so many places to go to, I go to Cotswolds for what?"

"True," Adam says, popping a puff into his mouth. "The Cotswolds are overrated."

"Adam!" Gemma says with mock outrage. "They are gorgeous, Mebs. They're like little fairy-tale villages. I live there, actually. You have to go." She turns to Alain. "You can take her next time you go."

"Aiya, no, he has better things to do," Mebel mutters, shooting Alain an apologetic look while at the same time glaring at Gemma.

Alain laughs. "Better things to do than showing a beautiful woman around a beautiful town? I think not."

The straightforwardness of Alain's words makes Mebel almost choke on her food. She quickly takes a gulp of wine to keep herself from coughing, and when she looks up, Alain has excused himself from the table and the next course is being served.

My goodness, her mind warbles. *These Western men are—are incorrigible!*

Unfortunately, as her mind spits out the word *incorrigible*, another part of her mind whispers: *Exciting!*

She barely tastes the smoked mackerel dish, though judging from the reactions of her friends, it seems to be life-changingly good.

"It's the cream of cauliflower for me," Bella says. "It's like they took the soul of cauliflower and concentrated it and crushed it and—god, how is cauliflower this good?"

"It's just roasted pureed cauli," Bruce says with a shrug. "Nothing to it. I bet I could re-create it."

This, at least, snaps Mebel back to the present moment. Nothing quite like a pompous comment from Bruce to snatch one's attention. Mebel takes a smidgen of the pureed cauliflower, and it is indeed life-changingly good, precisely because she's never once given a second thought to cauliflower. As far as vegetables go, it's one of the most unassuming, neither slutty like artichokes nor fashionable like the broccolini. But to take such a humble vegetable and turn it into what can only be described as something this sensual? My god. Mebel's loins are shivering with excitement, and Mebel doesn't even know what loins are and has been unconvinced, up until now, that she is in possession of any.

As the meal goes on, Mebel is surprised to find that she's actually enjoying the company of these youths. Even though they are a third of her age, they possess an unexpected amount of wisdom and self-assurance that Mebel definitely did not have at their age. Hell, she's not sure she even has it now. Part of her is jealous of their confidence. Mebel has only ever been confident of one thing: that she was raised to be a trophy wife and therefore things like her interests and her sense of humor won't be defined until she finds her husband, who will shape them for her. But here, Gemma and Bella chat with as much passion as the boys do, their faces lit up and animated, full of passion as they touch on everything from politics to family life. *How refreshing*, Mebel thinks.

"Mebs, what about you?" Bella says.

Mebel blinks. "What about me?"

"Well, while you've been sitting there dissociating," Adam says, "we've been talking about why we're here. I'm here because I've wanted to be a chef ever since I watched *Ratatouille*, and Bella wants to be a chef—"

"Since I won my county's baking competition at age nine," Bella says with a confident grin. Mebel winks at her. She likes Bella. Bella's smile widens before she turns to Bruce. "And Bruce here wants to be a chef because he didn't make it into uni."

Bruce, wineglass at his lips, sputters. "That is not true! I'm here because I want to learn how to cook."

They all give him incredulous looks.

"What?" Bruce says.

"The number of times you've called cooking 'menial labor' . . ." Adam muses.

"I've heard you calling chefs 'the help,'" Bella says.

Bruce looks like he's about to say something he'll end up regretting. Had Mebel been in her twenties, she would've gotten on the anti-Bruce ride, but as she watches Bruce's face turning red in the dim lighting of Le Provençal, all she sees is an insecure, scared kid. She sees Sammy at Bruce's age, his cheeks still retaining much of the buccal fat of youth that makes him look like a little boy. She recalls the terrifying sensation of free-falling that comes with graduating high school and not having a clear direction of where to go next. In a way, Mebel had been lucky precisely because she'd been prescribed such a clear goal that she'd only been too happy to comply with. Without one, she isn't sure how she would've turned out. And now, here is this young person flailing in an ocean, probably filled with self-doubt and wondering where the hell to go from here.

"Why you like cooking, Bruce?" Mebel says.

For a moment, it looks as though Bruce is about to argue or come up with some other response to save face. Mebel keeps her face earnest, hoping she is channeling motherly concern and zero traces of judgment. She sees the fight leak out of him. He sags a little, then says, "I don't know. I didn't do well enough on my A levels to get into any decent uni, and I didn't want to go to a technical school, so . . ." He shrugs. "I know it's not a great reason to go."

"Well, is better than my reason," Mebel says. "Mine is to win back my husband from our chef."

"What?" they all say in unison.

"Okay, there is so much to unpack here?" Adam says. "You need to tell us from the beginning."

Even Bruce looks like he's listening intently, his expression a cross between concern and curiosity. And so Mebel does tell them, going as far back as when they first hired Wendy. Mebel had been the one to find Wendy, and had been so proud of her decision to hire her. Wendy had gone to culinary school in Thailand and was adept at cooking everything from Asian food to Middle Eastern kabobs to lasagnas, and Mebel had been so happy with Wendy's dishes, had thought that hiring Wendy was yet more proof that she, Mebel, was the best wife that any man could hope for. "I thought maybe because I cannot cook, so okay, I hire someone who can," Mebel says, running the tip of her index finger along the stem of her wineglass. "But then turn out she can do more than cook."

"Shit, Mebel," Gemma says after a long pause. "That sucks."

"Yes, it does," Mebel says.

"You are out of this man's league," Adam says.

"How you know? You haven't see him yet," Mebel says.

"I don't need to," Adam says. "I've seen you. Have you seen you?"

"You are a snack," Bella says, nodding.

Mebel laughs. When she meets Bruce's eye, her laughter dies a little. Bruce is looking at her like he's slightly shell-shocked, like his understanding of her has shifted in some imperceptible way. "Your husband cheated on you?" he says finally.

Mebel picks at invisible lint on her dress. "Yes."

"And you're here to learn how to cook so you can win him back."

"Yes."

There is a pregnant pause, then Bruce says, "Well, that's rather pathetic, isn't it?"

"Bruce!" Bella snaps.

"What the fuck is your problem?" Adam says.

Mebel clears her throat, which, to her surprise, is somewhat thick with tears. "Yes, I think is quite pathetic if you look at it in certain way. I like to think of as me fighting for my happiness."

Bruce shrugs. "I dunno, I just think it's pathetic, is all. He doesn't want you."

"All right, that's enough," Gemma says. "Bruce, shut the fuck up. Mebel, you and I are going to the ladies."

"I'll go with you," Bella says.

As they stand, Adam hisses to Bella, "You're leaving me alone with him?"

"You can handle it," Bella says, then she and Gemma tuck their arms into Mebel's and lead her to the restroom.

Mebel, half-dazed by the wine, is only too happy to follow. She can't remember the last time she's had such a good evening. Even with the heaviness of the topics and Bruce's judgment, it's refreshing to be out with these people and not talk about the things she usually talks about with her friends back home. She tries to remember the usual topics of conversation she'd have with her friends. Ah yes, the subject of kids used to take up a huge chunk of their conversations, and when the kids grew up and started their own families, it turned to the subject of grandkids. Then there's the topic of where to go on vacation. Most Chinese-Indos travel at least twice a year—once at Christmas and once during Ramadan. Even though most Chinese-Indos are not Muslim, most businesses in Jakarta shut down during Ramadan, which makes it a good time for them to travel overseas. Even then, the topic of travel is often dictated by "Well, Henk would really like to go to Turkey this year" or "Henk has been wanting to go to Guangzhou" and the other wives are the same. And because Henk's choices have always been wonderful—who wouldn't want to go to Turkey?—Mebel has never felt the need to voice her own opinions.

Inside the bathroom, Gemma and Bella study their reflections and dab at their faces with tissue. Gemma glances over and says, "I hope you don't take what Bruce said to heart."

Mebel shrugs. "Aiya, my dear, you don't worry about that. If I take everything anyone say to heart, I won't be here."

Bella's mouth quirks up into a half smile. "Are you really here because you want to win your husband back?"

Mebel nods.

"I think that's kind of sweet, don't you?" Bella says, taking out lipstick from her purse.

"I do too," Gemma says. "But if you don't mind me asking, why do you want to win him back? You're fabulous all on your own."

At this, Mebel has no answer. Well, that's not quite accurate. She has too many answers. Because they've been married for forty years and that's something worth saving. Because what in the world is she going to do without Henk? Because she's spent her entire life being raised to become a trophy wife, and what is a trophy wife without a husband? Because of a dozen other equally compelling reasons. But somehow, none of them seems to suffice at this moment.

Bella finishes swiping her lipstick on, then offers it to Mebel. "I call this one siren red," she says. "I think it'll suit you."

Mebel dabs it on and stares at her reflection. "Siren red" is an appropriate name for it. She looks brazen, dangerous, a wild creature. Henk would be very scandalized by it. Mebel decides she kind of likes it. Maybe it's because of all that wine she's been drinking tonight. Whatever it is, Mebel finds herself wearing a coquettish smile as she and the two girls leave the restroom. God, just one month ago, if someone had used the word "coquettish" when referring to Mebel, she would've just perished. And look at her now.

As the kids would say, she does not hate it.

Chapter 12

THE REST OF THE MEAL IS JUST AS DECADENT AS THE starter, and by the end of it, Mebel is so stuffed that she can barely breathe. Gemma, Bella, Bruce, and Adam apparently feel the same way, as they all lean back in their chairs with glazed expressions, rubbing their stomachs. The server had switched to a red wine with the main course, and Mebel is not only full but quite tipsy as well. She smiles with quiet pleasure when Alain shows up with a small plate of chocolates.

"Did you all enjoy the meal?"

Though he says, "you all," his eyes are locked on Mebel.

"Alain," she says, "that was beautiful meal."

"It's going to cost us a fortune," Bruce hisses under his breath.

"Please don't worry about that," Alain says. "It's on the house."

"Oh, Alain, no," Mebel says, but she's flushing with pleasure at everything, the delicious food, the fun and varied company, and the way Alain is smiling at her. She already knows this is a battle she will lose, and lose quite happily too.

Everyone thanks Alain for the evening, and as they are walking out, Alain calls out to her. Gemma ushers the others out of the restaurant, throwing Mebel a wink over her shoulder as she does so.

Alain leads Mebel to one side of the foyer, where it's slightly quieter, and somehow, though there are people around them, Mebel feels the rest of the world melting away into the background. She looks up at Alain and her cheeks grow warm. She had boyfriends prior to Henk, of course. Well, a boyfriend, anyway, and they only went as far as chaste kisses lasting no longer than two seconds, so she's not sure if kids nowadays would even call him a boyfriend. Anyway, doesn't matter. The point is . . .

Goodness, but it's hard to get to the point when a handsome Frenchman is gazing at you like that. It's a wonder how French women get anything done, really.

With some effort, Mebel manages to say, "Well, thank you for wonderful evening."

"It's a shame we weren't able to converse much," Alain says.

"You have been busy with the opening of your restaurant. Which is gone so well, I see."

"I would like to converse with you in a more, ah, intimate setting."

The warmth from Mebel's cheeks travels down to places that she is sure respectable sixty-three-year-old women rarely think about. Her traitorous mind coughs up several "intimate settings," each one more inappropriate than the last. Giving herself a mental shake, Mebel beats away the urge to grin like a complete loon and instead smiles demurely. "Okay, can. I think it will be nice."

"Weekends are a madhouse for me because of the restaurant," Alain says. "How about next Wednesday?"

"I can do that," Mebel says, losing herself once again in those striking golden eyes of his and the way they stand out against the tanned brown of his skin. How is it fair that men age so much better than women do? It's an outrage, honestly. Also, is she talking coquettishly? She doesn't even know what talking coquettishly would sound like, exactly, except that she feels coquettish. *What does that even mean?* her mind says. *I don't know,* Mebel replies, *but I feel very coquettish right now.*

"Excellent," Alain says. "You are staying at the school, yes? I shall pick you up at eight o'clock."

Eight o'clock? Mebel wants to squawk. *What are we, in our early twenties?* Back in Jakarta, Mebel and Henk have dinner at six p.m., whether it's in the house or at a restaurant. By nine p.m., they are both in bed quietly reading—or rather, watching endless viral videos that have been forwarded to them via their numerous WhatsApp contacts. Being picked up at eight means they probably won't even start eating until nine. Unacceptable!

But when Mebel opens her mouth to suggest an earlier time, what comes out of her traitorous mouth is, "Perfect. I see you then."

My word, Mebel thinks. *Who is this person who goes out at eight at night? I have eight a.m. classes, and this face does not happen by accident. I need time to get ready!* But it's too late. Alain walks her out the door with a smile and waves to her friends, who are impatiently waiting for her on the sidewalk.

"Mebs!" Gemma says, looping her arm around Mebel's. "Did he ask you out on a date? Tell me you said yes."

"Can we go yet?" Bruce says. "I'm freezing."

"Our Uber is one minute away," Adam says. He turns to Mebel. "So? Did he ask you out?"

Mebel nods, and Gemma and Bella jump up and whoop before hugging her. She blinks, startled by their effusive joy. Back home, her friends are much more sedate. Shows of over-the-top emotions, whether good or bad, are frowned upon. Mebel even went to a funeral where the weeping widow was gently admonished by her relatives for crying too hard. Cheering and hugging someone because she got asked out on a date is unheard of.

Despite that, their excitement is catching. Butterflies, which have lain dormant for so long that Mebel has forgotten their existence, flutter their wings, hesitantly at first. Then the feeling takes over, and the butterflies flutter up and around inside her. She stops fighting the smile and lets out a girlish little giggle. *My god*, she thinks. *What has gotten into me*?

Excitement, pure and simple. And she feels so alive right now, standing on the sidewalk with these people who are a third of her age. She feels like a youth again, a girl barely into womanhood, giggling over a boy, overcome with the sensation that life is about to begin for her, that an entire sparkling galaxy is at her feet, and all she has to do is jump. What a terrifying, beautiful feeling.

Their Uber arrives then, and they all bundle inside. As it drives away, Mebel gazes out the window at the beautiful facade of the restaurant. She hopes she doesn't forget any details about this strange and wonderful night.

WEIRDLY ENOUGH, THE MORE COMPLICATED THE CLASSES get, the easier Mebel finds them. Well, not easy as such, but she is certainly no longer finding them as challenging as they used to be, despite the increased complexity of the things they are doing. They have begun the sauces portion of the class, which opens with Chef Clarke teaching them about clarified butter. Mebel, who has been on a strict diet ever since she was eight, is aghast at the amount of butter that goes into it. When she mentions it to Gemma, she gives her a look.

"The clue would be in the name, Mebs," Gemma says.

"I know. But I am saying, that is a lot of butter for people to eat. What's your LDL cholesterol level?"

Gemma laughs. "I don't know, but I'm sure yours is excellent."

"Extremely," Mebel says with pride. "My son Sammy tells me is the cholesterol level of Mediterranean fishermen."

"God, Mebel. How do you come up with these things?"

"Is not me, is my son."

Chef Clarke clears his throat in a very aggressive manner that makes it obvious there's nothing actually in his throat aside from a caustic remark. When he's sure he has their undivided attention, he says, "Right, as I was saying, you want to make sure the heat isn't so high that it burns the butter, and absolutely no stirring."

Mebel looks down at the pot she's been idly stirring and quickly lets go of her wooden spoon. It's obvious that Chef Clarke has spotted it, but to Mebel's relief, he chooses not to say anything. Fortunately, aside from the stirred clarified butter, the rest of the class goes well. They make a roux, and Mebel times hers perfectly to make three different batches—a light blond roux, a brown roux, and a dark roux. When their roux are done, Chef Clarke walks around the class with color swatches and holds them up against the various roux to ensure that they're the right color, and to Mebel's delight, he proclaims her roux the most accurately cooked ones.

"All right, Mebs!" Adam hollers, and the class breaks into soft applause.

Mebel, never one to shy away from a spotlight, gives a gracious curtsy. When was the last time she—

The thought makes her stop. Because she's only now realizing how often the thought has been recurring the last few weeks: When was the last time she felt X? When was the last time she did Y? When was the last time she thought Z?

"Earth to Mebs," Gemma says. "What are you thinking of?"

Mebel blinks and pulls her attention back to Gemma. She tries to process her thoughts. "I just thinking that life is very strange."

"Okay, I guess we're in a philosophical mood. So, hey, what are you going to wear on your date with Monsieur Alain?"

Mebel shrugs, trying to come off casual. "I will throw on something."

"He's picking you up at eight, right?"

"Yes."

Gemma nods. "Right. I'll be at your room at six, and we'll do a 'get ready with me' video for TikTok."

"What? TikTok?"

"It's a social media app."

"I know what TikTok is. I won't do one."

"Aww, Mebs, come on, it'll be fun! Tell you what, I'll shoot the video, and you can review it before I upload it, okay?"

Mebel narrows her eyes.

"Come on, we all know that the best part of a date is the getting ready part," Gemma says.

"I think you need to have better date," Mebel says.

"You are not wrong." Gemma taps on her phone and waves the screen at Mebel. "All right, it's in my Google Calendar. It's a date! I'm so excited!"

GEMMA SHOWS UP ON WEDNESDAY EVENING BEARING TWO bottles of cheap sparkling wine, three wineglasses, a shopping bag full of snacks, and an equally smiley Bella.

"We are going to make you even hotter than you already are!" Gemma says by way of greeting.

"Alain is going to die," Bella says.

"Not literally, I hope," Mebel says.

"Depends," Bella says, "does he have a heart condition?"

Gemma sputters with laughter. "Bella!"

Mebel finds herself cackling along with them. She'd been hesitant about this whole thing, but now that these girls are here, she has that wonderful feeling again, like she's about to step into something glorious and fun. They cheer when Gemma pops open the bottle of sparkling wine. She pours them each a generous glug and they hold their glasses up in the air.

"To Mebs," Gemma says. "Once a baddie, always a baddie."

"Aiya, I'm not sure I like this 'baddie.' It sounds like bad guy."

"No, it's not like a bad guy!" Gemma says.

"It's more like a bad bitch," Bella says.

"A bitch?" Mebel says in horror. "That is very rude word to call me!"

"Oh, we've reclaimed it," Bella says.

"What does that mean, reclaim it?"

Bella and Gemma look at each other and narrow their eyes as they consider it, then Gemma says, "Well, men use the word 'bitch' to penalize women for daring to disagree with them. We don't like that this word has so much power over us, so we took it and we made it ours. We took away its meaning from being something derogatory to something affectionate that we call ourselves and our friends. Now, when men use it against us, it no longer has so much power behind it."

For a long while, all Mebel can do is stare at them with her mouth slightly parted. Reclaiming something is such a foreign concept to Mebel that it takes some time for her brain to break it down into digestible pieces and absorb it. Mebel hasn't been called a bitch very many times in her life for two reasons: the first being that it's not a word commonly used in Indonesian culture, and the second being that pleasing people, and men in particular, has been so ingrained in her that she would never be capable of angering a man so badly that he would call her such a name. All Henk ever had to do was say, "I don't like that," or worse, "Why are you like this?" and Mebel would hit the brakes on whatever she was doing and do a desperate backpedal. Put quite simply, Mebel has never been considered a bitch, not because she isn't one, but because she is too well muzzled to be one. And she used to think it was a good thing, that she was always inoffensive to the men around her, but what if it's . . . not?

"Did we break her?" Bella says softly to Gemma.

"Mebs? You okay, babe?"

Mebel takes a deep breath and gives herself a small shake of the head. "You young people have many funny ideas," she says.

"Have more wine," Bella says, "then you won't find our ideas so weird."

Chuckling, Mebel takes another sip. She is disconcerted not just because of the whole concept of reclaiming slurs, but also by the realization that these young people are teaching her something. In Chinese culture, this would be unthinkable. Age is a hierarchy, and the older you get, the more respect you garner just by way of your age. Anything an elder says to a younger person is worth its weight in gold, even if what the elder says is: "Know what would be a good idea? Changing your name to Princess Underpants." Conversely, anything a younger person says to their elder is worthless and can be immediately forgotten, like a fart in the wind. And now here are these youngsters, younger even than Mebel's own son, and they're saying things that, really, Mebel should dismiss out of hand because these girls are barely out of their teens, but the things they're saying actually make sense, unfortunately. What is the world coming to when people under the age of fifty can speak sense and demand respect?

"Show us your outfit for tonight," Gemma says, clapping with girlish excitement.

As always, Gemma's effervescent joy is contagious. Mebel feels it infecting her as she pulls her outfit out of her closet, and for a moment, she chastises herself for being childish, but then she dismisses the self-consciousness. Maybe it's the wine. Whatever it is, Mebel wouldn't have traded this moment for the world, standing in her dorm room that is barely big enough to fit the three of them, drinking cheap sparkling wine, and poring over outfits with these two girls.

"Ohhh, Mebs," Gemma breathes. "That is divine."

"Mebs, has anyone told you that you are one posh broad?" Bella says.

Mebel preens. She has a feeling that "broad," like "bitch," is a reclaimed word. They are reclaiming a lot of things tonight. There is a moment of silence as they all admire her outfit. It is a sleeveless A-line dress from Fendi, with a demure high collar. The fabric, which is made of silk crepe satin, feels like water to the touch and shimmers liquidly under the light. The dress itself ends above the knees, and Mebel is pairing it with knee-high Louboutin boots and gold hoop earrings, as well as a patterned scarf from Hermès.

"To think," Gemma says, "we came here to help you get ready, but you clearly do not need us!"

"We're always needed," Bella says.

"That's true." Gemma pats the dress lovingly. "Okay, let's do your hair and makeup, then you can get dressed. Look what I brought." She turns around and lifts a bag from the table. "Ta-da! My makeup kit."

Mebel looks down as Gemma unzips the bag, brandishing the messiest collection of half-used makeup. "Oh no," she says.

"No?" Gemma looks like Mebel has just kicked her puppy.

"I'm sorry," Mebel says, "but later I will get pink eye from using your makeup."

Bella bursts out laughing as Gemma pouts. "I keep my stuff clean!" Gemma cries.

Both Bella and Mebel give her a look. Then Mebel says, "I show you my makeup set." With that, she opens the drawer at her dressing table, and the two girls gasp in awe.

"Oh my gosh, it's like a Pinterest photo," Gemma says.

Bella reaches out and caresses the neatly arranged rows of

makeup with admiration. "Chanel, Dior, Shiseido, La Mer . . . wow, none of this is from Boots." They both stare at the collection with such intensity that Mebel has to clear her throat to get their attention.

"If you want to use them, you can," Mebel says. Before Bella and Gemma can react, she holds up a finger and continues. "But only if you use carefully. Clean face and clean hands only, and wipe them down after you use."

Both girls nod enthusiastically. "I'm so excited!" Gemma says. "Okay, but right now, we're going to use this on you. I found the perfect look for you." She swipes a few times on her phone and brandishes the screen.

Mebel frowns. "I don't know, I think the eye is too much."

"Nonsense," Gemma says. She turns the phone to Bella. "It's good, right?"

"Mmm," Bella agrees. "We call that the 'draw a cat's eye sharp enough to kill a man' look."

"I don't want to kill Alain," Mebel says.

"You won't," Gemma assures her.

"But he will die," Bella says.

"Oh yeah, totally."

With a sigh, Mebel smiles and lets the two of them work on her face.

MUCH LATER, THE THREE OF THEM GO DOWN TO THE LOBBY, Gemma and Bella giggling the entire time.

Agatha glances up from behind her receptionist desk and smiles. "Going somewhere fun tonight, ladies?" she says.

"Well, Bella and I are staying in," Gemma says. She wraps

an arm around Mebel's shoulders and squeezes. "But Mebs here is going out on a date."

"Tsk," Mebel says, though she can't help but smirk a little at that.

"Ooh, a date!" Agatha trills. "Who's the lucky gentleman?"

"The handsome and oh so dreamy Alain," Bella coos.

Agatha frowns. "As in Chef Alain Moreau?"

"The one and only," Gemma says, pretending to swoon.

Agatha's frown deepens. "I don't know about the ethics of a student dating one of the directors of the school . . ."

Gemma gasps, her eyes widening. "Oh my god, Agatha's right. This is like a naughty schoolgirl and teacher situation."

"Except not gross because you're not underage," Bella adds.

Agatha sputters. "That's not what I meant. I don't know if it's entirely appropriate for a student to be seeing Chef Alain—"

"Oh, Aggie," Gemma sighs, "I know you've got our best interest at heart, but Mebs is a consenting adult!"

"And she *really* needs to get laid," Bella says.

Now it is Mebel's turn to sputter. She's pretty sure she's tomato red by now.

Agatha opens her mouth to say something, but Bella grabs Mebel's arm. "Mebs! I think he's here!"

Mebel has just enough time to say goodbye to Agatha before she is whisked out through the front doors of the school.

One look at Alain's face as he takes Mebel in is worth everything. She has to admit that the cat's eye look has turned out much better than she expected, and she really does feel like a bit of a femme fatale as she descends the stone steps outside the Saint Honoré School of Culinary Arts, aware that Alain's gaze is raking over every inch of her as she moves. The silk dress brushes over her skin, and she feels so sensuous and so utterly European. So far removed from the repressed Chinese-Indonesian housewife role she played for the last few decades. *Who is this sexy siren, and what has she done with Mebel?* she thinks.

When she reaches the sidewalk, Alain takes her hand, and to Mebel's utter surprise and delight, he brings it to his face and caresses it softly with his lips. The touch, so slight and so soft, is electric. Mebel feels the jolt traveling from her fingers up her arm, shocking all of her senses. Her entire body suddenly jumps alive, parts of her that she hasn't thought of in ages crying out for attention. *Stop that,* she scolds herself. *Such hussy behavior.*

"You look ravishing, ma chérie," Alain murmurs, gazing down at her with naked appreciation.

Okay, so maybe being a hussy isn't so bad. Mebel gives herself a mental shake of the head. "Thank you, you look nice also."

Alain looks over Mebel's shoulder, and his mouth stretches into a small smile. "Your friends?" he says with a nod.

Mebel turns around and sees Bella and Gemma standing in the doorway, waving and grinning. "Don't stay out too late!" Gemma calls.

"Bring her back in one piece," Bella says.

Alain raises his hand to them, smiling, then he opens the car door for Mebel. It's a small gesture, but it touches Mebel all the same because she isn't used to it. Opening the car door or any door in general isn't part of the culture in most Asian countries, and Mebel can't help but be charmed by this simple act. The only times Henk opened doors for her were when she had her hands full, and he certainly never did it with the magnetic charm and the intense gaze that Alain is now radiating. Aiya, if Mebel were watching another woman going through this right now, she would smack her over the head and tell her to keep her feet on the ground. So what if a handsome Frenchman is opening the car door for her? Are her standards so low that this is all it takes to sweep her off her feet?

Apparently so, because Mebel finds to her horror that she's having to bite down on her lip to keep from smiling.

Alain closes the door with a soft click, then goes around the car and slides into the driver's seat. He raises his eyebrows at her. "Ah, a beautiful woman in my car and a delicious meal to look forward to. What more can a man ask for?"

Mebel could have sworn that the tips of her ears have burst into flames. She manages to say, "You are too much smooth for your own good," in a mock stern way.

Alain chuckles and maneuvers the car onto the road. "How are you liking the culinary school?"

"It's okay. I never really like cooking. Is something I hire people to do."

Alain throws his head back and laughs, a deep throaty sound that affects Mebel in a very inappropriate way. "Mebel, you are a breath of fresh air."

"Because I don't like cooking?"

"Yes." Alain stops at a red light and turns his full attention to Mebel, making her insides flush. "Being a chef and a restaurant owner, I'm surrounded by people who idolize chefs. All day, every day, I am having to turn down requests for jobs or interviews or an endorsement for their restaurants."

"Oh," Mebel says. She ponders this for a moment. "So, you like me because I see you as helper?"

Alain's roar of laughter fills the car. "Yes, I suppose you could put it that way. I like you because you don't want anything from me. People always want something from me."

"Hmm. When you put it like that, I am thinking maybe I should ask for something from you."

"You can always do that. What would you like, ma chérie?"

The term of affection sends a tingle down Mebel's spine. "I think about it first. Because I have everything I want already." *Except Henk*, she thinks, but unfortunately Henk is not something Alain can give her.

Alain finds a parking lot in the heart of Oxford, and again, he opens the door for Mebel. This time, though, he also holds out his hand for her to take as she steps out of the car. *My goodness*, she thinks. She could get used to this, she really could. When she wins Henk back, she is going to ask that he does this for her all the time.

The night air is crisp, and there is a slight fogginess hanging low, which makes the city look dreamier, like something out of a fairy tale. Looking around at the antique architecture in the damp light, Mebel almost feels like she is stepping into an oil painting. As they walk, she leans into Alain and tells herself it's because she needs help to maneuver along the uneven cobblestones in her Louboutins, but she can't deny how much she enjoys feeling his sturdiness, the knowledge that he is propping her up.

"Here we are," Alain says as they reach a place that, to Mebel, looks like a literal castle. It even has a high stone wall surrounding it, including slots in the wall, probably for ancient soldiers to shoot arrows through. "This is Pemberton College."

They step through the large wooden gate and are greeted by a porter. The porter is dressed in an old-fashioned black suit with long coattails, and the look is completed with a tall black hat. "Good evening, sir, madam," he says, touching the brim of his hat.

"Good evening," Alain says to the porter. "We are here for a private dinner. I have arranged it with the head of the college."

"Mr. Alain Moreau?"

"Yes."

"Why yes, I have your name on the list. Go right in through that door and past the quad, last door to the right."

"Thank you."

Mebel looks around as they walk deeper into the college. "What is this place? What is Pemberton College? Are we in Oxford University?"

"Ah, you haven't been told about the oddities of the Oxbridge system. Oxford and Cambridge universities are divided into multiple colleges. There isn't actually a college called Oxford, Oxford itself is the collection of colleges. When students apply to the university, they have to choose which college they want to attend. Not all colleges are built equally, some are much harder to get into than others. Pemberton is one of their oldest and most prestigious, so it is very challenging to get a spot in here. Of course, I am biased because this is my alma mater."

"Oh!" Mebel says, completely taken by surprise. "They have culinary school in Oxford?"

"No," Alain says, smiling. "I studied chemistry here. I thought I was going to be a scientist, but it wasn't my calling, after all."

Mebel would be lying if she said she wasn't intimidated by

this piece of information. She'd thought about Alain as a chef all this time, and now it turns out he's an Oxford graduate who studied science.

"Are you having to recalibrate your opinion of me as the help?" Alain says.

"Yes!"

Alain laughs, the sound slightly muted in the damp night air, but lovely all the same. "God, I love your honesty."

Pemberton College is made up of two buildings, both wrapped around quads. They are built in the classic ornate Oxfordian style, out of yellow sandstone, with classical decorative pieces adorning them. It's a gorgeous, somber place that causes one to pause as soon as they get inside and think of the magnitude of its history. Alain leads Mebel into a doorway, and the sound of their footsteps turns from the crunching of gravel to thuds against old hardwood floors. They're inside a dark hallway, the wood-paneled walls hung with oil paintings. They walk up a flight of stairs, and Mebel marvels at the stained glass on these walls, depicting an angel carrying a sword surrounded by flowers. Once again, Mebel feels the weight of the history of the college heavy around her. She has never felt so far removed from Jakarta.

Then they step through another doorway, and Mebel's breath catches in her throat, because they are suddenly out in what seems like a secret garden. A garden full of flowers tucked into the side of the college.

"Oh my goodness," Mebel gasps.

There is a small table near the edge of the garden overlooking the city. The table is lined with a luxurious white tablecloth and is set with beautiful plates and wineglasses and a vase of white roses in the middle, alongside a steadily burning candle. A server stands at attention nearby, and as Mebel and Alain approach, he pulls out a chair for Mebel.

"Good evening, madam," he says.

Still in somewhat of a shock, Mebel sits down, her eyes wide as she tries to take in everything all at once. Right next to the garden is the Radcliffe Camera, and from this vantage point, Mebel can see the top of the dome and also the rooftops of the other colleges around it. She has a bird's-eye view of Oxford, and a prettier city she cannot imagine.

"What do you think?" Alain says, sliding into his seat across from her.

"Is magical," she says simply. She is at a loss for words, in both English and Indonesian. She doesn't know of another way of describing the scene before her aside from that it is pure magic.

The server hands them both flutes of champagne, and Mebel meets Alain's eye as they clink.

"To a beautiful evening with the beautiful Mebel," Alain says.

Mebel flushes. She will never get used to being called beautiful. Not because she isn't; any respectable trophy wife knows that it is of the utmost importance to keep oneself beautiful. But because it's not within her culture to vocalize it. Henk has never once told her she's beautiful; he shows his appreciation in different ways. He will tell her that her outfit looks nice or that a particular piece of jewelry suits her. He will even tell her that her hair looks pretty that day, or that she carries that Hermès bag really well, but he hasn't once told her *she* is beautiful. And Mebel has never minded, because again, it's not something men in her culture would say, and so she hasn't ever expected it from them. In fact, she even rolls her eyes when she watches

American movies and sees the male actors telling their love interests that they're beautiful. "Empty flattery," she'd say with a sardonic smile. "Who'd fall for it?"

Well, now she is learning that she would fall for it, because that word, "beautiful," applied not to her outfit or her makeup but to her, is making Mebel feel a warmth she has not felt in a long time.

The meal is, as expected, delicious, though not as sumptuous as the one at Le Provençal was. But Alain's company is so enchanting that Mebel barely notices what she is putting in her mouth. She thinks the starter might have had white asparagus in it, or maybe it was zucchini, she really can't remember. The everythingness of the night—the lights, the knowledge that she is surrounded by all of this history, enveloped in a place of learning, the sparkling conversation, and the bubbly champagne—it is all so much. Before long, Mebel finds herself opening up to Alain about, of all topics, Henk.

"We meet through our families," Mebel says. "Is how most people in my culture meet. We are sent abroad to school, many of us, to UK or US, and when we graduate, we return to Jakarta, and our families know we are in the market, so they help connect us to other people who are also in the market."

"Like matchmaking," Alain says.

"Yes, like that. But is not like how you see in the movies, so strict like that. It's not so formal, you know? We meet up with our families, and we can say afterward, 'Oh, maybe I don't really feel a spark for it, so maybe not this one.' And there won't be a fuss, everyone will understand, and we move on, try to find another more suitable person. Is all very casual."

"And you felt a spark with Henk?" Alain says.

Mebel cocks her head to one side, mulling this over. It's been decades since she first laid eyes on Henk, and it takes effort to remember that moment. "I don't know if there is spark, but I remember thinking: His name is spelled so badly, even worse than Mebel. It make me feel kind toward him."

Alain's gaze softens. "Are you saying you dated him out of pity?"

"No!" Mebel laughs. Then she pauses, because now she remembers that she did feel sorry for Henk over his unfortunately spelled name. "No," she says again, softer this time. "Is not pity, is more like, 'Ah, here is someone who can understand me.' It felt like we can understand each other better than other people can."

"All that over a name?"

Mebel's mouth purses into a small smile. "Ah, you see, to you is just a name, no big deal. But your name is so nice, and is spelled so nicely. My name is a misspelling. Everywhere I go, it mark me as someone who is not from here. It . . ." She pauses, trying to find the right words. "It makes me look stupid—"

"Stupid?" Alain says, his eyebrows rising. "I don't—"

"Yes, stupid. Because is like: 'Oh, you don't even know how to spell the name correctly. It shows you are not native English speaker,' and people immediately treat you a bit like—how to say it—"

"Condescending?" Alain says.

Mebel nods. "Yes, exactly. And they say, 'Why you talk like that? Didn't you go to USC?' Yes, I did, but I don't speak English most of the time. After USC, I go back home to Jakarta and live there for the next forty years. All our friends and family speak Indonesian to one another. Of course my English become rusty. And if you combine the rusty English with the misspell name, people automatically think: Oh, she is stupid. She is not educated enough. She cannot understand many things. Language is a gate to the world. It is a gate for your mind, and if that gate is broken, people think the mind is also not very bright. Is frustrating, because I know my mind has so many bright thoughts, I just don't know how to say in English, so then I end up not saying much."

"I see." Alain looks somber. "I'm sorry that you've had to go through that, Mebel. I think it's obvious that you are a very intelligent woman."

"Thank you." Mebel hides her smile behind her glass.

"Except maybe when it comes to Henk, because obviously he is not on your level, and you shouldn't even have given him a chance."

Mebel sputters with laughter. "You don't even know what he's like!"

"And I already know he doesn't deserve you. You say he is with a twenty-something-year-old now?"

The laughter dissipates from Mebel's face, leaving her feeling suddenly empty. "Yes. Our private chef Wendy."

"Ah yes, the reason why you are here. Well, let me tell you why he doesn't deserve you." Alain leans forward and holds up his thumb. "First of all, who would leave you for someone barely out of her teens?"

Mebel considers this. "I think many husbands do that, actually."

"Because they are boys, not men. There is nothing quite so

valuable than a woman who has gone through life and knows exactly who she is. What she likes, what she has no time for . . . What can possibly be more attractive than that?"

Mebel's eyes roam Alain's face, searching for a flicker of—well, she's not quite sure what she's searching for. A flicker of cynicism? A telltale sign that he's lying? Because of course he's lying. No man could believe that.

"Secondly, the way you have handled yourself throughout this whole thing . . . that tells me the kind of woman you are. You are a fighter, Mebel. Most people would go, 'All right, my husband is leaving me for a younger woman, I will divorce him.' But you? You go straight to France and attend culinary school to win him back. Is that not a fighting spirit?"

Mebel glances down and is surprised to find that her hand is in Alain's palm. When did that happen? She blinks, looking up at him. He's gazing at her with what can only be described as naked admiration. Her entire body is tingling, and she has the sense that she has just gone to the deep end of the pool. She needs to get a hold of herself, and fast. Clearing her throat, Mebel says, "Enough about me. You tell me about you now."

Alain smiles. "All right. What do you want to know?"

"Why are you not married?"

"Who says I'm not?"

The blood drains from Mebel's head. God, she feels stupid. She feels exactly the way she felt the night Henk told her about Wendy. She pulls her hand out of his and picks up her fork instead, not wanting him to see how upset this revelation has made her. The thing is, she also feels upset over feeling upset, which makes her feel even more upset. *Damn it.*

"It's not like that," Alain says, apparently reading her mind.

"We do not live together anymore. She has her own life, and I have mine."

"Oh." Mebel pokes at a slice of perfectly cooked duck. "Then, why not just divorce?"

Alain shrugs. "This is both of our second marriages. I think once you get to a certain point, things start to lose their meaning. She is my wife, but she lives in Lyon, I live in Paris, and our marriage serves us well on paper, so there's no need to change it. We are beyond such labels, we don't let them suppress what we want to do."

Mebel takes a long breath and gazes out at the city before her, a city full of young people with some of the brightest minds in the world. What would it be like to be one of them, knowing that you have a certain intelligence that surpasses most of the world's population? That your worth as a girl isn't just about pleasing your future husband, but rooted solely in what your mind is able to achieve? She senses her own mind bending, stretching to accommodate what Alain has just told her. If she had come across him just one month ago, before her own life fell apart, she would've recoiled at his lifestyle, scoffed at it and said something along the lines of *These Europeans, they don't deserve the sanctity of marriage!*

But now she's in a whole different place, having had her core beliefs about marriage completely shattered. Who's to say which way of living is better than the other? At least this way, both Alain and his wife are free to do as they please without hiding it. Neither party has had to go through something as traumatic as she's had to go through with Henk. Mebel sighs. She feels tired all of a sudden.

"Are you all right?" Alain says.

She nods. "I live my life a certain way this whole time, and then, poof. Everything is upside down, just like that."

"It's a lot to take in."

"Did you always know when you get married that you will live separate life from your wife?"

Alain considers this for a moment. "I don't know that either of us thought about it in such terms. We certainly never spoke about it."

"So, how you know that your wife doesn't want to be . . . you know, exclusive with you?"

"Well, she told me she is moving to Lyon and she didn't ask me to join her, so I felt that she made it rather clear," he says dryly.

Mebel can't help but smile at this. She likes the sound of Alain's wife, a woman who isn't afraid to make her own decisions in life. She wonders what his wife is like. She must be so different from Mebel. The thought saddens Mebel, and so she strives for a quick change in the subject.

"Why you go from studying chemistry at Oxford to becoming . . ." She gestures at him.

"The help?" he teases, laughing at her raised eyebrow. "To be honest with you, I was an idiot. I had no idea what I wanted to do with my life, and I happened to be quite good at chemistry, so I thought: *Why not?*"

Mebel laughs. "You come to the best university in the world because you think: *Why not?*"

"Yes, actually. I had no idea what you could do with a bachelor's degree in chemistry. But I was fortunate, because as it turns out, there is a lot of chemistry to be done in the kitchen. It's not just about chopping and frying things. Through my degree, I was able to learn about how the different chemicals in each ingredient work, how processing them in different ways can obtain a whole other taste and texture and look. If I had it my way, every culinary school would offer a chemistry degree, and it would be compulsory to take a few classes in it."

"Absolutely not," Mebel snaps.

Alain throws his head back and laughs, the sound filling the quiet courtyard, and Mebel wonders how she has found herself here, in this incredible little spot with this incredible man.

By the time Alain drops her off back at the Saint Honoré School of Culinary Arts, Mebel realizes that her cheeks are hurting from smiling so much. The last time she's felt this ache was maybe thirty years ago, when Sammy was born.

"Bonne nuit, Mebel," Alain says when they reach the doorstep.

And Mebel, full of wine and delicious food, reaches up and plants a soft kiss on his cheek. Perhaps to Alain, who is used to a European way of life, a peck on the cheek is nothing, but to Mebel, this is the most daring thing she has done since the time she was fifteen and stole out of her house to watch a late-night movie with her cousins. She leaves before he can say another word, her head buzzing, her mouth stretched into a lopsided grin, and traipses inside feeling as light as a butterfly.

Chapter 13

THE NEXT TWO WEEKS ARE SOME OF THE BEST TIMES IN Mebel's life. It isn't that she has found her purpose, since she's still unsure about the value of becoming a chef, but for the first time in a long while, she has a very defined goal and she is only too happy to work hard at it. Not to mention she now has an excellent group of friends—yes, even Bruce she is now considering a friend, albeit an irritating one she also sometimes wishes would not show up to class. She's even stopped wearing her custom-made Hermès chef uniform because she no longer wants to be seen as someone different from her classmates. She hasn't stopped wearing her makeup though. She's not an animal.

In the mornings, Mebel wakes up bright and early and, after a quick wash, blow-dries her hair and applies her makeup carefully. During this time, Gemma usually barges into her room and begs to use Mebel's Dior lipstick. The first time Gemma did this, Mebel was somewhat taken aback, hovering anxiously as she watched Gemma rummage through her makeup drawer. But after this happened for the third morning in a row, Mebel found herself expecting the intrusion. When Gemma doesn't show up the fourth morning, Mebel surprises herself by knocking on Gemma's door and demanding to know why Gemma is choosing to sleep in. Doesn't she know that they have Introduction to Soups today, which is, according to Chef Clarke, "one of the most important modules you could ever take"? Gemma rolls her eyes but smiles before prancing into Mebel's room.

Gemma has become a sort of honorary daughter to Mebel. Mebel has always thought of herself as a boy mom, grateful that she has Sammy as her son. But there is something so delightful about Gemma, both buoyant and comforting at the same time. She fills Mebel's room with a cheerfulness that Mebel finds both irritating and soothing in equal measure, and whenever Mebel tells her off, which is all the time, Gemma merely laughs and squeezes her arm affectionately. Once in a while, Bella pops by as well, and they stay in Mebel's room going through her closet and trying on various pieces of luxury clothing.

Their favorite topic to grill Mebel on is, of course, Alain.

"Have you fucked yet?" Bella says one afternoon.

They are getting ready to go out for dinner, and Mebel has generously allowed the girls to borrow her clothes. Mebel, who is carefully lining her eyes, almost stabs herself with the Shu Uemura liner. "Excuse me?"

Bella levels a flat gaze at her. "Mebel, you've gone out on, what, three dates now? It's a fair question to ask."

Mebel sputters. "Of course not! You think I am a—an easy woman?"

Gemma giggles. "Mebel, trust me, there is nothing easy about you."

Mebel harrumphs. "Good! Being easy woman is very bad. Premarital sex is very, very bad."

"Okay, but both you and Alain are technically married," Bella says.

"Not to each other!" Mebel cries.

Both Gemma and Bella share a look, then dissolve into wild peals of laughter.

"Aiya, both you kids are terrible!" Mebel snaps. "If you don't behave, you cannot wear my Ferragamo dress. You also, Gemma."

"Okay, we'll behave," Gemma says. "But, Mebel, Alain is going to want to do it at some point, you know."

Mebel wrinkles her nose. "Oh, if he want to do it, then he can go find someone else. I never like the sex. All that . . . skin."

Gemma and Bella are both staring at her like she's just started singing the German national anthem. After a thick silence, Gemma clears her throat and says, "Mebel, has Henk been with anyone else other than you?"

"Well, Wendy, I guess," Mebel mutters. Even now, the thought of it hurts, like a serrated knife biting into scar tissue.

"Aside from her," Gemma says. "Before you, I mean."

"Of course not! What part of premarital sex is bad you don't understand? In my culture, we stay virgin for our future spouse."

"Well, that would explain why you don't like sex," Bella says. "Have you ever had an orgasm with Henk?"

"I am not going to answer such question!" Mebel snaps.

"That's a no then," Bella says to Gemma, who stifles her laughter.

"This is so disrespectful!"

"Aww, Mebs, we're sorry. We're just trying to make sure that you're having a good time," Gemma says.

"Yeah, especially now that you're estranged from your philandering husband," Bella says. "It's time for you to enter your slut era."

Mebel feels as though her head is about to explode with a mixture of mortification, frustration, and strangely enough, laughter. "No slut era!" she snaps again. "Stop this nonsense now." With that, she strides out of the room. It's only when the door clicks shut behind her that she realizes she's just stormed out of her own room while only half-dressed, and of course, it is this very moment that Adam walks out of his room, which is two doors down from hers.

He sees her, takes in her bare legs, gulps audibly, and says, "Good day, Mebs." Then he turns and goes back into his own room.

"Aiya," Mebel mutters before marching back into her room and pointedly ignoring the two giggling girls while she finishes getting dressed.

When she goes down to the reception hall, Agatha calls out to her. "How are you doing?" Agatha says.

"Okay. You?"

"Good, good," Agatha says. She tucks her frizzy hair behind her ear. "Ah, I was wondering, how are things going between you and Chef Alain?"

"Oh!" Mebel feels her cheeks warming. If Agatha, like Gemma and Bella, asks her for intimate details about her relationship with Alain, she is going to melt into a puddle right here, she knows it. "They are going okay." She turns away to signal that she is done with the conversation, but Agatha calls out to her once more.

"Only"—Agatha pauses, wringing her hands—"I just wanted to make sure everything's, you know, kosher?"

What is she trying to say? Mebel wonders. What does "kosher" mean in this sense? With a sense of growing horror, she realizes that Agatha, like Gemma and Bella, might be referring to Mebel's sex life. Is she about to ask Mebel if they are practicing safe sex? *Oh my god, this is mortifying.*

"Oh yes," Mebel chirps. "Everything very good. Very healthy!"

Confusion crosses Agatha's face. "Healthy?"

"You know, all kosher. Very organic!" Mebel's brain, it seems, has hit a wall and is now choosing to throw random words out.

"I don't quite follow . . ." poor Agatha says.

"I have to go. Bye!" With that, Mebel rushes off, her heart thundering, her face melting from sheer embarrassment. Once she is round the corner, she has to stop and take a few deep breaths to recenter herself before heading to the front door.

LESSONS ARE GOING SWIMMINGLY. MEBEL FINDS THAT SHE IS adept at the soup module. The first day, they learn to make consommé, and Chef Clarke is surprised by how clear and deeply flavorful Mebel's consommé is. They also learn to make leek and potato soup, which Mebel doesn't quite understand because leeks and potatoes seem like two of the most boring ingredients one could put into a soup. When the soup is done, Mebel has to admit that it is far more delicious than one might have reasonably expected. Her favorite is the cream of spinach and kale soup, which comes out in a beautiful, vivid shade of green and tastes both healthy and decadent at the same time.

After the second day of soup class, Mebel goes out to dinner with Gemma, Bella, Adam, and Bruce. It is now a regular thing for them to do, and at least twice a week, they all go down to Cowley Road for a casual meal. Their favorite place is a pub that serves mediocre food but decent cheap cider, and Mebel has developed a taste for English pear cider, which is both refreshing and dangerously gluggable. Their conversation flows easily, and they've all accepted Mebel into their inner circle, even Bruce.

Sometimes, they ask her for advice, something that Mebel is always ready to give. A typical example might go something like this:

MEBEL: "Bruce, you seem even more bad temper today than usual."

ADAM: "Thank god someone's noticed."

BRUCE: "Mind your own business."

GEMMA: "Why don't you tell us what's on your mind, Brucey?"

BRUCE: "It's nothing, just family drama."

MEBEL: "With your parents? Tell me, I know how to fix. I am a mother."

BRUCE: "You can't fix this, Mebel. My parents don't want me to go to culinary school. That's all there is to it."

MEBEL: "Ah. Why they don't want you to go to culinary school?"

BRUCE: "They're both doctors, they wanted me to be a doctor, simple as that."

MEBEL: "Oh, no. You cannot make it as doctor. You have terrible bedside manner."

BRUCE: "Thanks, Mebel. Very helpful, as always."

MEBEL: "But you are a very good cook. I see your cooking in class, you always get good marks. I remember the daughter sauces class? Your bordelaise and Mornay sauces were perfect."

BRUCE: "Thanks, Mebel."

MEBEL: "Is not so easy, making these sauces. I never use to think cooking is complicated until I start this course, and now I see is actually very difficult. You should ask your parents to come visit you at the school, then maybe they will see how hard you are working."

BRUCE: "They won't wanna come. But I appreciate the thought."

On a different occasion, Mebel finds Adam pacing in the hallway outside his room, obviously upset at something. When she asks him what's wrong, he tells her, "I think my boyfriend's about to break up with me."

Mebel is, for a moment, taken aback by the revelation that Adam has a boyfriend. She has heard of homosexuality, but in her culture, it isn't something that most people would be comfortable talking about openly. But when she looks at Adam, it seems silly to care about such things, when she cares about him like he's a nephew to her.

"Why do you think he is going to break up?" she says finally.

"Lately when I text him, it takes him ages to reply. He'll tell me he's busy or tired or whatever. He used to reply right away, and we used to FaceTime each other every night but the last three, four nights he's told me he's too tired."

"Where is he? Can you see him on weekend?"

"Nah, he's in Manchester Uni, it's too far away. We have to wait until the holidays." Adam wraps his arms around his body, and the act makes him look so young that Mebel's heart clenches painfully.

"You come into my room now," she says, and leads him inside, where she makes him sit at the foot of her bed while she boils the kettle for him. As she starts making tea for him, she tries to think of the right thing to say. From what it sounds like, Adam's boyfriend is distancing himself, probably because he's met someone else, and why wouldn't he? A young man at university, chances are he would meet other people.

"We were high school sweethearts, you know," Adam says forlornly. "Together for three years now. We were voted Most Likely to Get Married."

Mebel smiles at him. The kettle boils and she pours it out into two mugs, adds a splash of milk and some sugar, and hands it to him. "He sounds like a nice boy. Like you."

"What if he does dump me?" Adam looks at her with wide, scared eyes.

"Well, then you will cry. It feels like the world ending, and tomorrow is scary and big, and you feel like your life is . . . no meaning."

"Mebel!" Adam cries. "That's not making me feel any better."

"But it will pass," Mebel says. "Every day will be easier to live through, and then one day you wake up and you go on your day and then you realize, 'Oh! Is three in the afternoon and I haven't thought of him!' And then next day maybe you think about him at four o'clock, and so on. And one day you don't even think about him at all."

"But that sounds like really hard work," Adam moans.

"If I can move on after my husband of forty years leave me for younger woman, I think you can move on from a three-year relationship, yes?"

Adam rolls his eyes. "Okay, you can't use that as your trump card every time you want to make a point."

"Why not? I think I earn it already."

"Technically, you haven't moved on, because aren't you here at culinary school because you wanna, like, cook him a really good meal and win him back?" Adam raises his eyebrows at her.

Mebel searches her mind for a good retort, but now, of all times, her mind is choosing to remain silent. Finally, she says, "You don't talk back to your elders, so disrespectful."

They sip their teas in silence for a while, then Mebel says, "The problem for me is if I am not Henk's wife, I don't know who I am."

Adam tilts his head to one side. "Aww, Mebs! That is the saddest thing I have ever heard. Now I can't even be sad anymore because your thing is so much sadder."

"Good, I am glad I make you feel better."

Adam puts his arm around Mebel's shoulders and squeezes her before letting go. "I hope you know that even without Henk, you'd still be you. The Mebel we all love."

Mebel smiles. When Adam leaves her room a while later, he does so with his head held high, no longer drooping like a wilted flower. Mebel watches him leave with pride fluttering in her chest. This young generation is so vibrant and strong, and yet vulnerable at the same time. She thinks of what Adam said about her being the Mebel they all love. It's a curious feeling, to be loved by strangers. Well, not strangers. They are her friends now. And somehow, it feels like they are the only people who truly know her.

Henk has always known her as someone orbiting his life—first his girlfriend, then his wife, then the mother of his child. Sammy has always known her as someone who as a mother lives to cater to his needs. And her friends back home in Jakarta knew her as Mebel the trophy wife, just like themselves. She has never once talked to any of them about her own dreams and goals. She had no dreams, or goals, other than to be a trophy wife. This strange little group of friends she's made here is the only one to talk of such things, and they're filling her head with new ideas. Ideas that are exciting and scary and strange and so impossible to shake off.

The third day of the soup module, they learn to make lobster bisque, and Mebel doesn't flinch this time at the task of taking apart the lobster. She handles it with confidence, uttering a short apology before plunging the tip of her chef's knife into its head and ending its suffering. The rest she dispatches easily before working on the broth. Her lobster bisque comes out tasting so incredible that after class, Mebel suggests a picnic to Alain.

She brings a pot of her lobster bisque, as well as freshly baked baguettes that she filches from the bread baking class, and a punnet of nectarines she bought at Tesco a couple days ago. Alain brings a little jar of pâté, a jar of freshly made raspberry jam from Le Provençal, and a bottle of crisp wine. They go to the University Parks and find a relatively secluded spot away from the Frisbees and the joggers, and Alain unfolds a blanket. He watches as Mebel lowers herself gingerly onto it.

"Have you never been on a picnic?" he says after a while.

Mebel shakes her head. "Jakarta doesn't have many parks. Well, it has some, but the parks are not so nice, not like this. The grass is patchy, lots of spots where it's muddy soil, and people smoking in there. And it's so hot and humid because Indonesia is a tropical country, so it's not so nice staying outside. You just sweat all the time."

"Ah, I see. So, this is your first picnic?" Alain straightens up, his eyes dancing. "Take off your shoes."

"What?" *Oh god*, Mebel's brain gibbers. *This is it. This is his fetish. He is going to ask if he can suck on your toes right here, in the middle of the Oxford University Parks.* And to Mebel's horror, she isn't completely turned off by the thought. She is 99 percent horrified and 1 percent excited. Wait, no, she has more dignity than that: 99.5 percent horrified and 0.5 percent excited—no, not excited. Curious. Yes, let's go with that.

"You need to dig your toes into the grass, Mebel. Feel the beauty of nature."

"Ah, okay." Mebel gingerly takes off her Ferragamo shoes and tries to swallow the teeny tiny pang of disappointment she feels at the realization that Alain wasn't trying to get her to go barefooted for some sex thing. God, those silly girls are such a terrible influence on her.

But when Mebel extends her legs and lets her bare feet rest on the damp Oxford grass, all thoughts of deviant sexual activity evaporate from her mind. Why hasn't Mebel done this sooner? She did it before, so many years ago, at USC, didn't she? Yes, she remembers now, sitting on the quad, unwrapping a sandwich, enjoying the warm Californian sun on her skin. And then what happened? Then she went back to Jakarta and got caught up in the whirlwind of finding the perfect husband, and she never thought to sit barefoot on the grass anymore.

For a while, they are both quiet. She senses that Alain is letting her have this moment to herself, and she appreciates him for it. She has never been with anyone like him before. As a real estate tycoon, Henk proudly wears his business like a cloak. He is always on the go with two different cell phones, and they're both always dinging with important messages he has to tend to right away. And Mebel admired him for it. She didn't like men who were idle, because of course there's always something to take care of, isn't there? But Alain is teaching her to slow down, to touch the grass, literally, and what a strange feeling it is.

Mebel takes a deep breath, surrendering herself to this beautiful moment. She takes in her surroundings, the various different trees and plants around her in different shades of lush green. The trees in England are so different from the tropical ones that are found in Jakarta. The ones here are softer, dreamier somehow, their colors muted like a watercolor painting. She accepts a glass of wine from Alain, and as they clink their glasses, their eyes meet, and a shot of electricity travels all the way from her head down to her toes. They curl into the grass as Mebel's cheeks redden.

"I would like to make love to you, Mebel," Alain says.

Wine bursts out of Mebel's mouth. She doubles over, coughing. When the coughing stops, she can barely meet Alain's eye. "Sorry, I think I hear you wrong."

"I don't think so. Look, Mebel, you are a beautiful woman, I am a man who is very attracted to you, and we enjoy each other's company very much, non?"

Mebel's mouth opens and closes. "I—but—"

"Take your time and think about it. I do not expect an answer now." Alain puts a spoonful of bisque in his mouth and his eyes close as he savors it. "You made this in class today?"

Mebel nods, still not trusting herself to speak. Did he just mention wanting to, uh, do intercourse and then swiftly change the subject to talking about her lobster bisque?

"It's perfect. Mebel, you have a talent for cooking. Chef Clarke is very pleased with your progress."

"He is?" Mebel says, momentarily forgetting the awkwardness of the moment.

"Oui. He says you have improved massively, and I can see that he is right."

And maybe it's the wine or the grass on her bare toes or the praise for her lobster bisque or the talk with Bella and Gemma about orgasms. Or maybe it's just that Mebel is sick of doing whatever is expected of her. Her whole life, she's followed the road laid out before her, no questions asked. She'd studied hard(ish) at school, gotten good(ish) grades at USC, restricted her diet mercilessly her entire adult life, and been as good a wife as possible, and look where that has gotten her. Barefoot at a park in Oxford, England, having a picnic with a handsome Frenchman.

Well, when put that way, it's not so bad.

Wait, no, her mind snaps. *It's bad. It's really bad. This is not how life is supposed to turn out.*

Well, maybe life can shove it. Maybe it's time for Mebel to let loose and have a bloody orgasm, damn it. Okay, maybe not a bloody one, that sounds rather dangerous, and like something that would hurt her back.

Whatever it is, Mebel turns to Alain and says, "Okay. Let's do it. Let's have the sex."

Alain's face breaks into a smile so wide the corners of his eyes crinkle. He clinks his glass to hers. "Wonderful. Let's have the sex."

THE SEX.

Oh, the sex. Or rather, should she say: *Ooh la la, the sex!*

Mebel always wondered why people made such a big deal about sex. Every time there was a sex scene in a movie, she always wrinkled her nose with distaste and wondered what the big deal was all about. And why were people always so out of breath afterward, anyway? Mebel was never out of breath after sex. A slightly elevated heart rate, perhaps, but certainly nothing that left her gasping for breath. She decided that breathless sex, much like coffee after four p.m., was a European thing, best to be observed from a very far distance.

Now, Mebel lies in Alain's bed, her legs tangled in the duvet, staring up at the ceiling, and she is very definitely, very much so, out of breath. So out of breath, in fact, that she can barely keep a single thought in her head. Her mind, usually so quick with catastrophic thoughts, is blissfully silent for once, except for the occasional *Oh my.*

Next to her, Alain has lit a cigarette. Smoke curls up from the tip, and the rank smell of it snaps Mebel out of her dazed state. She flaps her hand over her face and makes an obnoxious coughing sound.

"I'm sorry, would you like me to put this out?" Alain says.

"Yes. Smoking is very bad habit," Mebel says automatically. "In my culture, the only people who smoke are bad people, like gangsters and politicians."

Alain smiles. "In my culture, those two are the same." He stubs out his cigarette and slides close to Mebel, gesturing at her to lay her head on his chest.

Mebel is hesitant at first. She and Henk had cuddled for a bit during the first handful of years of their marriage. Over the decades, the cuddles had dwindled, slowly at first, then the rest of it disappeared so fast that Mebel didn't have time to miss them. They were simply too busy to cuddle. At night, when they went to bed, both of them picked up their phones and scrolled mindlessly through cautionary reels before turning off the lights and going to sleep. And Mebel has certainly never cuddled while sweaty after a round of what can only be called vigorous, life-changing, mind-blowing sex.

Who am I? she thinks to herself. *I am a hussy, I am. Imagine if Meimei or Natalia or any of the other ladies from the country club back home see me now.*

The thought makes her shudder with a touch of excitement. She leans into Alain's open arms and rests her head on his chest. It's not as sweaty as she'd feared, merely a little damp, and much hairier than Henk's. Mebel has never spared a single thought for men's body hair, but it is with much surprise that she finds herself liking it. She places her palm gingerly on his chest, feeling very awkward at first. When Alain chuckles, she feels it vibrating through his chest.

"Have you never been held, Mebel?"

"Of course I have," she says as a knee-jerk reaction.

"Have you been held recently?"

She doesn't bother with a reply. He can extrapolate from her silence what he wants to. Mebel's mind wants to start racing like it usually does, but what she has just experienced moments ago is still luxuriating through her body, still flicking at her pleasure sensors. She relaxes, melting into Alain's arms, marveling at what her body is capable of.

"What are you smiling about?" Alain says, looking down at her.

Mebel wrinkles her nose. "Don't face me when you talk. You smell like cigarette."

"Okay," Alain says good-naturedly, turning his face away from her. "Now tell me what you are smiling about."

"Sex is not really an open thing in my culture."

Alain nods slowly, his expression contemplative. "Not what I thought you were going to say, but okay."

"Is not something we talk about. I think the young people, they talk about it openly, but my generation? Never. We don't talk about such thing. We treat it like something we need to do, you know? Get married, have children. The sex happen somewhere in between that. And after children, finish. Maybe have it once in a while, on birthday and anniversary, but that's all."

"Ah. I see. Very different from my culture then."

"Yes. We see it as something embarrassing. You know, my mother, she used to be so proud that she didn't have sex with my father after my siblings and I are born and they are done having children. She used to say, 'Hah, you think your father and I do anything anymore? Of course not. Ugh.'"

"What did your father have to say about it?"

Mebel shrugs. "Not much. He never say much."

"And your relationship with Henk was like that?"

"Yes." And now the sadness comes over her like a wave, soft but unrelenting. She takes a sharp breath. "I wonder if he secretly want more, but maybe he doesn't know how to ask me."

Alain's fingers stroke up and down her arm and he murmurs, "Well, then he's an idiot. If he wanted it, he could've talked to you about it."

Mebel sighs. "I don't know. I don't make it easy for him, you know? I always say things like, 'Ugh, sex is so unhygienic,' or 'Oh, what a bother, and is such a hot day.' And this and that. I think maybe is because I am so bad at it, I don't know what to do, you see. Nobody ever talk to me about sex and how to do it right."

"You're not so bad," Alain says. "I quite enjoyed it."

"You have had many sex?"

"I've had a few."

"And you think I'm not so bad?" Mebel holds her breath, suddenly feeling vulnerable. She tries to convince herself that it doesn't matter what Alain thinks, but she knows she would only be fooling herself.

"Better than that. You have a natural instinct for it."

The blush spreads across her entire body, and for a second, Mebel nearly starts giggling uncontrollably. Fortunately, she is of sound enough mind to wrestle the giggles into submission. There is also a tiny bit of shame inside her at being told that she has a "natural instinct" for something as lascivious as sex. It goes against every part of her moral upbringing as a CHIP.

Then again, CHIPs rarely turn into professional chefs, so

maybe Mebel is only finding out now, at the ripe age of sixty-three, that perhaps she is not a CHIP, after all. Maybe she is something entirely different, though what it is, she has no idea. But as Gemma and Bella would say, she does not hate it. Not in the least.

Chapter 14

MEBEL SHOULD HAVE KNOWN THAT NOTHING GOOD can last. It has been over two months since she arrived at Cowley, England, and she has made the best of her time there. She has gone to an appropriate number of events that require her to dress up in luxury attire, which, for someone who is unfortunately living in Cowley, is quite the feat. She has a clear goal that she is working steadfastly toward, she has a solid group of friends who broaden her horizons every day, and she has a lover who broadens her . . . horizontally. Oho! And she is in such high spirits that she makes little dirty jokes now and again, which says a lot, really.

She should've known that things were going too well and life was about to swoop in and shit all over it, just as it is wont to do.

It happens on a Thursday, which feels doubly offensive because all bad news should arrive on a Monday, everyone knows that. But, no, this piece of bad news not only has the audacity to swoop in on a Thursday but also has the cheek to come in parading as good news.

"Attention, everybody," Chef Clarke says that cursed morning. "I have a rather exciting announcement to share with you."

Mebel and her classmates stand a little straighter. In the past couple of months, Mebel has been bitten by the culinary bug, and she now finds herself being motivated by silly things like being praised for making the perfect consommé (she is still glowing over that one) and removing the beard off a scallop efficiently.

"For the first time in the history of the Saint Honoré School of Culinary Arts, we are proud to present an exciting end to the year." Chef Clarke spreads his arms wide open. "We will be catering the prestigious Pemberton College Ball at the end of the Michaelmas term. Oh, that's the end of the fall term for those of you not familiar with Oxford terms."

An animated whisper rises from the group of students. Gemma raises her hand, her face bright and lively.

"Gemma?"

"Chef, are you saying we will be cooking the food for the Pemberton Ball?"

"Yes, and not just cooking it, but you will be designing the menu."

A handful of gasps rises around the room.

Chef Clarke raises his index finger. "Now, to make things even more exciting, this will be a competition. You will be pairing up with a fellow classmate to design one course of the menu. The students who come up with the winning course will win a cash prize and a spot in the kitchen of Canard et Vin, the restaurant in Paris with three Michelin stars."

Everybody gasps this time. Even Mebel does so, because by now, she knows the importance of Michelin stars and how they are coveted with the same amount of fervor that a CHIP would covet a crocodile-skin Birkin. The students begin to chatter animatedly among themselves.

Gemma catches Mebel's eye and points to her, mouthing: *You and me?*

A flush of pleasure washes across Mebel's body, and she nods. Designing a course with Gemma sounds like a dream come true. But then she looks over at Bella, Adam, and Bruce, and her smile wanes. There is an odd number now, and she wonders, for a moment, if she should step aside and let one of them partner up with Gemma instead.

But then Chef Clarke calls out their names and assigns them their partners, and Mebel is partnered up with Gemma anyway. Well, she's not about to complain about that. She exchanges a glance with Gemma and throws her a smile, which Gemma returns with a full-on sun-at-midday grin.

After class, Gemma goes to Mebel's room, where she immediately makes herself comfortable by trying on Mebel's extensive shoe collection.

"Yes Gemma, you can try on my Manolo Blahniks," Mebel says dryly.

"They kind of pinch my toes," Gemma says, trying on different poses in the mirror.

"That is Manolo for you. I don't think he likes women very much." Mebel hands Gemma a cup of tea.

"Neither does Jimmy," Gemma says.

"You mean Jimmy Choo or Jimmy in our class?"

"Both, come to think of it."

"Yes, I think you are right." Mebel sips at her tea. She isn't a big tea drinker in Jakarta, mainly because it's so hot and humid there that to drink anything warmer than tepid water is asking to be bathed in sweat. But here in England, she has found a taste for the hot beverage, and now she can't go five minutes without holding a hot cup of tea in her hands. "So, what are you thinking for our course?"

They'd been assigned the poultry course for the evening's menu.

Gemma takes a long slurp of tea and ponders the question. "I'm thinking roast pigeon, what do you think?"

"Okay," Mebel says simply.

Gemma frowns at her. "Mebel, you've got to tell me your honest opinion."

"I think pigeon is good."

"Okay, or what about duck? We could do duck, or even turkey, since it's close to Thanksgiving?"

"Thanksgiving? Isn't that American holiday? To celebrate freedom from . . . you?" Mebel says.

"Well, yes, but it's become popularized, and it's less of a 'Yay, we got away from the English' and more of a 'Ooh, let's eat a load of food' type of holiday now," Gemma says. When Mebel continues to look skeptically at her, she says, "All right, not turkey. But what about duck?"

"We can do duck," Mebel says agreeably.

"Mebel!" Gemma cries.

"What?"

"Don't just agree with me. What do *you* want to do?"

Mebel pauses, thinking hard. It's yet another moment when she's having a mental block because she realizes she hasn't been in a situation where she's had to think about what she really wants. "I—ah—" She's always just gone along with whatever Henk wanted. It seemed much simpler that way. She gives herself a little shake of the head, trying to clear her thoughts. "I want—ah—"

Gemma looks expectantly at Mebel.

"Maybe we throw a coin," Mebel says.

"Mebel!" Gemma snaps. "Just make a decision. Right now! Duck or pigeon? Duck or—"

"Duck!" Mebel shouts.

Silence rings for a moment, then Gemma breaks into a laugh. "Yeah, way to go, Mebs! Look at that, you made a decision for yourself, for once. You are a baddie!"

Mebel looks at her, stunned, then the smile slowly takes over her face. "Yes, duck."

"All right, duck it is. How do you feel?"

Mebel takes a deep breath. "I don't know. Is very strange. Who cares about duck or pigeon or chicken or what? Nobody cares. I don't care about such thing, but . . ."

"But it turns out you do care?" Gemma says.

"Yes." Mebel cups her mug of tea and looks down at her lap. "But is like—it feels silly to care about such thing."

"It's not though, is it?" Gemma says. "Because you are spending so much of your time and effort to excel at this thing."

Mebel struggles to try to explain her reticence about accepting the importance of this event. "You know, this kind of thing, in my circle of friends and family, is like a silly hobby.

Unless is something that make a lot of money, then otherwise it has no value to us."

"I understand," Gemma says.

"You do? I thought you young people are all about, 'Oh, I love to do this, that is all that matters.'"

"Okay, I'm gonna ignore the ageism there," Gemma says. "Thing is, Mebs, we're all raised in this capitalist society. I mean, I wish we could all be like, 'Fuck money, we're doing this purely for the love it!' But at the end of the day, I need to have enough money to be able to pay rent and buy myself some food to eat. So, yeah, I get what you're saying and why your culture would place so much importance on ventures that earn you money."

"You young generation are very wise," Mebel says.

"Thank you. We are, aren't we? It's because of social media."

"Mmm, I don't know if that is true."

Gemma grins. "Okay, let's brainstorm on duck dishes. I'm thinking we do something like a confit, cook it in its own fat."

"Maybe a combo between duck confit and Peking duck?" Mebel suggests.

"Ooh, I love the sound of that! So, like, confit of duck but served in a Chinese crepe with hoisin sauce?"

"Something like that, yes." Mebel feels the excitement fizzing inside her. She can tell already that their dish is going to be amazing, and the thought of it fills her with so much happiness that it quite bowls her over. She's so unfamiliar with this feeling.

"I love it," Gemma says. "We can crisp up the skin really well—"

"You know what I am thinking?" Mebel says. "I am thinking of fish skin, is very popular in Asia."

"Fish skin?"

"Yes, we fry it until it is crispy like potato chips, and then we season with salted egg powder. Is so delicious, very addictive."

Gemma looks dubious, but she nods anyway. "Okay, I'll take your word for it."

"I wonder if maybe we can do the same with the duck skin. Sprinkle some salted egg yolk powder onto it. Give it that umami taste."

Gemma continues to look dubious. "I mean, I'm not gonna knock anything until I've tried it. I've tasted some combinations that I thought wouldn't work, but they ended up pairing beautifully, so I'm keeping an open mind."

Mebel smiles, struck by how much affection she feels toward this girl. "I think we going to win this competition."

"Oh, heck yeah, Mebs. We're going to crush it!"

APPARENTLY, THE OTHER TEAMS FEEL EXACTLY THE SAME way, like they're going to destroy the competition, because the following day, when Mebel goes to class, everyone is staring down everyone else with obvious animosity.

"Good morning, Bruce," she says as she passes by Bruce's workstation.

In answer, Bruce merely snorts and turns away. Mebel doesn't think anything of it, because Bruce behaves like a wounded Chihuahua most days. What catches her attention is Adam, who, when she greets him, merely spares a quick glance in her direction and says, "Hey," before turning back to study his notes.

Mebel ignores the alarm going off inside her and greets Bella.

Bella has been partnered up with Adam to do the red meat course, and Mebel has no doubt that between the two of them, they are going to come up with something genius. But now, Bella just turns away from Mebel with a muttered "Morning."

Mebel takes her spot at her workstation. As she sharpens her knives, she scans the room, taking note of all of the students in there. The atmosphere in the kitchen this morning is tense, everyone lost in their own worlds, scowls being worn and nothing being said. She can't wait for Gemma to arrive so she can talk to her about it. Or at the very least, she can make very obvious looks aimed at Gemma to communicate the strangeness of the morning.

"All right, class," Chef Clarke says. "This morning, I would like you to go over your proposed dish and present a description of it to me."

At this, everybody gets to work, going into their respective partnerships and murmuring in low voices, as though deathly afraid that anyone is going to listen in on their conversations. Mebel swears that not even CIA operatives would behave in such a secretive manner. Whenever she turns her head to look in a certain direction, the students in that vicinity hunch their shoulders more and lower their voices while glaring at her.

My goodness, Mebel thinks. *What is everyone's problem?*

Well, it's obvious, really, isn't it? her brain replies. *They're all scared that you're going to steal their ideas.*

But we all have different courses assigned to us, she argues.

Yes, but even within each course, you could use similar methods to cook your ingredients. And you could deliberately ruin the taste of the next course, for example, by serving artichokes in your dish when you know the next course is going to be a white fish, which would alter its taste.

I wouldn't do anything like that, Mebel thinks furiously.

I know that, but do they know that?

Mebel looks around at the toxic atmosphere in the kitchen and sighs. No, she does not know that, and worse still, she does not know that no one else in the class would stoop so low, especially when the prize is this meaningful.

She settles back in her seat, twirling her pen for a while, gazing at the door, willing Gemma to come through it. It is now fifteen minutes since the class officially started. It isn't like Gemma to run so late to class. Mebel stares down at the blank piece of paper in front of her. She writes *Duck* at the top, then underlines it. After an excruciating minute crawls by, she writes *Confit/Peking* underneath it. When she looks up, she jumps. Chef Clarke is right next to her.

"Mebel," he says by way of greeting.

"Chef," she replies. She hooks her arm over her notepad, trying to cover it from view without being too obvious.

"What've you got there?"

"Well, just preliminary notes for our dish, not anything official or anything like that."

Chef Clarke nods. "What poultry are you and your partner thinking of doing?"

Mebel gestures at the empty space next to her. "My partner not yet arrive, as you can see. So I don't want to make any decision without her."

"Mm. Yes, I see that. However, because of the time crunch we have surrounding this event, you do need to come up with a proposed course by the end of the day, with or without your partner."

That's not fair, Mebel wants to wail. But she merely gives Chef Clarke a smile and says, "I think we decide on duck."

"Wonderful. One of my favorite meats. And how will you be cooking it?"

"Ah," Mebel says, frantically working through her memory. She and Gemma had had a cursory discussion, and in theory it sounded delicious, but they have no idea if it would work in practice. "We are thinking maybe a duck confit—"

At this, Chef Clarke's smile wanes, and Mebel's senses go into overdrive to compensate. Her only purpose right in this moment is to come up with a duck dish that would prove to Chef Clarke that she belongs in the school. "But we are going to do something special with the skin!" she says loudly.

Heads look up and turn toward her. Now she has not only Chef Clarke watching her, but most of the class as well. Wonderful.

Mebel makes an effort to lower her voice. "We are thinking maybe something like Peking duck, with the crepe, but the duck itself is cook in the own fat like a confit."

Chef Clarke nods, his lips thinning as he considers this. "Bit of a fusion dish then? I suppose it could work. But what are you doing with the skin? Peking duck is traditionally roasted, which gives the skin that beautiful golden brown shade and subtle crunch. Are you going to fry your duck skin?"

Mebel, who has no idea what the fuck they're going to do with the duck skin, nods vigorously. "Yes, sure, yes."

"All right," Chef Clarke says. "Well, I look forward to it. Let Gemma know when she arrives."

With that, he stalks off, on the lookout for his next prey. Mebel is so limp with relief she practically melts across the kitchen worktable. She hurriedly writes down as much as she can remember Chef Clarke saying. She likes the sound of her and Gemma's dish, and as she tries to work out a recipe for it, she wonders for the hundredth time where Gemma is. It really isn't like her to disappear like this.

Mebel checks to make sure Chef Clarke is out of earshot before reaching over and tapping Adam on his back.

He turns around, wearing a look of mild irritation. "What is it, Mebel?"

Mebel notes with a pang that he's calling her Mebel and not Mebs. "I—ah, have you hear anything from Gemma? I am worried about her, why she not come to class yet, is not like her to be this late and—"

"Right, yeah," Adam says distractedly. Bella gives him a pointed look, and he says, "Okay, Mebel, I get that you're worried, but I can't do anything about that right now. We can check on her after class, all right?" With that, he turns his back on Mebel.

A sense of loneliness threatens to overwhelm her. *Don't be silly,* she tells herself. *This is nothing. Gemma probably overslept, like young people usually do, or maybe she has a cold, or is hungover. Ah yes, probably the last one. These English kids drink a lot, much more than Chindo kids, that's for sure, and there have been many a morning where they've shown up to class bleary-eyed, their hair greasy and pulled back from their faces in a hasty ponytail. Yes, that's probably what happened to Gemma.*

Mebel just needs to—hmm. Well, she just needs to work on this stupid recipe. She looks around at the paired-up students who are murmuring quietly to each other. She catches bits and pieces of their conversations, and it all intimidates her. Terms like "sous vide" and "foam" are being thrown around. She recalls what Alain said about how chemistry is vital to the culinary arts, and she jots down *Chemistry*. She stares at it, her mind blank. Or more accurately, her mind is whizzing with a dozen random ideas, gibbering uselessly at her. A quick snapshot of the many thoughts crowding her mind would show something like this:

Chemistry, that means mixing potions.

The act of firing up the stove and cooking a piece of raw meat is chemistry, isn't it?

Can you foam duck? Oh, maybe you could foam the duck fat!

I could use a Nespresso foamer on liquid duck fat maybe.

And I-ee-I will always looove youuuu, and I—

All of the thoughts are voicing their opinions at the same time, while one of them is always singing a random song in the background. Once in a while, one of the thoughts would actually be an okay one, and Mebel would try her best to pluck that out of the sea of useless thoughts and jot that down. She does so now, writing *Milk frother + duck fat*. She leans back and tries to envision it. It sounds like an idea that might turn out to be absolutely brilliant or absolutely revolting, but at the end of the day, she won't know unless she tries it.

By the time the class ends, Mebel is a frazzled mess. She hurries out of the kitchen and up the stairs, taking them two at a time, which just goes to show how worried she is about Gemma, because at her age, her knees are no longer of the two-steps-at-a-time caliber. She briskly walks down the hallway and knocks sharply at Gemma's door, then steps back and tries to catch her breath.

No answer.

Mebel raps her knuckles at the door again, a little bit harder this time. Not quite at the level of *Open up, this is the FBI and we know you've got several dead bodies in there!* but at the level of *Open up, I am a Chinese mother and I can smell wrongdoing in there!* which is pretty close.

Still, there is no answer.

"Gemma?" Mebel calls out. After checking to make sure there's no one else in the hallway, Mebel presses her ear gingerly to the door and tries to pick out any sounds from within the room. Any guilty shuffling? Held breaths? But there is nothing.

And now, Mebel's brain switches from irritated concern to paranoid worry. As a mother, she excels at paranoia. When Sammy was a newborn, Mebel woke up several times through the night to check that he was still breathing. Sometimes, if he was sleeping too deeply, she would reach into the cot and poke him gently just to make sure he stirred. It drove Henk crazy, because sometimes, Sammy would fully wake up and start to cry. "Leave him alone," Henk would say. "Haven't you heard of the saying 'Let sleeping dogs lie'?"

Like hell am I going to leave anything alone, Mebel thinks now. What if Gemma was in an accident? Maybe she was crossing the street and got knocked over by a car in a hit-and-run. Or maybe she was eating a pastry she'd filched from the patisserie students and choked while swallowing, and now she is lying dead in her room. The thought of this is so vivid that Mebel can almost see Gemma lying on the old maroon carpet in the bedroom, her eyes wide open with shock, her mouth frozen in a silent cry for help that nobody heard.

With a cry, Mebel rushes down the hallway, nearly falling over on the stairs in her haste to get to the first floor.

"I think Gemma is dead!" she cries as she runs toward Agatha at the front desk.

Agatha, who had a cup of tea halfway up to her mouth, freezes. Then she gently places the tea back down on the table and says, "I'm sorry, what was that?"

"I think Gemma is dead," Mebel says, gesturing madly. Her thoughts are so frenzied her mouth is having a hard time forming the words and putting them into a coherent sentence. "She not show up to class today, and I just go to her room and knock the door, but she didn't reply. I think maybe she choke on something when she snacking last night and—aiya—quick, we need to open her door!"

"Oh dear," Agatha says. She looks somewhat saddened by this, though nowhere near alarmed enough, in Mebel's opinion.

"Quickly!" Mebel snaps. My goodness, what is wrong with Agatha? Why isn't she doing anything?

"It's okay, Mebel, Gemma is not dead."

"How you know?" Mebel cries.

"She withdrew from the course this morning. She's no longer enrolled at the school, that's why there was no answer when you knocked on her door. She's not here anymore."

For a moment, all Mebel can do is stare blankly at Agatha. Then the words slam through her skull and sear themselves onto her brain and she shouts, "What?"

"Shh," Agatha says, flapping her hands at Mebel. "Good grief, there are classes going on right now, and you are being quite distracting. Gemma dropped out, it happens all the time. Every semester, there will be a handful of students who find that they can't actually cut it at culinary school and drop out."

"No," Mebel breathes.

"Oh yes, it happens very frequently. The problem is, these kids are young, and they're not used to hard work, and they watch too many TikToks and think that cooking is fun and easy to do. Have you seen cooking videos on TikToks? Some of those content creators are out there cooking the most complicated dishes, things that would take six, seven hours to make, and they do it all and then edit it into a thirty-second video, and so kids think the dishes are easy. Then they come here and they're dismayed to learn that, actually, it is really bloody hard to make a boeuf bourguignon fritter, and they're like: *This is no fun, I quit.*" As Agatha speaks, she grows more and more impassioned, and it becomes clear to Mebel that this is perhaps something Agatha has had a long history with.

"But you don't understand," Mebel says. "Gemma is not like that. Gemma is very responsible student. She knows all the things already, how difficult everything is, she knows that."

Agatha throws up her hands. "I don't know what to tell you, Mebel. Gemma came to me first thing this morning and told me she no longer wants to be a student here."

"She come to you this morning . . ." Mebel muses, more to herself than to Agatha. "How she look? She look sad? Angry?"

"I don't know, she looked normal, I guess," Agatha says with a shrug.

Mebel shakes her head. "I don't know why you are being so—so 'I don't care.'"

"I'm sorry," Agatha says, and she truly does seem apologetic.

"I guess I don't have much sympathy for students who drop out of their courses because, well, I've been saving up to take a course here, and seeing students take the courses for granted is just not very nice, is it?"

"Oh." Mebel pauses. She hasn't spared a thought for Agatha. To her, Agatha has always been just a receptionist at the school, and now she feels ashamed for not being more thoughtful, because of course Agatha has her own goals and dreams. Agatha is a person, not just a pleasant face at the front desk. Just like how Mebel isn't just a trophy wife, but a complete human being with her own hopes and dreams.

You're getting carried away again and making this about you, her mind says.

Right, Mebel thinks, snapping herself out of her derailed train of thought.

"Is there anything else I can help you with?" Agatha says.

"No. Thank you." With one last look at Agatha, Mebel walks out of the school building. Outside, she takes out her phone and calls Gemma. She should've done this earlier, now that she thinks of it.

The call doesn't go through. Instead of ringing, it immediately goes to an automated message that says: "The number you have dialed is not in service."

Mebel checks to make sure she has tapped on the right contact, then tries again, with the same results this time. Frowning, she goes back indoors.

"Agatha?" she says.

Agatha gives her a tight smile. "Yes?"

"Does Gemma have another number?"

"I don't know, I'm afraid. We're not allowed to give out contact information for privacy purposes."

"Because I just try calling her number, but it says disconnect. Then how?"

Agatha sighs. "Yeah, well, I can't help you there, I'm afraid."

"What about her email address? Maybe you can give to me?"

"I can't do that, sorry."

Mebel is about to ask for Gemma's home address in a last-ditch effort when Agatha holds up her hand. "I can't give you any information about Gemma unless she expressly tells me I have permission to do so."

A deep sense of sadness overtakes Mebel. Now that the initial panic has ebbed away, Mebel is left feeling, well, really lonely. And what in the world is she going to do about the dish she was supposed to cook with Gemma? She doesn't have what it takes to come up with an impressive duck dish worthy of a Michelin-starred restaurant on her own.

After thanking Agatha, Mebel walks to the chefs' offices, where she knocks on Chef Clarke's door. "Come in," he calls out. His eyebrows rise when he sees Mebel. "Oh, hello, Mebel. This is a nice surprise. What can I do for you?"

"My partner Gemma drop out of the course."

Chef Clarke sighs. "Ah, yes. I saw the email when I came out of this morning's class. That's a real shame."

"What email? Gemma send you email?" Mebel says.

"Yes. It was quite brief. It only said how sorry she is to have to drop out in the middle of the semester."

"She didn't say why?"

"No."

"And you don't ask why?" Mebel says, her voice rising. *Aiya, what is wrong with these people? How can they not see that something isn't right? Why don't they care enough to ask what has happened?*

Chef Clarke frowns at her. "No, because, quite frankly, it's none of my business, and neither is it any of yours. Now, what can I do for you?"

Mebel struggles with the urge to tell him off for not caring about his students. It won't go well, she knows. She just needs to let it go for now. Taking a deep breath, Mebel forces herself to focus on something she knows he can fix. "Well, I lose my partner. What should I do for the banquet? I cannot do the course by myself. It's not fair." She regrets the words "It's not fair" as soon as they come out of her mouth, because even though they're true, they also have the maturity of a whiny toddler. If she were speaking Indonesian, she would be so much more fluent, but, no, she is held back by her broken English. *It's not fair!* Her mind says petulantly.

"You're right," Chef Clarke says with a sigh. "It is most definitely unfair. Now, I can't pair you up with anybody else since everyone is paired off—"

"Maybe I can join a pair? Make it a three-person group?"

"I'm afraid not. It wouldn't be fair to the others."

Mebel glowers at him. "So is okay to be not fair to me, but not to everyone else? This is discrimination!"

"How about this: you are allowed extra prep time on the day of the banquet to make up for the lack of a partner, and you can come to me to brainstorm your ideas. Those things should give you a good bit of advantage to get ahead." He looks hopefully at Mebel.

"How much more prep time?"

"Thirty minutes."

"Impossible. Two hours."

"One hour extra."

"One hour and a half," Mebel counters. Inside, she is crowing. This Caucasian man thinks he can outbargain her? A Chinese mother? Hah! Even his ancestors would be shaking their heads and saying, *My dear boy, you need to know your own limits.*

Sure enough, Chef Clarke seems to have realized this as well. With a defeated nod, he says, "All right. One and a half hours extra time on the day of the banquet."

"And you give me brainstorm also."

"That too, yes."

They shake hands, and Mebel leaves the room feeling, if not quite victorious, then at the very least somewhat mollified that she has evened out the playing field a little.

Back in her room, Mebel sits at her desk and drums her fingernails on the wooden surface. For the first time, her tiny room feels big. She looks around the space and realizes what it's missing: Gemma. If this were any other normal day, Gemma would be in here, rummaging through Mebel's closet shamelessly, putting on her dresses and her shoes while talking nonstop. Mebel used to think it was irritating as hell, but now, the room feels painfully silent without Gemma.

With a sigh of frustration, Mebel gets up and goes to Bella's room. She'll invite Bella over for a cup of tea and a very animated discussion about Gemma's sudden disappearance. She knocks at Bella's door and hears footsteps. A moment later, Bella opens the door a crack.

"Oh, hey, Mebs," she says.

"Bella, come talk to me. I want to come in."

Bella opens the door wider, letting Mebel in. Her room is pristine compared to Gemma's. She doesn't own as much stuff, for one, and whatever she does own has been lined up neatly. "What's up?"

Mebel perches on a chair while Bella sits at the foot of her bed. "Did you hear about Gemma leaving? Is very strange, right?"

"Yeah, I heard from the grapevine."

"What grapevine?"

Bella shrugs. "I dunno, people were talking about it. Like you are."

It hurts Mebel to think of people talking about this without telling her. Weren't they friends? Fortunately, she has enough presence of mind to not ask that aloud, since it would most definitely make her sound like a petulant teen. *Move on from this part of the topic*, her mind warns her.

"Have you hear anything from her?" she says.

"Nope. And I'm kinda mad about it. She should've said something. Who leaves just like that, without even so much as a goodbye?"

"Is strange, right?" Mebel cries. "I try to message her and look, only one tick. I try to call her and it says her number is not in service. I am very worried, I think something happen to her."

Bella blows out her breath through her mouth. "I dunno, Mebs. I think she's just a flake. My guess is she got tired, she wanted to quit the school, and she was too embarrassed to tell us."

"No, that doesn't sound like Gemma. Why are you so—" Mebel shakes her head, trying to find the right words to call out how uncaring Bella is being without offending her. Her gaze lands on Bella's laptop, on which is a document. Without meaning to, Mebel reads it. She gets as far as "Venison with rosemary and truffle essence smoke" before Bella snaps the laptop shut abruptly, making Mebel jump.

"That's private," Bella says.

"Sorry," Mebel says, flustered. She really hadn't meant to snoop; her eyes had settled on the screen without her brain telling them to. But then again, why the big secret? It's not like Mebel had stumbled upon a diary entry, for goodness' sake. "Why so secretive?" she blurts out. "Is for the banquet, right? Who cares if I know what you are making? I am happy to share with you what I am making for my course."

"Mebs," Bella groans. "Do you really not get it?" She glares at Mebel, who looks back with all the innocence in the world. Grumbling, Bella says, "Look, you're here on a bit of a lark, aren't you?"

"What you mean?" Mebel is trying really hard not to feel offended, but it is somewhat of a challenge in this moment.

"Well, you're here to learn to cook fancy dishes so you can win back your philandering husband," Bella says.

"We been married forty years," Mebel says. "Is it so bad that I want to win my old life back?"

"I mean . . . I wouldn't have made that choice myself, but whatever, not the point. The point is," Bella says, "you're not here to become a chef. But the rest of us are. This is all I've got, Mebs. I was terrible at school. Failed all my subjects. I barely scraped by with my A levels. I don't have any prospects. If I flunk out of culinary school, I'm fucked."

Mebel gapes at Bella. Bella, who with her sullen nature and

straightforward, no-nonsense attitude, had led Mebel to believe that she is the most confident kid Mebel has come across. "Bella, you have such bright future ahead."

"I really don't. I took out loans to come here. My parents could've helped me out with it, but they didn't, and you know why?" Bella crosses her arms in front of her.

Mebel shakes her head.

"Because they know I'm a fuckup. They fully expect me to do exactly what Gemma has just done and drop out in the middle of the school year. They told me they've 'invested enough in me.'"

"Invested in you?"

"Yeah, like put me through school and all that. It is a sort of an investment when you think about it."

Mebel supposes Bella has a point, but it seems callous to her, all the same. She has never once thought of Sammy as an investment.

"So, this banquet? The chance for a position at Canard et Vin's kitchen? Do you even know of the place? It's one of Paris's most celebrated restaurants. Three Michelin stars. You don't even know how hard it is to even get a single star, Mebs. It is, like, nearly impossible to get three stars, especially in a city as competitive as Paris." Bella gestures animatedly, her eyes shining with passion. "It's the only chance I've got to prove my parents wrong. To make a good living for myself. Once you've worked at a place like Canard et Vin, you can basically find work at any restaurant of your choice. That's what's at stake for us with this banquet. That's why we're taking this shit so seriously."

Mebel is overcome by a mix of guilt and embarrassment, because Bella's right. She hasn't even spared a thought for what the reward would mean for her classmates, because it means nothing to her. Even if she wins, she won't take the job, because she's never going to become a chef anyway. Her path will always lead back to Jakarta to reclaim her spot as Henk's trophy wife, to be placed back on the shelf, all shiny and even more impressive now that she can cook a mean steak. She can already see it—she and Henk will throw dinner parties. They'll hire caterers, because of course they will, but Mebel will be in charge of the star dish, something impressive with a complicated French name, and when she brings it out of the kitchen, everyone will applaud. Henk's friends will clap him on the back and say, *You got lucky with her, didn't you?* and Henk will smile smugly and nod.

"I'm sorry," she says quietly. "You are right, I don't realize how much pressure you young people are under."

Bella gives a forlorn nod. "It's a lot."

"Yes, is sound very tiring. But, Bella, you are very talented young woman. You will make it out there, even if you don't win this one competition."

Bella sniffs. "I don't know about that. We'll see, I guess."

Mebel leaves Bella's room with her head spinning, too much information swirling around inside. She takes out her phone and sees that there is a text from Alain. For a second, Mebel's spirits lift, but then she reads the actual message.

> ALAIN: Ma cherie, I am going to be in London to check on my restaurant for the next few days. x

What the hell kind of message is that? Mebel thinks huffily. No apologies, no reassurances about when they will see each other again. For a moment, fear slices through her like a rusty knife. Her immediate thought is: *This is because you gave the sex to him. He has had the sex, and now he is satisfied and he is bored of you and now he will meet his lover in London and have the sex with her instead.*

Stupid, she scolds herself. She should've known better. Isn't that what her upbringing was all about? Withholding sex from men so that the power remains with her? Women who give it up too soon are used and then discarded. Doesn't Mebel know that? Every good CHIP worth her salt knows that her value lies in her sex, and that once given, she also gives her worth to the man. Mebel could just scream at the thought of how foolish she's been.

Shame overwhelms her, and she hurries back inside her bedroom, locking it behind her. She takes her shoes off and climbs into her narrow bed, pulling the covers over her head and cocooning herself in its soft darkness. For a long while, Mebel lies there listening to the sounds of her own breathing, trying to calm the whirlwind of emotions rushing through her.

Don't be so dramatic, she tells herself. *So, Gemma has quit the course abruptly. You've talked to people about it, and everyone agrees this is just what young people are wont to do, which is true. When you were in your early twenties, you started a ton of projects that you left halfway through. You picked up tennis and piano, remember? And now you play neither. And so what if Alain has left you just because he has slept with you? It's not the end of the world. You're here to win Henk back. Your little tryst with Alain was never to go anywhere, not really. It was a fling. What the youths would call a rebound.*

Am I the sort of person to have rebounds? she wonders.

Apparently, yes.

God, she thinks. *If Henk ever finds out, he will be livid. There will be no taking me back then.*

What a double standard, her mind seethes. *So he gets to do whatever he wants and leave you for another woman, but if you then have a little tryst of your own, he thinks you're soiled goods?*

Well, yes, Mebel thinks. *That is, unfortunately, how the world works, isn't it?* Or at least the part of the world that she's from. *Argh, this is impossible.*

Life, it seems, has decided to throw yet another monkey wrench into her plans, and this time, Mebel is too exhausted to try to pull it out.

Chapter 15

THE ONLY THING THAT HAS ALWAYS CHEERED MEBEL UP when she feels this way is to binge-watch *Sex and the City*. These women's lives are so far removed from Mebel's that it is a complete escape from reality for her. And she loves knowing that even with the freedom that comes with being a career woman in New York City, Carrie and her friends' lives remain disastrously messy. Mebel likes to imagine Samantha growing up as a CHIP and being told no sex before marriage.

Now, as Mebel watches her eighth episode of *Sex and the City* in a row while eating a caramel Cadbury bar and sipping a glass of white wine, she imagines herself as one of these women. Carrie, Miranda, Charlotte, Samantha, and Mebel. Why not? Their names even go great together. She imagines confiding in them about sleeping with Alain and thinks of how each woman would react. Samantha would nod at Mebel over her martini glass and give her a proud wink. Come to think of it, even Charlotte would be proud of her.

In contrast, her friends back in Jakarta would be absolutely horrified. Their mouths would drop open, aghast, and then they'd catch themselves and force polite smiles onto their faces. Then, one by one, they would come up with some excuse to leave the gathering, after which they would furiously gossip about Mebel the hussy over WhatsApp.

Mebel watches forlornly as Carrie learns to eat at a restaurant on her own. She snorts. What's the big deal about eating on her own? Mebel does it all the time. People do it all the time. But then she watches as Carrie sits down at a table and tells the waiter that she is there alone. She doesn't take out her phone or a book or a newspaper or anything. She merely sits there and eats on her own, enjoying her own company, and that's when it hits Mebel that although she has eaten on her own plenty of times before, she has never done it without the aid of a book or, in recent years, her phone to distract her from the fact that she is eating alone. And when she thinks back to all the people she's seen eating alone in restaurants, they too have always been immersed in their phones. And it is very different, isn't it, to sit there and be on one's phone versus sitting there and being fully in the moment.

Mebel checks her watch. It is seven o'clock. She didn't plan on doing anything for dinner because everything that's happened today has killed her appetite, but now, she sits up, puts aside her half-eaten chocolate bar, and gets out of bed. She throws on a pair of jeans and a comfortable sweater. A glance in the mirror tells her that she looks haggard, most of her makeup wiped away, and she doesn't bother reapplying it. Why bother when she's only got herself for company? She picks up her phone and is about to slip it into her handbag when she pauses. Why tempt herself? Drawing a deep breath, she places the phone carefully on her table, then with one last look at it, she leaves her room.

Minutes later, Mebel is out on the street, breathing in the cold night air and making her way to Cowley Road. Without her phone to look at, she is forced to pay full attention to her surroundings. For the first couple of blocks, Mebel's mind rebels against the boredom. Maybe she should turn around and grab her phone. What if Sammy messages her? What if Gemma tries to call her?

The urge to go back to the dorm and snatch her phone off the table is almost overwhelming, but Mebel forces herself to keep going. *You can be without your phone for an hour or so,* she tells herself. *If anyone tries calling you, you will see the missed call when you get back and you can call them back then. No one is going to die while you are away from your phone, and even if they were and you were at your phone, there's nothing you can do about it.*

The realization that the world won't fall apart just because she doesn't have her phone on her for an hour releases a tension that she didn't realize existed inside of her. She looks around her and takes in a deep, slow breath. The houses are still as gray and gloomy as the day she arrived, but now, she notices the plants. She notices how one house on this street has a huge rosemary bush in their front yard that has grown so large that it hangs heavy over their fence. Mebel reaches out and snaps off a tiny sprig, and as she walks, she brings it to her nose and inhales. The spicy scent of rosemary fills her nostrils and soothes her mind, and she smiles to herself. How had she not noticed this house before?

Another house has a gorgeous hydrangea bush growing in their front yard. Mebel doesn't snap any off, but she pauses for a second to admire the purplish-blue flowers, marveling at their simple beauty. By the time she reaches Cowley Road, she's in a far better mood than when she first left the school. She steps inside a casual Taiwanese restaurant and is seated at a booth. The place is only half-full, and after ordering herself a bowl of spicy beef noodle soup and a boba milk tea, Mebel looks around, taking in her surroundings.

Taiwanese pop music plays softly in the background, and the decor in here reminds Mebel not of Indonesia but of LA, particularly San Gabriel Valley. When she moved to LA for college, she'd sometimes get homesick, so she and her other Chindo friends would make the drive east to SGV, where they'd get dim sum and then hang out at a local boba tea place. It's been decades since Mebel has thought of LA, and she smiles at the nostalgic feeling it's bringing back. A couple tables over, one of the patrons, dining on her own, happens to glance up from her phone and meet Mebel's eye. The girl, who looks about in her early twenties, studies Mebel for a moment, probably feeling sorry for her. She gives Mebel a small smile, then she goes back to staring at her phone. The moment is over, just like that. But there is a newfound peace in Mebel. Being out here without her phone is a whole new experience that she hadn't thought she'd be able to go through, but here she is, doing exactly that.

The food arrives and Mebel slurps up her noodles, marveling at how good they taste. She hasn't realized just how much she's missed Asian food after weeks of cooking creamy, rich French food and eating heavy British fare. She's missed spice, and clear broths that are not cream-based, and springy thick noodles that can be slurped up easily. The boba milk tea is strong and sweet and comforting, and without her phone, Mebel is forced to pay attention to every bite, every slurp of her food and drink. She can't remember the last time she's been so aware of what she is eating. Every mouthful is a revelation of flavors, and the classes at Saint Honoré have made Mebel more appreciative of how chefs use different methods to bring out the best flavor profiles from each ingredient.

When she finishes, she feels like she has nourished not just her body but her soul as well. She's just had a meal with nothing else to distract her from her food and the pleasure of her own company, and Mebel is delighted to find that, in fact, her mind isn't as intrusive as she'd thought it would be. When she gives it the time and space to revel in its own thoughts, the usual frantic anxiety quiets down and mellows out into a steady stream of thoughts that are actually bearable and not always self-destructive.

You're not so bad, Mebel tells herself.

Thank you, her mind responds, *neither are you*.

THE NEXT FEW DAYS, MEBEL DIVES INTO DOING THE RESEARCH necessary for her to come up with a duck course that would blow everyone's mind away. She likes the idea of a Peking duck–inspired dish, but by now, after hearing bits and pieces from her fellow classmates, she also knows that she needs to do something truly special to ensure that her dish lives up to expectations.

It isn't that Mebel wants to steal the prize away from her more deserving classmates, but for once in her life, it's no longer enough to simply get by. She wants to excel. In between classes, she goes to Chef Clarke's office and runs her ideas by him.

"I have decide the duck needs to be aged," she announces one day.

Chef Clarke smiles and nods. "Excellent idea. I quite agree. Duck meat is absolutely divine when it's aged. Now, have you thought of what spices or herbs you might want to age it with?"

Beaming from his enthusiastic response, Mebel says, "I am thinking maybe orange peel and ginger."

Chef Clarke tilts his head to one side and ponders this. "I fear the ginger might be overpowering. Ginger is something that strengthens over time. No, it will ruin the duck."

Mebel sighs. She was so close. She tries asking him for a suggestion of what to use instead of ginger, but Chef Clarke gently reminds her that this is something she needs to think up on her own. They end the discussion with her agreeing to put more thought into the aging process. She spends the rest of the day walking aimlessly, muttering to herself and rejecting various ingredients.

The answer comes to her as she sips yet another boba milk tea from the Taiwanese restaurant on Cowley Road, which has become her favorite haunt now that her friends have all become fully absorbed in their tasks. The next day, she hurries into Chef Clarke's office beaming with excitement. "Orange peel and brown sugar syrup. The sweetness will be very subtle, more aroma than actual taste. It go perfectly well with the savory spiced brine."

"Brown sugar syrup?" Chef Clarke says with a frown.

"You know, like the one we are using in boba milk tea."

"Ah." Chef Clarke frowns for a while, then he raises his eyebrows. "Well, maybe. Yes, I can see that working. And how will you be cooking it?"

"So after I dry-age it with the orange peel and brown sugar syrup, I will do it in a confit style, cook it in its own fat. That way the meat becomes so tender and falling off the bone."

Chef Clarke nods. "That sounds good to me. Good work, Mebel. I will arrange for some duck to be delivered here, and you can start practicing once it arrives."

Mebel can't remember the last time she felt so proud of herself. She walks all the way back to her room with a huge smile, and once inside, she notices that she hasn't even put her makeup on today. She looks a frightful mess, but for once, she doesn't care. She's designed her own dish all by herself, and none of this process involved her blow-drying her hair in a meticulous fashion. There's something so incredibly satisfying about that knowledge.

Alain, who has returned from London, takes her out that night, and listens with a look of quiet amusement on his face as she walks him through her duck dish.

"I like the sound of this dish," he says.

"You do?" Mebel says, her eyes lighting up. Then she stops herself. Of course he would say that he likes the sound of it. He's her—well, not boyfriend, it seems ridiculous to refer to someone as one's "boyfriend" when one is in her sixties. Goodness, what is he? Her lover? Her paramour? Mebel bats the question away. Doesn't matter. What matters right now is the fact that he is kind of obliged to like her dish because they are sleeping with each other.

The thought makes Mebel uneasy. Is she cheating on this competition because she's sleeping with Alain?

"Is it okay that we are talking about this? I don't want to cheat the competition and win just because you have the sex with me."

Alain's eyes dance with laughter. "Do you think that's what I'd do? Have you win the competition and start working at my highest-rated restaurant just because we are lovers?"

Mebel blushes at the word "lovers" coming out of Alain's mouth. Despite the intimacy of their relationship, she still hasn't quite come to terms with the fact that she is the sort of woman to have a "lover." "I don't know. Men always think with their penises, not their brains."

"Well, that's not incorrect. But, no, Mebel, to put your mind at ease, you are not behaving in an unethical way, and I can guarantee that, because I won't be the one judging the competition. The students at Pemberton College will cast a vote for the best dish at the end of the meal."

"Ah." Mebel sags with relief. "I am glad."

"Good, now let's enjoy—"

"But is it cheating because I discuss my dish with you and you give me advice when you are such famous chef?"

Alain puts down his fork and knife and regards Mebel closely. "Is it cheating? No, I don't think so. The other students are free to approach me or Chef Clarke for our input. And I certainly won't be giving you any information that I wouldn't tell your classmates if they asked. Now, before you ask another question, let me ask one of my own: Why do you care so much if it's ethical or not? The culinary industry is a cutthroat one. Backstabbing happens every day, especially when the stakes are as high as this."

"I know," Mebel sighs. "I don't like this backstabbing thing. My friends and I have good relationship, and then this competition come along and ruin everything. They need this prize badly, some of them. More badly than me."

"Not really," Alain says. "Once they graduate from the program, they'll be snapped up by restaurants all over the country, just like that. They don't have to work at Canard et Vin. They want to, but that is a choice. Just like you have a choice to do the best you can for this banquet."

"I see," Mebel says, nodding slowly, trying to parse through his words. Alain has a tendency to speak softly and fast, and sometimes Mebel has trouble understanding him. Like now, for example. All she got from his speech is that nobody needs to work at Canard et Vin, which seemed extremely obvious to her, but she has since begun to understand isn't true for most of her classmates.

"You need to make a decision for yourself, Mebel," Alain says. "I see the way you have been working so hard on your dish. It's not the way someone who only wants to be a housewife would work. You are applying yourself very hard. Are you sure you are only here to win back your husband?"

"Yes, of course," Mebel says, irritated by the question. Why do people keep asking her this question? They simply don't understand what is at stake for her back in Jakarta. It isn't just about losing Henk, it's about losing her entire life, her social circle, her home, her way of being. She can't imagine being invited to any meals or events if she were to be a divorcée. Society would slice her out neatly, and she would be forgotten in no time. And here Alain thinks she would give all of that up just because, what, she's into her duck course?

Fortunately for Alain, the sex later that night more than makes up for the dicey dinnertime conversation. Mebel is beginning to see the value in having lovers. She can't see a future with Alain, a man who is married, who thinks nothing of having multiple lovers, but she enjoys his company very much, which would've confused Mebel the CHIP. But Mebel the worldly culinary school student is adept at compartmentalizing parts of her life. It is as though she has split into two different selves.

Mebel the CHIP would never have a meal alone without a phone to keep herself company.

Mebel the worldly culinary school student not only is happy to have meals alone, but sometimes even prefers it, sitting there slowly eating with only her thoughts for company.

Mebel the CHIP is a one-man gal, devoting her entire life to her husband.

Mebel the worldly culinary school student is here to have fun before she returns to the company of her husband.

Mebel the CHIP spends her days working on making herself look fabulous, going for regular facials and having all sorts of chemicals injected into her face to boost collagen production. When she isn't working on keeping her face looking as youthful as possible, she is shopping to make sure her outfits are as flattering as possible.

Mebel the worldly culinary school student looks, quite

frankly, like shit. She spends her days perspiring heavily in the kitchen, her hair trapped in an unflattering hair net. For once, the way Mebel looks isn't the most important thing about her.

DESPITE THE JOY THAT COMES WITH WORKING HARD IN culinary school, Mebel's life is far from perfect. As they get nearer to the banquet, the tension among the students grows thicker, until it lies heavy in the air like a poison cloud. The classes are no longer an easygoing camaraderie. Mebel longs for the days when Adam would turn around and give Mebel a cheeky wink in the middle of class or when Bella would exchange an eye roll with her at Bruce's antics.

They still go out for meals sometimes, but the meals are a far cry from what they used to be. All Adam, Bruce, and Bella want to do is discuss what they think the other groups are cooking for the banquet. Bruce in particular is in a bad mood because, apparently, he and his partner, Chris, are in a disagreement over their dish, but of course he is unwilling to talk about it.

"Did you hear what Kate and Matt are making?" Bella says one evening.

They all look at her in anticipation.

"Miso-smoked cod accompanied with blanched asparagus and shiitake mushrooms."

Bruce's mouth falls open. "She can't do that."

"Why not?" Mebel says, feeling like she's missed something.

"Because Chris and I are using shiitake mushrooms in *our* dish. Are you sure about this?" he says to Bella.

Bella nods. "I overheard her talking to Chef Clarke about it."

"I'm sure is okay if she does mushrooms too, so what?" Mebel says.

They all stare at her like she's just said the dumbest thing in the world.

"So what?" Adam echoes. "You can't have two courses with shiitake mushrooms in them."

"Why not?"

"For fuck's sake," Bruce says, standing up so abruptly that his chair screeches across the floor. "I need to talk to Chris. We're going to have to scrap our entire dish and start over." He strides off, tapping on his phone furiously.

"We can't have the same ingredients in our dish, Mebel," Adam says. "It's tiresome on the palate, and given Bruce has the sixth course and Kate and Matt have the third course, it'll look like Bruce and Chris copied them."

"Ah." Mebel chews her pasta slowly, considering what Adam just told her. It makes sense, she supposes, though she still thinks they're all overreacting a little.

"Especially when it's something as distinctive in flavor as shiitake mushrooms," Bella says. "Can you imagine having two shiitake dishes in the menu? Awful."

Mebel doesn't see the big deal in having two shiitake dishes in a menu, but she wisely decides to keep her mouth shut.

Then Bella says, "Tell you what, though, their dish actually sounds really good. They're marinating the cod with miso, orange peel, and brown sugar syrup."

That's when the dagger of doubt plunges deep into Mebel's belly. Orange peel and brown sugar syrup? That's exactly what she was planning on doing with her duck. The duck meat that

Chef Clarke had ordered for her arrived two days prior, and Mebel had gotten to work on it immediately, marinating it in a spiced brine overnight before coating it with her brown sugar and orange peel syrup. Could it be a coincidence that her classmates have picked out the same ingredients as she had?

"You all right, Mebs?" Adam says.

"I am using orange peel and brown sugar syrup in my dish," Mebel blurts out.

Adam and Bella both stare at her. "What," Bella says, "like, exactly that combination?"

Mebel nods, not trusting herself to talk.

"Well, fuck," Bella mutters.

"What does this mean?" Mebel says.

"You've got the poultry course, right?" Adam says. When Mebel nods, he says, "That means you're right after fish. You've got to change your dish. It's going to look so bad if you go right after them and your dish is exactly the same flavor profile as theirs."

Anxiety claws at Mebel's chest, making it close up. "But I work so hard to come up with the combination."

"They must've overheard you talking about it or seen your notes or something," Bella says.

"But why they want to copy it?" Mebel cries.

"Mebs, I told you, this is a big deal. Everyone wants to win," Bella says. "And brown sugar syrup? That's pretty fucking brilliant. That'll go really well with miso and orange peel. I can see why they'd copy it."

"Do I really have to give up on my idea?" Mebel says in a small voice. She feels so lost right now.

Adam and Bella exchange a glance before nodding sadly at her. "Sorry, Mebs," Adam says.

"It sucks. You need to be more careful."

Mebel can't stomach the thought of staying through to the end of the meal. She tells them she is done and leaves the table. Outside, she walks past Bruce, who is arguing animatedly into his phone. How ironic that only minutes ago, she'd judged Bruce for getting upset over his dish, and now here she is, upset for exactly the same reason. Life really does have a way of getting you.

Mebel walks briskly down the street, hugging herself. She feels at once angry and hurt and vulnerable. Not to mention foolish, because how many times have people tried to warn her about the stakes in this competition, and she'd failed to take any of them seriously. To her, all of this has just been an amusing game, but now that her dish is being copied, everything has suddenly turned very real for her. It is only in this moment that she realizes, despite the compassion she feels for her classmates and how much they have at stake, she really, really wants to win this competition. Not so much for the position at Canard et Vin, but to prove to herself that she is capable of it. She is capable not just of doing decently well but of excelling. She is capable of being more than just a trophy wife.

But now, she is going to lose it all, and isn't that just classic Mebel?

As she walks, she goes through a list of ingredients that she might be able to substitute for the orange peel and brown sugar syrup. Maybe instead of brown sugar, she could use Javanese sugar? It's her favorite sugar, made out of palm instead of sugar cane, and has a caramel taste that is very distinct. No, that's the problem with Javanese sugar, it's too distinctive. It'll overpower the entire dish. Perhaps wild honey? That could work, but it isn't as exciting as brown sugar syrup though. And what about the orange peel? What can she substitute that with? Lemongrass? Maybe. But lemongrass wouldn't go with the Peking duck–inspired dish. It's too strong and would overpower the hoisin sauce. *Argh, this is horrible!* And why must Mebel go through this ordeal all by herself? It's so unfair, especially when everyone else has a partner they can bounce ideas off.

She should storm inside Chef Clarke's office and demand—what? What should she demand at this point? The banquet is only two weeks away. What can Chef Clarke do? He's hardly going to call the whole thing off, and there's no way he can get her a new partner. And anyway, Mebel doesn't want any other partner, she wants Gemma, her first-ever friend at the school, the girl who loves cooking and secretly works overtime to shoot cooking videos for her social media account.

Mebel gasps. Foolishness! The answer was right in front of her all this time and she'd missed it. She scrambles for her phone and opens up Instagram. She's messaged Gemma on there several times, of course, but Gemma hasn't bothered to reply. The messages show as "Seen," however, so she knows that Gemma is still alive, even though she has stopped posting videos since she disappeared from the school.

But now, Mebel realizes there is a ton of valuable information to be gleaned from Gemma's IG account. She scrolls through the videos, looking for the ones she's thinking of. Ah, here we go. Here's one where Gemma bakes a honey cake using "locally sourced honey." In the voice-over, Gemma says, "I am so lucky to live within walking distance to the Clover Lover Farm. Their honey is just the absolute best. Look how thick this clover honey is, and it smells heavenly. Oh, I wish you could smell it through your phone screen."

Mebel had known that Gemma lived in the Cotswolds, but when she previously looked up the Cotswolds, she'd been surprised to find that it's a huge area. There is no chance of Mebel finding Gemma just by driving around the entire Cotswolds.

Now, Mebel hurriedly taps the words "Clover Lover Farm" into Google, and the first hit is a farm located in an area called Northleach, which, according to Google, is a small market town located in the Cotswolds district in Gloucestershire, England.

"Aha!" Mebel says. Several passersby turn to look at her, but she ignores them. Her heart races with excitement as she keys "Northleach" into Google Maps. She's not sure if it's small enough for her to go door-to-door until she finds Gemma, but she sure as hell is going to try.

Mebel goes to her contacts list and taps on Alain's name.

"Hello, Mebel, I wasn't expecting to hear from you tonight," he says when he picks up the phone.

"Alain, you want to go to the Cotswolds with me?" Mebel says.

There is a pause, then he says, "Uh, why?"

"Well, you remember my classmate Gemma?"

"Yes," Alain says carefully.

"She disappear and I am worried about her. So I am going to look for her there. She lives there."

"I don't know about this, Mebel. Maybe she just wants to be left alone, no? She is a grown woman, if she wants to talk to you, I'm sure she'll reach out."

Mebel sighs impatiently. "Okay, I take Uber."

"Wait—" Alain pauses again. "All right. I will take you. But, Mebel, I think you're overreacting."

Mebel ignores the patronizing tone in his voice. "I see you tomorrow. Nine o'clock."

She is done with people telling her she's overreacting.

ALAIN SHOWS UP AT TWENTY PAST NINE THE NEXT MORNING. Mebel is irritated, but she's also aware that she needs him to drive her to the Cotswolds, and so she bites her tongue when she sees him. He greets her with a hug and a kiss on her cheek, then he says, "How about a day trip to London instead? Lunch at the Ritz? You'd love that."

Mebel swallows yet more irritation. What is it about her that makes people think they can just ignore what she wants and try to push their own agenda onto her? "I have lunch plenty of time at the Ritz. Is okay, nothing special."

"All right. What about—"

Without waiting for him to open the car door for her, Mebel opens it herself, slides in, and closes it. She smiles at him through the window and sees his chest heaving in a sigh. When he's inside the car, she looks at him askance. "Why you don't want to go to Cotswolds? I thought is your favorite place in England."

"Oh, I love the Cotswolds. I just think the reason you have to go there is rather suspect. We are intruding on someone who'd rather be left alone. I want to respect her privacy. Now, if you wanted to go to the Cotswolds to have a nice day out, that's an entirely different matter and I'd only be too happy to oblige."

Mebel snorts. "That is nice, but I am Chinese mother, I don't respect anybody's privacy. Start the car."

With that, Alain seems to realize that the decision is final, and he does as he is told. Mebel turns away from him and looks out of the window to hide the smirk that's taken over her face. What is she? She has never spoken to Henk like this before, and it is exhilarating. She could get used to this.

The drive to the Cotswolds is a peaceful one. For Mebel, that is. For Alain, it seems to be a different story altogether. Once or twice, he mutters under his breath in French, but when Mebel says, "What?" he says, "Nothing, ma chérie."

Maybe he is irritated at having been coerced into driving her there, or maybe he is turned off by Mebel's insistence at finding Gemma. Mebel decides that either way, she doesn't actually care. She knows that their relationship has an expiration date, and the knowledge is liberating.

When they get to the Cotswolds, Mebel's spirits lift even higher. She has never been to a place quite like it before. Whenever she and Henk and their friends have traveled, they have always stuck to glamorous big cities. Paris, Shanghai, Dubai, places dominated by shiny towers. The Cotswolds is an entirely different place. The houses are cottages straight out of a fairy tale, with steepled roofs and flowerpots overflowing with blooms under the windows. Alain finds parking near the center of Northleach, and they climb out of the car.

"I think we should go to market square, ah, there it is," Mebel says, hurrying ahead.

The town, already charming on its own, becomes straight-up enchanting when Mebel arrives at the market square. Since it's a Saturday morning, it's bustling with people going around, perusing the locally made goods. The stands are all selling things one would expect at a local farmer's market. There's fresh produce, with some of the biggest heads of garlic and glossiest bell peppers that Mebel has ever seen. There's freshly baked loaves of sourdough bread and baguettes, and there are baskets of fresh fruit and berries, and for a good while, Mebel is distracted by all of the goodies she's surrounded by.

Finally, she arrives at a stand selling pots of honey. She looks up at the stand's name, and sure enough, it says "Clover Lover Farm."

"Hi, would you like to try some of our clover honey?" the lady behind the stand says when she spots Mebel.

Mebel nods, and the lady unscrews a jar of honey that looks like milk and has the consistency of a paste rather than the usual golden syrupy honey that Mebel is used to. She dips two wooden spoons into the jar and hands them to Mebel and Alain. Mebel puts it in her mouth.

"Mmm," she says, not expecting the texture at all. It's a lot more solid than normal honey, almost like a chewy candy, and she can taste the subtle flavor of clover in it. The sweetness is soft and gentle rather than an over-the-top kind that hits your tongue at once. "Ah, is delicious."

"Yes, it is," Alain says. "The flavor notes in this are very distinct."

The honey seller beams. "Thank you. It's my family farm. It goes back three generations."

"I will buy ten jars, thank you." Mebel takes out her wallet.

"Oh my! Lovely," the seller says, packing up ten jars for them.

"Do you happen to know my friend," Mebel says, "her name is Gemma Stevenson, and she is a—"

"Oh, Gemma! Yes, of course," the honey seller says, her eyes lighting up. "Such a sweetheart. She buys honey from us all the time. She came up with the most delicious recipe for a honey cake that we sell here, actually." She points to a cake stand on which, sure enough, is a pale yellow cake with the sign: Honey Cake, £5 a piece.

"Oh!" Mebel says. Her heart twists at the sight of it. She hasn't realized just how much she has missed her friend. "Can I buy a slice?"

"Of course." The lady packs up a slice and hands it to her. "It's a crowd favorite. We've gotten so many orders for it since we started putting it on the market."

"Gemma live nearby, right?" Mebel says, trying to look casual. If this lady, like Agatha, is all about privacy, then Mebel will have no choice but to go knocking on every house door until she finds Gemma's house. She glances up at Alain and sees his tense expression. He probably feels awkward standing there listening to her. A quick flash of inspiration makes Mebel add, "Actually, I am just on my way to see Gemma. I'm buying some groceries for her—I think she say her house is over there, right?" She points down a random side street and does her best to look innocent.

"No, actually, she lives on Grace Drive, over there. Sorry, what did you say your name was?"

"Mebel. I am very good friend of Gemma. Okay, thank you for honey and cake, I tell Gemma you say hi." Before the honey seller can say anything else, Mebel grabs Alain's hand and walks off. Once they are out of sight, she takes out her phone, opens Google Maps, and types in *Grace Drive*. "Okay, this way."

Alain shakes his head as they leave the market. "I can't believe you did that."

"What?"

"You got her street address from that woman so easily."

"Oh?" Mebel says with doe eyes. "Is it easily? I don't know, I just speaking normally to her, just making chitchat."

The left corner of Alain's mouth rises into a smirk as he gazes down at her. "You are something else, Mebel."

Mebel bites down on her lip to keep from smiling. What most people don't know is how vital it is for trophy wives to be able to finagle information out of anyone. Having wiles and infallible charm is essential for any self-respecting trophy wife. She could probably teach CIA operatives a few lessons in how to dig information out of an unsuspecting victim.

It is a beautiful walk down crooked lanes lined with cobblestones, and Mebel is so glad that they made the trip here. Even if she fails to find Gemma, it would have been a nice little day trip out. When they make the turn onto Grace Drive, Mebel brushes her hands down the front of her outfit and takes a deep breath.

"You're not really going to knock on every single door here, are you?" Alain says.

"Why not?"

"Because—" Alain rakes his fingers through his hair. "It's kind of intrusive, don't you think?"

"No, is not," Mebel says with all the confidence in the world. Before Alain can argue, she holds up the bag of clover honey. "Because I give these out." She grins at Alain's shocked expression, then turns and walks down the lane. At the first house, she rings the doorbell and stands there holding a jar of clover honey.

The door opens and an old man peers out. "Yes?" he says, looking suspiciously at Mebel and Alain.

Mebel holds out the jar of honey. "Hello, I am here to give out free sample of Clover Lover honey. Is our best product, here you go."

The old man takes the jar from her, then stands there looking a bit confused. "Are you looking for a donation?"

"No. Is a free sample. I hope Gemma enjoy it."

"Gemma? She doesn't live here. She's down at number four."

"Thank you. Enjoy the honey!" With that, Mebel walks away.

Alain hurries after her. "I can't believe that just happened," he says in amazement. "Who are you?"

"I'm Mebel."

"No, but"—Alain catches her hand—"are you an MI5 agent?"

"If I am, why I tell you for what?"

"True," Alain says. "Hang on, you've got nine jars of honey left, what are you going to do with those?"

"I give to Gemma. She like this honey." Mebel finally locates house number 4.

It's a small terraced house sandwiched in the middle of a row of houses, its stone walls bare. The front yard is tiny but well maintained, with a row of asters growing along the fence. The door is painted a navy blue and the knocker is in the shape of a cat. The house number has been hand-painted onto a ceramic plate that is decorated with painted flowers. Everything about it screams Gemma, and the sight of it unexpectedly makes Mebel nervous. What if Gemma isn't here? Or worse still, what if she is, but she doesn't want Mebel here? There is, after all, a reason why Gemma has chosen to leave the school without a single word.

"It's not too late to turn around," Alain says, reading her mind.

"Nonsense." Mebel doesn't give herself time for second thoughts before reaching up and ringing the doorbell. The sound reverberates through the house, and as Mebel stands there waiting for the door to open, her heart rate doubles, then triples. She forces herself to take a long, deep breath for six seconds. Then she holds it for another six seconds before releasing it slowly. She's read somewhere (or watched a reel, more likely) that this is how snipers slow their heart rate down.

The door clicks open and there, finally, is her dear friend Gemma.

Chapter 16

GEMMA!" MEBEL SAYS, RUSHING FORWARD AND ENGULFing the girl in a hug. She's missed Gemma so much, and also, she doesn't want to give her the chance to slam the door in her face.

"Mebel," Gemma says, shock apparent in her voice. "What are you doing here?"

"I come to find you," Mebel says. She releases Gemma and takes her in. To her surprise, she feels tears moistening her eyes. After all this time, she can't help but see Gemma as an honorary daughter, and the sight of her standing there is bringing up so many emotions.

Gemma's expression softens for a moment, but then she glances over Mebel's shoulder and tenses. "Look, Mebs, I left because I just—the atmosphere at the school just got so toxic, and it was wreaking havoc on my mental health. I don't really want to talk about it."

"What?" Mebel's head is swimming. She tries her best to parse through these terms that Gemma is saying. Toxic? Mental health? Sammy has said these words before, but Mebel has always dismissed them as a "young people thing." She scours her mind for any signs of toxicity in the culinary school. Well, she can't deny that there's certainly a lot of it recently, but it only happened after the competition was announced. Before that, they were doing just fine, weren't they? They'd created their own little friend group, and the camaraderie was wonderful.

"I don't understand," Mebel says. "We talk about it over tea. I got clover honey for you, I know you like it." She hands Gemma the bag of honey and takes off her shoes before letting herself into the house. "Oh, and Alain is here also."

"Uh—" Gemma says, struggling with the bag of honey and hurrying after Mebel. "I really don't think—"

"This is a nice place, is very you," Mebel says, plopping down on the sofa and looking around her appreciatively. It is the tiniest house Mebel has ever been in. The ceiling is so low that if Mebel were to stand on tiptoes and reach up, she would be able to touch it, and she is barely five foot two on good days. The living room can only fit a two-seater sofa plus a chair and a coffee table the size of a wine crate. In fact, Mebel realizes, the coffee table is made out of a wine crate. Gemma has taken care to put a vase of fresh flowers on it, which makes the whole thing look rather charming. The walls are painted a muted dusty pink and hung with watercolor paintings.

"Um, thank you. Sorry, it isn't very big. It's not a very good place for guests, I'm afraid." Gemma stands there, her wide-eyed gaze bouncing back and forth from Mebel to Alain. "Mebel,

I just don't think there's very much to discuss. I'm quite a lot happier since leaving the school."

"Why?" Mebel says, confused.

Alain sits down next to her. Gemma glances at him, and Mebel kicks herself for bringing Alain in here. She should've told him to wait in the car. Of course Gemma wouldn't want to talk bad about the school in front of him, especially with the knowledge that he holds so much power there.

As though sensing their discomfort, Alain says, "I'll wait outside. Take your time." He stands and plants a kiss on Mebel's cheek. As he leaves, he reaches out and gives Gemma a single pat on the shoulder. "I hope you work out whatever it is that's been bothering you." With that, he leaves the house.

Mebel turns back to Gemma. "Well? You explain yourself."

Gemma hugs the bag of honey to her chest. "Wha-what's there to explain?"

"You leave without telling anyone!" Mebel cries. "Why you don't even tell me?"

Gemma's eyes roam the room, as though searching for an escape route. "I don't know—I just—it all got too much. I struggle with anxiety, and it was getting worse in the school."

"Anxiety?" Mebel says. She has no idea what "anxiety" means in this sense. "You mean like stress?"

"Something like that, but more persistent. It's something I feel most of the time, whether or not there's something worth getting anxious over. Obviously it gets worse when there are triggers, like the competition," she says, her words coming out faster and faster as she speaks. She stops herself, and as she looks at Mebel, her face falls. "I'm sorry, Mebs. Oh, I hope they let you partner up with someone else after I left."

"They don't," Mebel says. "I am doing the duck course all alone. You need to come back. This anxiety thing, I will give you some Chinese ginseng, it will cure for sure."

Gemma laughs, but there is no humor in it. "I don't think it's something that can be cured with ginseng."

"How you know? You never try before."

"I just know, okay, Mebel?" Gemma cries, frustration bleeding through her usually soft voice.

The anger in Gemma's voice reminds Mebel of Sammy when he says things like, "Ma, you just don't get it, okay?" She's always felt so hurt when he says stuff like that, because she's always prided herself on being understanding, on being one of the more open-minded parents in her generation. She listens when he tells her things, she got herself familiarized with social media so she can have a peek into the lives of youths nowadays. She really does try to keep her mind flexible so it can accommodate the new generation's needs and quirks. The ones who don't get it aren't her; it's them. They don't get that old dogs can learn new tricks, if the old dog is appropriately motivated, and Mebel is very much motivated. She digs deep and draws from her experience with Sammy, draws from the times where she did manage to reach past their generational gap and get to him.

"You're right," she says to Gemma. "Maybe I don't understand. But I know one thing, and that is you belong at the culinary school. You are talented cook, Gemma. Everyone knows. Your technique is very smooth, you learn all the method so well, and you have good instinct for flavor."

Gemma looks like she's about to burst into tears. "You're just saying that to be nice."

Mebel snorts. "I have never been accuse of being nice."

Gemma rolls her eyes, but she looks like she's suspiciously trying to hide her smile. "That's true. Look, Mebs, I appreciate you coming all the way here—although, hang on, how did you find my address? Did the school give it to you? Because that's a serious breach of privacy."

"No, I have my ways," Mebel says with a flippant wave of her hand. "Are you sure you not coming back?"

Gemma nods, not meeting Mebel's eyes. "I'm sure."

"Okay," Mebel says.

Gemma's eyebrows rise up into her hairline. "Okay? Just like that?"

Mebel shrugs. "Yes. I accept your decision. If you say you not coming back, then, okay, you not coming back."

"Wow, okay. That's surprisingly accepting of you. Thank you."

"But I still need your help."

Gemma frowns. "What with?"

And so Mebel tells Gemma about her duck course being pirated by Kate and Matt.

"Oh, those bastards!" Gemma cries. "I knew they weren't trustworthy. Kate's always got this shifty look about her, and Matt—"

"Matt look like he is drug dealer," Mebel says.

Gemma laughs. "Oh my god, he really does, doesn't he? Ugh, how could they do this? Well, I know why they did it, because orange peel and brown sugar syrup? That's brilliant, Mebs. I can't believe you came up with that all on your own. That's amazing."

"Thank you, yes, it is, but now I don't know what new thing to come up with."

"Hello, earth to Mebel, you're with Chef Alain? One of the

most well-regarded Michelin-star chefs in the world? Why don't you ask him?"

Mebel shakes her head. "Because if I do, then people say, 'Oh, you win just because you sleeping with Chef Alain.' No, I need to do this myself. Or with my partner, which is you. You owe me, Gemma."

"Okay." Gemma taps her chin for a moment, then gets up and leaves the living room. When she comes back a minute later, she's carrying a notebook. "All right, let's see."

Mebel leans forward. It's a book containing all of Gemma's notes on anything food-related. There are recipes, notes on different methods of cooking, musings about different ingredients, and so on. The entire thing is very impressive, and Mebel has to bite her tongue from using it as proof that Gemma belongs at a culinary school.

"How about dry-aging the duck with butter that has Chinese spices mixed into it?" Gemma says. She glances at the bag of honey and adds, "Oh! That'll go really well with clover honey, actually, won't it?"

Mebel considers this for a second before nodding. "Ah yes. Chinese five-spice powder, star aniseed, cloves, soy sauce, and sugar. I love this combination, I always eat Chinese boiled peanuts for snack, and they use this combination."

"Yep, except instead of sugar, I think you should use the clover honey."

Mebel nods more enthusiastically. "Yes, it go so well with the Peking duck confit dish. But you don't think is too traditional?"

Gemma grins. "No, because you are going to top the dish with this." She holds up the open notebook and points to a page filled with barely legible writing.

Mebel squints at it. "I need my reading glasses to read your chicken scratch writing, Gemma."

Gemma laughs. "I came across a review of a Michelin-starred restaurant that tops their duck dish with crumbled crunchy duck skin. How amazing does that sound? I haven't eaten there, obviously—can't afford to—but I did my own research and experiments, and I think I've got it. Here's my recipe for crumbled duck skin. It is divine, Mebs."

"Crumbled crunchy duck skin," Mebel muses, shaking her head in awe. "I don't know how people think such things. And you figure out how to do yourself?"

"It took a while, but yep."

As Gemma continues to come up with a sauce to accompany the dish, Mebel stares at her, this bright young woman who has folded under the pressures of culinary school despite her brilliance. The thought of it fills Mebel with a tangled mix of sorrow and admiration. It is clear to Mebel that she is in the presence of a gifted person, and her motherly instincts are going haywire, wanting to help Gemma somehow. *It is not your place*, she reminds herself.

By the time Mebel is ready to leave Gemma's house, she has an entirely new recipe for her duck dish, something she's confident is completely original.

"And be more careful this time," Gemma says at the doorway, hugging Mebel. "You can do this, Mebs. I believe in you."

Mebel returns the hug, closing her eyes for a moment. "Are you sure you not want to come back with me?" she says as she pulls away, her hands still on Gemma's arms.

Gemma's smile wavers. "I am. Let me know how the banquet goes. I hope you win."

"You must reply to my messages, no more ignoring them!" Mebel scolds.

"All right, Mebs. I promise."

Outside, Alain is looking at his phone. He looks up as Mebel leaves the house and gives Gemma a small wave before turning to Mebel. "Did you figure out a new recipe?"

"Yes, but I not telling you. I don't trust anybody from now on."

Alain laughs. "You can't tell even me? But I'm not in the competition."

"Sure, but how I know if you are good at keeping secret or not?" Mebel says breezily, walking ahead of him.

"Oh, I'm good at keeping some secrets," Alain murmurs, snaking his arm around her waist and pulling her close.

Mebel's cheeks heat up. She is suddenly eager to leave the Cotswolds and go back to Oxford, where she and Alain will no doubt tumble into bed like a pair of overgrown teens.

AFTERWARD, MEBEL LIES LANGUOROUSLY IN ALAIN'S BED, luxuriating in the creamy rich bedsheets and the wideness of the bed. God, what she wouldn't do to have a bigger bed than the sad little single in her dorm room. Then again, because her room only has a sad little single, it's made her far more appreciative of a proper king bed.

After kissing her temple, Alain gets out of the bed and goes into the bathroom to shower. Mebel remains there, smiling lazily and going over the events of the day. She's found Gemma, who seems okay(ish), and she's come home with a brilliant new recipe. The thought of the recipe makes Mebel jolt upright in bed. Where did she put the recipe? She clambers out naked and grabs her handbag, rummaging through it. There it is, tucked safely into the inside pocket of her Dior. She sighs with relief. She knows better now, and she is going to guard this baby with her life.

As Mebel puts her handbag to one side, she notices a sheaf of papers on the table. She wasn't planning on snooping; she really isn't the type to do that. She's merely curious, that's all, and can anyone blame her? After all, she's gone through several huge life changes the past few months, and given her relationship with Alain, it's only natural for her to want to know more about his life.

Stop trying to justify it, her mind mutters.

Okay, so she is snooping. And she's not even sorry about it.

Glancing at the bathroom to make sure Alain is still in the shower, Mebel riffles through the papers. They don't seem to be anything particularly interesting. Contracts for his various restaurants. Then she catches sight of the words "Saint Honoré Oxford banquet," and some strange instinct makes her pause. In the bathroom, the shower has turned off. Mebel hurriedly grabs her phone and takes photos of the contract before replacing the stack of papers to their original position.

By the time Alain comes out of the bathroom with a towel wrapped around his waist, Mebel is back in bed, looking as innocent as someone who definitely would not think of riffling through his private documents. She smiles as he kisses her cheek, then takes her phone into the bathroom, where she glances over the photos of the documents, trying her best to parse through the words. English is a confusing enough language on its own, but when paired with legalese, it becomes absolutely diabolical. She feels silly. What is she even looking for, anyway?

This is nothing but a bunch of papers talking about stuff she knows nothing about, so after a minute or two, Mebel gives up and climbs into the shower.

When she comes out of the bathroom, Alain serves her a freshly made cappuccino.

"Thank you," she says. She studies him as he moves around the room, though what she is looking for, she isn't sure. It's just that . . . the thing about being cheated on after so many years of marriage is that it has utterly broken up her confidence. She used to think she was smart. She used to think that if Henk was hiding anything, surely she would know. Her instincts would kick off alarm bells and she would sniff out the truth. But she hadn't, not ever. Not until Henk himself was the one who lifted the veil, and then Mebel realized that she was nowhere near as smart or perceptive as she'd thought. And now, those painful feelings of doubt are crowding in once more. She'd seen Alain as a romantic Frenchman, a gifted chef, and a good businessman, and she hadn't spared another thought about him as a person, but now she finds herself trying to get a better grasp on who Alain is as a human.

"Are you all right?" Alain says as he buttons up his shirt.

"Yes," Mebel says, with a start. She blushes at the thought of him catching her staring. Lifting her coffee mug, she takes a long sip. "I think I go back to school now, work on my new recipe."

"Sounds good. I will order a car to take you."

And for the first time, Mebel is glad to leave Alain's company.

AS SOON AS MEBEL OPENS THE DOOR TO THE FOYER OF THE school, Agatha looks up and says, "Oh, Mebel! You've got visitors."

Mebel's first thought is that Gemma has changed her mind and reenrolled back in the school, but she doesn't even have time to say, "I do?" before a painfully familiar male voice says, "Mebel?"

She turns around, and it is as though she has just been plunged into a dream world, because there, standing in the reception area of the Saint Honoré School of Culinary Arts, Cowley, is Henk. And behind him are Sammy, Hannah, and their children: Luciana, Freydis, and Aegilfu.

"Ama!" Luciana says, rushing forward and wrapping her little arms around Mebel.

It takes a second for Mebel's senses to slam back into her body, and with a cry of joy, Mebel hugs Luciana tight. "Oh my goodness," she says in Indonesian. "You've grown so tall in just a few months!"

Sammy and Hannah hug her as well, then Mebel kisses the twins, making a huge fuss over them. And the entire time, she is achingly aware of Henk standing to one side, hands in his pockets, looking awkwardly at her. When she is done greeting her family, she catches Henk's eye, and a pregnant silence descends on all of them before she says, "I can't believe you are all here! What—why? How?"

"We all missed you very much, Ma," Sammy says. "It's not the same without you there."

"Yes," Henk agrees quietly.

A lump forms in Mebel's throat, and she blinks rapidly. "Okay, well, where are you staying?"

"At the Old Bank Hotel," Sammy says. "Shall we go up to your room so we can all have a chat?"

The thought of all seven of them crowding into her tiny

dorm room makes Mebel bark with laughter. They look at her, probably taken aback by her unladylike reaction.

"Sorry, it's just that my room is so small that we won't all fit in there."

"I'm sure it'll be fine," Sammy says.

"No, really," Mebel says. She wonders if her son has always been this cocky. "Let's go to a restaurant or your room at the Old Bank Hotel, and we can talk there." She heads for the front door, but Henk calls out.

"Mebel, did you not want to change?" he says.

Mebel looks down at her outfit. She'd thrown on her most casual clothes this morning—sweatpants and a sweater—because she was going to the Cotswolds and did not want to stand out by wearing designer clothes, and she'd worn her sneakers because she'd been expecting a long walk hunting down Gemma's house. It's something she never would have considered wearing back home in Jakarta, and certainly not something she would've worn out of the house. To make matters worse, she recalls with a flush of shame that she's just come back from a session of enthusiastic sex with Alain, and her hair must be a complete mess. She hadn't bothered to wash it at his place. Her makeup, too, is mostly undone.

Embarrassment crawls down her spine as she takes in the way her family is looking at her. A mixture of uncertainty and pity on their faces, as though they're all wondering how she could've fallen so far. She wonders, with increasing horror, if they can sense the sex on her, and she feels inexplicably guilty at the thought of what she was just doing less than an hour ago. *My god,* she thinks, *if they ever find out . . .*

"You know what?" she chirps manically. "You're right, I do need to change. I was just out walking for exercise, but I am going to change into something more appropriate right away. Give me ten minutes. Be right back!" She doesn't give them a chance to respond before hurrying up the stairs and into her room, where she double-locks the door behind her. She leans against the door, breathing hard, and catches her reflection in the mirror. "Well," she mutters, "shit."

Chapter 17

THE OLD BANK HOTEL IS ONE OF THE NICER HOTELS IN Oxford, a place where Mebel feels instantly at home. She feels more like herself as well, now that she has dressed herself in a Hermès silk dress and YSL shoes. She spent more time working on her makeup, and though her hair remains stubbornly flat since she chose not to spend two hours blowing and primping it into the usual puffy hairdo, she feels appropriately glamorous.

The hotel offers a fancy English teatime every weekend afternoon, so they opt for that. The sandwiches and petit fours are served on tiered trays, which delights Luciana, and for the first few minutes, the conversation is minimal as they focus on the aesthetic food placed before them.

"So, whose decision was it to come all the way here?" Mebel says as she works her way through a cucumber sandwich.

"Mine," Hannah says at the same time as Sammy. They look at each other.

"Actually, it was Pa's idea, remember?" Sammy says.

Hannah shrugs and bounces Freydis on her knee. Or maybe it's Aegilfu. After such a long time away from the twins, Mebel finds it even harder to tell them apart.

"It was your idea?" Mebel says, turning to Henk.

He clears his throat, looking embarrassed.

"Pa misses you, Ma," Sammy says. "Right, Pa?"

Henk straightens his suit and tugs on his shirt collar. "Well, I was talking to Sammy and I said, 'I wonder how your mother is doing.' And then—"

"I suggested coming here and seeing for ourselves," Hannah says.

"Right," Henk says.

"And how is Wendy?" The words are out before Mebel can stop herself. The moment they are, she feels such a virulent wave of anger toward herself that she almost pinches her own leg. Why had she said that? They're having a perfectly nice time, and now she's gone and ruined it all.

Henk blanches.

"Aduh, Ma," Sammy says, "does it matter? She's not in our lives anymore."

"She's not?" Mebel says.

Henk shakes his head. "I made a mistake." He opens his mouth as though to say more, but then he glances up at Hannah, then looks meaningfully at Mebel. "Can we talk about this later?"

Mebel is about to say, *Yes, of course,* when she stops herself. That's what the old Mebel would've done. The old Mebel would've swallowed her anxiety, ignored her own stress signals, and agreed that, yes, of course they can table the conversation until later so that nobody else feels uncomfortable. And now that Mebel thinks about it, she feels annoyed at Sammy for questioning her. Does it matter? Of course it fucking matters! This is her marriage she's talking about.

"I'd rather talk about it now," Mebel says.

Henk tenses up, and Sammy looks irritated. Before he can say anything, Mebel turns to him and says, "And, yes, it does matter. Maybe not to you, but it matters to me, and I think having it matter to me is enough for it to matter in general."

Sammy's mouth drops open.

"Papa, what is Ama talking about?" Luciana says.

Sammy glances down at his daughter, then back at Mebel. "I really don't think we should talk about this in front of the kids."

Mebel looks into Luciana's wide eyes and trusting face and extends her arm to the little girl. "Come here, darling." Luciana does so, climbing up and sitting in Mebel's lap. "We are talking about marriage, sweetheart. They are all complex and deep, and sometimes people make mistakes, and it's important to talk about them," Mebel says, and directly meets Sammy's eye, "instead of brushing them under the rug and pretending everything is okay. Do you understand?"

Luciana shakes her head. "Not really." She jumps off Mebel's lap and goes to her mom. "Can I have screen time, Mama?"

"Sure." Hannah takes out a tablet from her handbag and hands it to Luciana with obvious relief.

Sammy is shaking his head, looking even more irritated than he'd looked moments ago. "Can you take them to the room?" he says to Hannah.

Hannah glances at Mebel, and Mebel gets a hint of . . . something. She has always regarded Hannah as the ideal daughter-in-law—obedient and respectful. And she still sees those qualities in Hannah now, but at the same time, there is a flicker of something underneath. A sense of curiosity. *It's because of me,* Mebel realizes with a start. *She senses a change in me and she is curious.*

"Okay," Hannah says to Sammy.

"Wait," Mebel says. "Do you want to stay?"

Hannah's eyes widen like a trapped rabbit, and she looks back and forth from Sammy to Mebel, obviously afraid to say something wrong. "Um," she says after a while. "Would you like me to stay?"

"I think you should take the girls up," Sammy says through gritted teeth. "This is not a conversation that is appropriate for them."

"First of all, we're talking about relationships, which is simply a part of life," Mebel says. "And second of all, Lulu isn't even paying attention, and the twins are too young to understand anything. So I don't see the problem. If you want to stay, Hannah, you can stay."

Mebel and Sammy both turn to face Hannah, who looks like she wishes the ground would open up and swallow her. Mebel decides to put the poor girl out of her misery and adds, "Listen to Mami, I want you to stay." There. She has played the mom card, which trumps the husband card, and Hannah visibly relaxes, settling back in her seat and picking up a scone.

With that little derail settled, Mebel turns her attention back to Henk. "So? What is happening with you and Wendy?"

Henk scrunches up his mouth and scratches his chin, a nervous tic Mebel has always hated. "Nothing is happening between us," he says, as though it were the most natural thing in the world, as though Mebel has made the whole thing up in her head and he is now here to wake her up from her self-made nightmare.

"Did she dump you then?"

"Mami," Sammy sighs.

Henk's hyperfocus on his lap tells Mebel enough. She snorts. "Right, so she left you. Why? Did she find someone else? Someone her own age, perhaps?"

"It doesn't matter!" Henk snaps.

"It does to me!" Mebel snaps back. "Because what you are telling me is that if she hadn't left you, you wouldn't be here right now. You'd still be off in your own little happy world without a care for me."

"That's not true," Henk says. "Of course I care about you. I've been worried sick about you."

Mebel frowns. "Why would you be worried about me?"

"Why wouldn't I be?" Henk says. "When Sammy told me you've moved to England to attend culinary school—I mean—what is that all about? I thought you'd lost your mind, Mebel. I didn't even know what to tell our friends. They've been asking about you, and—"

"Our friends?" Mebel laughs. "Why don't you tell them the truth? That you left me for a woman forty years our junior and I decided to come to England to go to culinary school so I could win you back."

For a moment, Henk's eyes widen. Then his expression softens, melting into affection. "And, Mebel, I want you to know how much I appreciate that you did that. I made a mistake. You are the love of my life, the one woman I want to be with forever." He reaches out and takes Mebel's hands into his. "You moved all the way here just to learn how to cook so that I would take you back. That's an incredible sacrifice, Mebel. And I see you. I see how much you have done for me over the years, and I love that."

Mebel gazes down at his hands wrapped around hers. They feel so foreign, and she realizes it's not because she's been away for months now, but because they haven't held hands in the last . . . what, two decades? When they were dating, they held hands all the time, so much so that it became something they did without much thought. Then they had Sammy, and they held *his* hand, or they held his diaper bag, and somehow, they stopped holding each other's hands. And now she feels his hands so acutely that the touch is overwhelming.

And not in a good way, her mind whispers.

She has to resist the urge to pull her hands out of his grasp. The thing is, it's not just the hands. It's Henk's expression of love. No, not of love, but of sympathy. And he melted only when Mebel said she'd come here with the sole purpose of winning him back. Because that's just it, isn't it? Henk loves seeing Mebel as someone whose sole purpose in life is to please him. Everything she has done her whole life has revolved around meeting Henk's needs. She can't remember the last time she had an opinion of her own that wasn't shaped by him. And now, after over two months away from him, Mebel feels like she's finally thinking clearly for the first time in her life.

"Actually," she says, "I would like to stay here and finish my course."

Henk smiles the smile of a doting parent whose child has just said something immensely adorable. "Oh, Mebel. Why? It's not worth your time."

"My time?" Mebel says with a snort. "My time back home is spent going to salons and perusing new clothes and finding new things to gossip about. It's really not that valuable. But I am making it valuable here. I'm learning an actual skill."

Henk's smile becomes a tad less adoring. "Don't be silly. An actual skill? What are you going to do with that skill? Work as a cook? You think you can make a good living doing that? Look at your lifestyle. It's not going to support even a tenth of what you're used to."

Mebel's gaze flicks for a split second to Hannah and Sammy, who are watching them with rapt attention. "You're right," she says finally.

Henk breathes a sigh of relief.

"Working as a chef isn't going to pay me much," Mebel continues, "but I think the settlement from our divorce will tide me over."

Sammy groans out loud. "Mami—"

"Divorce?" Henk cries. "Don't be crazy, Mebel. We're not getting divorced."

"Why not?" Mebel says. "You were the one who asked for one."

"That was different," Henk says vehemently.

"Oh right, that was when you had a girlfriend. Now that she's left you, you want your wife back. Well, I have thought about it, and I'd like to go ahead with the divorce."

"Oh my god, Mami, you're being so crazy," Sammy says. "You've made your point, okay? You need to think about how this is going to affect everyone. It's humiliating for all of us. We get it, you want Papi to beg you to come back. He's done that. Can you just get over yourself and admit that a divorce isn't going to happen?"

Mebel turns to face Sammy, and he must've caught the full force of fury burning bright on her face, because his mouth snaps shut. "No," Mebel says slowly, enunciating every word. "He hasn't actually done that. I haven't heard him beg. And how come when your father was the one demanding a divorce, you were all for it, but now that I'm the one asking for one, you call me crazy? What's the difference? Is it just that he's a man, so he has the right to want a divorce, whereas for a woman to want one, it's unthinkable?"

Sammy's mouth parts as he sucks in a breath, but he doesn't say anything.

Mebel turns to Henk, who looks like he's about to explode. "You thought that you'd come here and I would be swept back into your arms and come home and be a good trophy wife to you. That I would want to save face and sweep everything under the rug, that's what you thought. You thought an apology would be enough to make everything right, but it's not. So what if you said you're sorry? So what if you think you've changed? I do hope you have changed, Henk. I hope you're not the same old person who would think nothing of destroying forty years of marriage without so much as a backward glance. I'm glad for you, if you have changed. But that doesn't mean I am healed. What about the impact that your selfishness had on me? On my self-esteem? My trust? You think 'sorry' will fix all of that?" She snorts. "You know why you fell for Wendy?"

There is a moment of silence, then Henk shakes his head hesitantly.

"You fell for Wendy because, yes, she is young and full of life and so on, but I think you were attracted to her because she was also a woman with her own career. She didn't exist merely to be a decorative piece to some man's life. She had her own purpose in life." Mebel meets Hannah's eye before saying the next sentence. "I never had my own purpose. My parents raised me to be a wife and nothing more. And I don't know if cooking is my purpose, but I do know that it's something I myself own. It's the only thing that's all mine."

Hannah bites her lip, and Mebel wonders what Hannah would've been like if she hadn't been brought up in their culture. If she'd been told by her parents that the purpose of her life isn't solely to find a good husband, but to find a career she loves, what would Hannah have chosen as a job?

"And," Mebel continues, "yes, you will all absolutely lose face when we divorce. It's an unfortunate part of our society. But don't forget that you were the one who wanted one in the first place. And I have learned something about losing face. It hurts, but after a while, it will pass. You'll survive."

"You're being so selfish," Sammy says.

"Shut up!" Mebel snaps, and the rage oozing out of her is white-hot as she turns to glare at her son. "I am your mother, don't you forget that. Just because I have doted on you all these years, you think you can treat me with disrespect?"

Sammy leans back as though trying to increase the space between him and her rage.

"I have spoiled you," Mebel hisses. "You want to talk about selfish? I have raised you to be a Chindo boy, and there is no one in the world as selfish and self-centered as a privileged little boy, and that is what you are. I am telling you right now, son, treat your wife better than how your father has treated me. If you don't, you will regret it one day. Just look at your father if you don't believe me." With that, Mebel gives a small nod to Hannah, another searing glare at Henk, and stands up. "Come give me a kiss goodbye, Luciana darling. I will see you back in Jakarta after my semester ends." As she embraces Luciana, Mebel catches Hannah's eye and says, "You raise these girls right, not the way you and I have been raised, you hear me?" Hannah gives a nod so tiny it is almost imperceptible, but Mebel catches it all the same.

After hugging and kissing her granddaughters, Mebel strides out of the Old Bank Hotel, her head held high. She takes in her surroundings as she walks, breathing in deeply. She wears a confident smile until she rounds the corner, when the reality of what she's just done slams into her like a speeding truck. Mebel staggers into the side of the building and clutches the wall, panting, her mind reeling with dizziness.

A passerby walking her dog stops next to her. "Are you all right?"

It is all Mebel can do to make herself nod. She waves limply at the woman to leave her alone, and fortunately, she gets the message and carries on her way. Mebel stands there for a while, slumped against the wall, her chest heaving. *My god*, she thinks, *what the hell did I just do?*

You asked Henk for a divorce, her mind answers. *Actually, you demanded a divorce from him.*

She could scream with frustration right now, she really could. *Why did I do that? It's this stupid fucking temper of mine. Look at me, sixty-three years old, and I still don't know how to control my emotions.*

For a few moments, her mind is silent. Then it says, *Well . . .*

Well, what? Mebel thinks.

Well, is it actually your temper though? Or is it that a divorce is what you secretly wanted?

That's crazy. She doesn't want a divorce. She wants her old life back.

Mebel imagines a life in Jakarta as a divorcée. It is an awful thought. No friends, zero invitations to social events, and a shitty house that she'd have to downsize into.

Then again, says her traitorous mind, *do you even want to move back to Jakarta? Cowley is perhaps not the best city in the world, but you're doing well here, enrolled in the culinary school. I think what you should do is . . .*

Yes? Mebel asks her mind expectantly. *What should I do?*

Maybe move to New York City and work there as a chef?

Mebel rolls her eyes. "I'm way too old for that," she says out loud in Indonesian.

A father walking with his toddler gives her a weird look and walks faster away from her. Mebel has never been the kind of person who strangers would avoid. She has always been highly regarded because she's always dressed to the height of perfection and has always been so well composed her entire life. But look at her now, scaring away grown men. She snorts at the thought. In a way, it's kind of liberating.

I have no fucking clue what I am going to do with my life, she thinks. And though it is a terrifying thought, it also comes with no small amount of excitement. She senses that feeling again, the one she used to have back at USC, the sensation of being at the doorstep of the universe, looking down and seeing an entire galaxy at her feet, distant planets glimmering invitingly, and all she has to do is keep walking forward. And this time, her life path isn't one that has been prescribed to her by others. It is going to be one that she paves one step at a time, all on her own.

Chapter 18

THE NEXT FEW DAYS, MESSAGES CONSTANTLY POUR IN from Mebel's family. They are all along the lines of:

SAMMY: Mami, you need to come to your senses.

SAMMY: What is our whole family going to say? All the aunties and uncles and cousins? You're not going to live this down. It's going to destroy us.

SAMMY: You know, it'll affect the girls too. When they are old enough to find their matches, people will talk about how their grandparents were divorced. You are damning them out of good society, and for what? Just to be spiteful to Papi?

HENK: I am sorry, okay? I am sorry for everything.

HENK: Mebel, pick up your phone.

HENK: You know you've never worked a day in your life. You're not cut out to work. Who's going to want to hire someone in their sixties?

HENK: I bought this for you.

A picture of a beautiful Birkin Faubourg Tropical was sent.

Admittedly, that last text message does give Mebel pause. She taps on the photo of the Birkin and zooms in, sighing with need at the meticulous embroidery of a lush jungle on the iconic Birkin bag. What a whimsical design, so utterly Mebel, she loves that Henk gets that she is—

No, stop that. Henk doesn't understand any part of you, her mind hisses. *All he did was probably walk into the Hermès store in London and ask what Birkin they have available.*

That's true, Mebel thinks, sighing. She makes herself delete the photo. Out of sight, out of mind. Though the thought of turning down a Birkin really does hurt.

Instead, Mebel devotes all of her time to practicing her duck dish. Now that she has experienced the betrayal of her classmates, she is far more secretive than before, saying nothing about her course during class and throwing dirty looks at Kate and Matt when their backs are turned to her. After school hours, Mebel goes back into the kitchen on her own and spends hours working on her dish.

These solitary evenings spent in the darkness of an empty kitchen soon become Mebel's sanctuary. She grows to love the silence of the space, how every single noise she makes becomes magnified in the still air and how it sometimes feels to her like she is the only person awake in England. Without the distraction of her classmates, Mebel's movements become more smooth and certain, as if she were a dancer onstage. She has dry-aged three pieces of duck meat using three different mixtures, each one with the same ingredients but with the quantity of each ingredient slightly altered, and tonight Mebel cooks the duck legs in separate pans, filling the kitchen with an aroma so savory that her mouth starts watering.

When the legs are cooked, Mebel calls up Gemma.

"Hey, Mebs, how's it going?" Gemma says, smiling at the camera.

"I just finish cooking the duck legs," Mebel says.

"Ooh! Okay, tell me how they taste." Gemma leans forward, her eyes dancing with excitement.

"Okay, this first one is with less clove," Mebel says, cutting into the leg and popping a piece of the meat into her mouth. Her eyes flutter closed on their own accord. *My god*, she thinks. *Amazing.*

Dry-aging meat makes the natural enzymes in it break down connective tissue, which tenderizes the meat. In addition to that, it also intensifies the natural flavor, so instead of tasting like duck, this piece of duck leg tastes like *duck*.

"Oh, so good!" Mebel says when she finally swallows the mouthful of duck.

"Yay!" Gemma cheers. "Okay, try the others."

Mebel does so, and declares the second piece the winner.

"The one with less star aniseed?" Gemma says.

Mebel nods. "You are right, the star aniseed too overpowering. I can actually taste the clover honey in the second one. Is very subtle."

"All right, Mebs! Well done!" Gemma raises her hand and they do a virtual high five.

Mebel continues working on the dish, perfecting every component. The crumbled crunchy duck skin turns out to be a lot harder than she had expected to master. Her first attempt is a major fail. When she bites into it, oil gushes over her tongue, so utterly disgusting that Mebel has to spit it out. The second attempt results in a tough crumble. "Like trying to chew sand," Mebel describes to Gemma, who suggests drying the skin for twelve hours before frying it. The third attempt is better, and the fourth attempt is so delicious that Mebel tears up.

The more days pass and the more hours Mebel spends in the kitchen on her own, the more at peace she becomes. She has never known this joy before, the joy that comes with being satisfied by your own handiwork. She has never had such a long-term project to devote herself to before. No one had expected this of her. Certainly she never expected it of herself.

Each morning, Mebel wakes up with a renewed sense of purpose. When she gets dressed, she finds a spark of happiness as she ties her apron around her waist and places her chef's hat on her head. She no longer bothers doing her hair since she knows there won't be any chance of her saving it after wearing a chef's hat for ten straight hours, and she has stopped wearing most of her makeup, since there is also no saving makeup after rushing around in a hot kitchen for ten straight hours.

Sometimes, she will grab a meal with Bruce, Adam, and Bella, but the meals are short and tight-lipped, and as they get nearer to the day of the banquet, they stop going out altogether. Mebel is sad, but at the same time, she understands that this is a natural occurrence when a group of passionate people are pitted against one another. She hopes that once the competition is over, they will go back to their old camaraderie.

She sees Alain once in a while, and her rising awareness of the nature of their relationship empowers her. When they first started seeing each other, Mebel was swept off her feet by Alain, who is so charming and larger than life itself. But now, she sees that he is human, just like her. Like her, he shows signs of aging; the skin on his arms and his legs is slightly loose, and she knows there are certain positions he can't do in bed due to them being too harsh on his knees. His imperfections do not turn Mebel off; rather, they remind her that at the end of the day, they are all human and flawed, crashing into each other's lives by pure chance and enjoying each other's company when they can. She knows that the relationship with Alain won't go further than what they have, and this, too, is a new experience for her. She has never dated a guy without marriage as a goal, and there is a certain degree of liberation that comes from that knowledge, that she isn't here to convince him to put a ring on it. That there is nothing for her to convince him to do other than pick a good restaurant for dinner. Part of Mebel is certain that she will pass away much later in life as an unmarried woman, and for that, she is grateful.

Three days before the banquet, Mebel finally completes the entire dish. The dry-aged duck meat has been cooked to perfection before being placed on top of a soft Chinese crepe brushed with the most delectable duck sauce. She places a sliver of cucumber and a sliver of scallion on top of the duck meat before sprinkling it with a generous amount of crumbled crunchy duck skin. Then she rolls the crepe up, picks it up with her chopsticks to take a bite, and pauses. She looks at the crepe. There is no doubt in her mind that this is the most delicious thing she has ever made in her life, and her mouth is watering at the sight and smell of it, but she doesn't want to experience this moment alone.

Before Mebel can change her mind, she assembles the remaining ingredients, making ten rolls in total, then packs them all up in a plastic container. She cleans her workstation up, and as she leaves the kitchen, she orders an Uber. Minutes later, Mebel is in a car, the duck crepes sitting safely on her lap.

"Mebs!" Gemma says when she opens the door. "What are you doing here?"

Mebel holds up the container. "Ta-da!"

Gemma's eyes widen. "Is that . . . ?"

"Yes, I finish it. This is final dish." Mebel slides into the house without waiting for Gemma to invite her in.

"How does it taste?" Gemma says, locking the door behind her. "Is it just the most divine thing ever?"

Mebel sits down at the couch. "I don't know. I haven't taste yet."

"Why not?"

Mebel gestures at Gemma to sit down next to her. "Because you create the dish. I want to try it together."

"Oh, Mebs," Gemma says. She sits down on the sofa and tucks her feet under her. "I didn't create the dish. This is all your hard work."

"Nonsense. You give me the recipe. Now, no more talking. I want to eat." Mebel opens the container, and a delicious aroma fills the room. They each pick out one roll.

"Smells amazing," Gemma says. "Cheers." They tap the rolls against each other and then take a bite.

It is, indeed, the most divine thing Mebel has ever tasted. She is probably biased, but she doesn't care. Both she and Gemma close their eyes and moan out loud as they chew through the different textures of the dish. There's the soft crepe, followed by the crunch of the salty crumbled skin and a pop of refreshing flavor from the cucumber and scallion, and finally, there is the star of the dish, the duck meat. It is so tender that it almost falls apart at first touch, but retains a satisfying chew, and the taste of it is so intense, it's like eating meat in its purest form.

"Oh my god," Gemma says. "Mebs, you are going to win this competition, hands down."

"I agree," Mebel says shamelessly. She takes another roll and bites into it. My god, but she has surpassed her every expectation.

"This is worthy of a Michelin restaurant," Gemma says, picking up another roll. "This is so good. Oh man, seriously? They are going to beg you to work at Canard et Vin."

"Yes, they will," Mebel agrees happily, "but I won't go. Because you deserve to go."

Gemma's smile withers, and she puts down her half-eaten roll. "No, Mebs. I don't want to. I'm happy where I am, shooting cooking videos for my channel."

"I don't understand," Mebel says, frustration coloring her voice. "You are such gifted chef. Why you quit the program halfway through? What a waste of money. And no offense, Gemma, but you clearly don't have money to spare." Mebel gestures around her at the tiny house.

"Wow," Gemma says, and now, finally, she looks angry. "No offense? Why is it that people only ever say 'no offense' when they know they're about to say something offensive as hell? That hurts, Mebs. Sometimes, the things you say are really mean."

"Sorry," Mebel says in a soft voice. "I don't mean like that, like not having enough money is shameful or anything. Is not. Let me tell you something. I am wealthy."

Gemma rolls her eyes. "Yeah, we all know that. The wardrobe full of Gucci and Fendi and all that other stuff was kind of a dead giveaway."

"I never work a day in my life. My parents send me to school, I don't really work hard, I just work hard enough to get by, and then I marry rich man for rich family and done. My son, he works for his father. I don't think he knows what is like to work for a living. We are all soft. If one day our money goes away, we won't be able to pick ourselves up and rebuild from the ground."

Gemma purses her lips, her eyes softening as Mebel continues to talk.

"But you are different. You are not brought up like that. I admire you. You work so hard, you put yourself through school, and I don't think is easy to save up enough money to go to culinary school, am I right?" Mebel says, her eyes searching Gemma's.

Gemma gives a small shrug. "I mean, this house was left to me by my grandmother, so it's not like I'm starting from absolutely nothing."

"Yes, and that is very valuable, but what about culinary school? How you pay for it?"

"I worked different jobs and saved up."

"You see?" Mebel says triumphantly. "You do it yourself.

You work hard and you save up. So why you suddenly just throw it away like that? What happen?"

"Nothing happened," Gemma says, and her voice trembles, threatening to break.

Mebel pushes harder. "Something must have happen. You leave so suddenly, you don't even tell me, or anyone else, and when you leave, everybody go crazy. Doesn't make sense, you tell me right now what happen, why—"

"Chef Alain hit on me!" Gemma cries, and it is so loud in the tiny space and so sudden and unexpected that there is total silence for the next few moments.

Then reality crashes back, and Mebel says, "What?"

Gemma bursts into tears. "I'm sorry!" she sobs, covering her face with both hands.

"Aiya, why are you sorry?" Mebel says, moving the container of food off the couch so she can sit next to Gemma. She strokes the young woman's back. "Why are you sorry? There's nothing for you to be sorry about, silly girl."

"Because you're so in love with him?" Gemma wails. "And isn't this exactly what happened between you and your husband? He left you for a much younger woman? Someone my age?"

"Well . . ." Mebel bobs her head sideways. "Got some similarities, yes. But I'm not in love with him. And you are saying that Alain hit on you? Did you have relationship with him?"

"No!" cries Gemma, her head snapping up. "God, of course not. I could never do that to you. And no offense, Mebs, but he is way too old for me."

"Hmm, you know, someone wise once say: Why do people always say 'no offense' before they say something offensive?"

Gemma laughs through her tears. "Sorry."

"But you are right, he is too old for you. He is too old for me, even."

Gemma laughs again. "God, I don't know how you're able to make me laugh right now. I feel like shit."

"Why you feel like shit? I don't think you do anything wrong."

Sighing, Gemma pushes her hair back from her face. "I did do something wrong. The truth is, I was so eager to prove myself in the school that I was seeking out Chef Alain privately to ask for his advice on the lessons. I have all these recipes, you know—"

"Oh yes, in your notebook," Mebel says.

"Yeah. I like creating new recipes, and I'd go to him and ask if he could look them over and give me some input."

"What's wrong with that?"

"I was sucking up, basically."

Mebel shrugs. "So? People do it all the time. Is part of business, you smile and pretend to be nice and all that. So what?"

"Well, I think I went overboard and gave him the wrong impression. One night, he just leaned over and kissed me—" Gemma pauses, wincing at the memory of it. "I kind of pulled away, and he looked so confused. He asked me what's wrong, and I said I wasn't looking for that kind of relationship, and"—tears well up in her eyes once more—"and he got so angry. He said I'd been leading him on for days and I was trying to take advantage of him by seducing him—"

"What?" Mebel yells. She holds up her hand. "No."

"But Mebs—"

"No!" Mebel says again. "You are twenty-year-old student, and he is—I don't know how old he is, sixty-five? He is a boss at the school and he owns multiple restaurants, and at least one of them has three Michelin stars. He is so rich and so powerful until you cannot imagine, and he says you giving him the wrong impression and taking advantage of him?"

"But—"

"You think he get so far in life by being stupid? You think Alain is stupid?"

Gemma gulps. "Um, no?"

"That's right. He is not stupid. Nobody get to where he is without understanding how people relationships work. He told me so many times already that everywhere he goes, people are always sucking up to him. They want him to endorse this, stock that in his restaurant, they want him to hire them, blah blah blah. Everywhere he goes, people do this, and he see right through them. So why you think you are so special that he got tricked by you?"

"Um." Gemma gnaws on her lower lip. "I don't know."

"You know what I think?"

"No, but I have a feeling you're about to tell me," Gemma says.

"I think Alain is full of shit. He try to have the sex with you and you turn him down, so he is so embarrassed—oh no, his manhood is threatened—so he turn around and bully you. He feed you all this bullshit about how you lead him on, et cetera," Mebel rants. "And he make you feel like is your fault."

Gemma doesn't say anything.

Mebel takes a deep breath, trying to clear the chorus of angry voices in her head. "And that is why you quit?"

Gemma shakes her head. "Not quite."

"Oh?"

"Well, after he told me off for taking advantage of him, Chef Alain told me that I'll never find work as a chef in any respectable restaurant in the whole of Europe." At this, Gemma bursts into a fresh wave of tears.

Mebel is incandescent with rage. The anger inside her is boiling so hot that she feels as though she might combust into literal flames. "He blacklist you?" she hisses.

Gemma nods through her tears.

"Oh, that wang ba dan," Mebel says. "I will kill him."

"No," Gemma sobs. "It's okay, I mean, like I said, I'm perfectly fine here. I shouldn't have gone to culinary school. I'm just not cut out for it."

"Rubbish! You are the best student there. You are made for culinary school. All we have to do is deal with Alain, then it will be fine. Your position will be restore."

Gemma sniffs and wipes her eyes with the back of her hand. "Okay, when you say, 'deal with him,' what do you mean? I don't think we should, like, kill him, you know? I don't have it in me to chop up a body."

"There is meat slicer at school," Mebel points out.

They meet each other's eyes, then both of them start cackling. Mebel doubles over with laughter, and there is something so wonderful about this moment, a release that both women desperately needed. She laughs until tears leak from her eyes and she runs out of breath. When they finally stop, the awful tension in the air is gone, and Mebel feels like she can think halfway clearly once more.

"I don't know what to do about Alain yet," Mebel admits. "But I know one thing, and that is we have to clear your name.

Doesn't matter if you decide to be food influencer or work in restaurant, you don't deserve to have your name blacklisted like that."

"He's one of the most powerful chefs in the world," Gemma says. "I'm sure anyone who crosses him would be blacklisted."

Mebel harrumphs. She's had just about enough of powerful men. Powerful men, she is coming to realize, are some of the neediest, most insecure human beings she has ever met. The more power and money they amass, the more fragile their egos become. Maybe she should just hit Alain over the head with a cast-iron skillet and be done with it.

"I take care of it," Mebel says.

"How?"

"You don't worry. You let me take care of it."

Mebel leaves Gemma's house with her mind racing. The whole drive back to Cowley, Mebel goes over all the events of the past two months. Because despite the bravado she showed to Gemma, the truth is, finding out about Alain's evilness has shaken her. How could she have been so bloody stupid? This is Henk all over again, isn't it? Oh, it's different in the way that Alain was so forthcoming about him being married, and his honesty that they are not exclusive ironically lulled her into a false sense of security. She put more faith in him because she thought she could trust that they were simply two consenting adults enjoying each other's company, with no strings attached. She was so confident in that, so smug in the knowledge that they come with an expiration date, that she didn't see this one coming at all. And now, she has failed to keep her friend safe from her predatory lover.

Tears roll down Mebel's cheeks, and she lets them, crying

softly in the back seat of her Uber. Despite everything, she has to admit that she does feel hurt. She does feel betrayed. And above all, she feels utterly foolish. When is she going to fucking learn?

She allows herself to feel sorry for herself for a few more minutes, then she sniffs and wipes her tears away. It is important, she thinks, to let one mourn, even for a bit. And now, on to revenge.

Chapter 19

When Mebel gets back to the school, the first thing she sees is Agatha's sour face. She sighs when she spots it. It is so tiresome to see another woman turn cold toward her just because of—

She gasps inwardly.

Just because she started seeing Alain.

Mebel stands at the reception hall for a second, unmoving, staring at Agatha until the other woman starts looking around uncomfortably. Finally, Agatha says, "Everything okay, Mebel? Is there anything I can help you with?"

Mebel narrows her eyes. "There is, actually."

"Yes?" Agatha looks wary.

"Why you start acting so strange to me?" Mebel demands.

Agatha's mouth drops open, but no words come out.

"When I first arrive here, you are so nice to me, you even

help me bring my luggage in, and my luggage is very heavy. Lots of heritage leather in it."

Once more, Agatha's mouth opens and closes, though no words come out.

"And then all of a sudden, poof, you become very weird. Why?"

Agatha finally says, "I don't know what you're talking about."

"I think you do," Mebel says. "I think it has to do with Chef Alain."

From the way that Agatha's mouth snaps shut into a thin line and the way her cheeks tighten, Mebel knows she's hit the nail right on the head.

"You don't like him," Mebel says.

Agatha's nostrils flare, but she manages to keep herself from saying anything.

"And you are worried about me, but you can't say anything because you don't want to lose your job," Mebel says, "so you have to continue seeing me go out with him when you know what a dog he is." Mebel leans forward, her face inches away from Agatha's. "Yes or no?"

Agatha's mouth presses into an even thinner line, as though she is barely holding herself back from exploding.

"I know Alain is a bad person now," Mebel says. "You don't have to be keeping secret anymore. I want to take him down."

At this, Agatha leans forward until her nose is practically touching Mebel's. "He is the most disgusting snake I have ever come across, and he is a blight to this school. There have been many female students here who suddenly left the week after Alain comes for a visit. He needs to be removed from the culinary world." Having said all this, Agatha retreats, her hand over her mouth and her eyes wide in horror, as though she can't believe what she just blurted out.

Mebel grins. "I agree."

"You do? But you're sleeping with him."

Mebel waves a hand flippantly. "Is just sex, not a big deal." *Hah!* Her mind crows. *Look who's talking.* Mebel ignores it. "The really important issue is, I think Alain is using his power to pressure people to sleep with him, and I think that is not right."

"You're damn right it isn't, but who's got the balls to stand up to him?"

"I think you mean who got vagina to stand up to him," Mebel says. "I have idea, but I need your help."

THE NEXT COUPLE OF DAYS, MEBEL IS BUSY RUNNING AROUND and meeting all sorts of people. People who Agatha is putting her in touch with. Women who are rightfully angry. Her phone doesn't stop dinging with messages, and she is constantly picking up phone calls and getting into heated discussions with the callers. She feels both undone and yet at the same time ready to take on anything. When she has a free moment, she opens up the photos she took of the contract she found in Alain's room and reads through them slowly, her index finger trailing across the screen as she plods through the document one slow word at a time.

At the end of each day, she calls Gemma to unload everything, and the young woman absorbs everything Mebel tells her and shares her thoughts with her. At one point, when Mebel is ten minutes into a rambling tirade, Gemma says, "Mebs, have you ever considered getting assessed for ADHD?"

Mebel pauses in mid-sentence. "What?"

"ADHD. It stands for attention deficit hyperactivity disorder."

Mebel thinks about it for half a second before saying, "No." Then, before Gemma can ask why, she says, "I think you young people coming up with so many disorders, everyone has disorder this, disorder that. I don't see why the need for having a name for everything. And anyway," she adds, "I am not hyperactive."

"I think it might be worthwhile to look into it," Gemma says. "The condition expresses very differently between boys and girls, and I don't think you should take 'hyperactive' quite so literally. I read that in girls, it could be expressed in symptoms like being a chatterbox or tapping your feet or twirling a pen, and all that. It doesn't actually have to be jumping off the walls or anything as dramatic as that."

Mebel scoffs. "No. I don't have that. I am not Gen Z."

"All right. I thought it was worth mentioning anyway."

"We focus now on the banquet."

"There's that ADHD hyperfocus," Gemma jokes.

Mebel sighs, her eyes rolling up to the ceiling. God help her, but she really needs this scheme to work.

THE BANQUET TAKES PLACE IN THE PEMBERTON DINING hall, which is probably the most magical room that Mebel has been in. It is a dining hall of epic proportions, easily seating three hundred people comfortably at long tables. On one side of the room, torches are attached to the stone walls, filling the cavernous space with ambient light. On the other side of the walls are stained glass windows depicting various scenes from the Bible. At the far end of the room is an altar, which is now filled with huge towers of flowers. Mebel is impressed by the place, not because of the fancy parts, which she is more than used to, but because of the ancient history steeped into its very walls. The presence of its history serves to remind Mebel of the precariousness of life itself, and she resolves to make the best of her time here in Oxford.

They are allowed into the kitchen three hours before the banquet begins, although Mebel, of course, has been allowed an extra ninety minutes prep time back in the school kitchen. By the time she arrives at the Pemberton kitchen, she's done as much initial prep work as she can in the allotted extra time, and she thanks her lucky stars that Chef Clarke had been amenable to her request, as she clearly needed every extra minute of it. All of the students assemble in the Pemberton kitchen, apron strings double-knotted and knives sharpened. They are all wide-eyed and so nervous that the tension is palpable in the room.

"All right, listen up, everybody," Chef Clarke says. He is standing next to Alain, who is scanning the room with a somber expression. When his gaze gets to Mebel, he pauses for a second. Mebel squirms. She hasn't seen him since the night Gemma told her the truth, and seeing him now fills Mebel with both disgust and rage. How dare he stand there in his suit with his hair slicked back, looking so confident, so comfortable in his own skin!

"Tonight is the night you will cook like you have never cooked before," Chef Clarke says. The students shuffle in place, their eyes shining bright. "I have reviewed all of your recipes and I know how creative they are. You are going to blow everybody's socks off. This is the day you put your practical skills to the test. I know it is nerve-racking, but you've got this. Before you get to work, I'd like to remind you to please respect other people's spaces and don't forget to have a bit of fun while you're at it. Let's go."

The moment Chef Clarke finishes talking, the students disperse to their various workstations. Because of the nature of the competition, every pair has been assigned a specific workstation to concoct their dishes from start to finish. They have all been instructed to make enough portions to feed fifty people. Though the banquet itself will have over two hundred guests, the rest will be catered by the college's chefs, while only the VIPs will be eating food cooked by the Saint Honoré students.

Mebel goes to her workstation, trying to close her mind off from noticing how everyone else is working in a pair. Next to her are Adam and Bella, who have switched into silent work mode, Bella working a potato down a mandolin while Adam chops up some garlic.

Deep breaths, Mebel tells herself. *You've done this many times over. You can do it again now.*

She removed her duck legs from the dry-aging unit earlier, and now she gets to work cutting the crust off. She inspects the meat and nods, satisfied with its color, texture, and smell. She sets it aside and starts to mix the dough needed for the crepe. Chinese crepe is one of the simplest things to make. Its ingredients consist merely of flour and boiling hot water. Mebel sprinkles in a touch of salt as well as a dash of stock powder that she made days in advance for this very purpose, then she starts mixing it. When the dough forms, she lets it rest before shaping it.

Even though they have all gone through every aspect of their dish meticulously, the act of actually doing it, of making every single component and putting it all together while also making sure there is enough for fifty portions, is a massive change. Mebel has only ever made enough for five portions at a time since she is limited by the amount of ingredients she can get her hands on, and it is the same for the others as well.

As the first and then the second hour pass by, the stress levels mount up. The students go from confident well-prepared machines into flustered, irritable messes. One by one, mistakes are made. Cries of "Shit!" and "Oh crap!" are heard all over the kitchen, followed by a mad scramble to salvage the dish.

By the final thirty minutes of the scheduled prep time, there has been such a huge accumulation of adrenaline in there that walking into the kitchen is like walking into a lion's den. Nobody is happy and everyone is in full stress mode, rushing about and crashing into one another. After about five minutes of this, Mebel is this close to screaming at them all and telling them to calm down, but somehow, through some miracle, she is able to stop herself from doing that. *Good job, me,* she thinks.

She manages to force herself to concentrate on her dish. The duck legs are out of the oven, and she has sliced into one and found it to her satisfaction. The crunchy duck skin is nicely crumbled, and she has managed to keep it from absorbing too much grease during the frying. Her first attempt at the duck sauce results in a broken emulsion, but it isn't the end of the world.

And the whole time, as Mebel is rushing about putting her dish together, she is constantly having to fight distractions that her mind conjures up. Now and again, it spits out a sudden image of Henk, then of Sammy, then of Hannah, and so on. Each time, Mebel gives herself a small shake of the head, as though literally trying to shake the thoughts off, and forces herself to focus on the task at hand. She is also painfully aware of Alain's presence. He's taken a few phone calls outside the kitchen, but the rest of the time, he's stood there lurking, his eagle eyes taking in every workstation. Mebel keeps her eyes glued on her stuff, but her body, so attuned to Alain's presence, is practically vibrating with tension.

"Ten minutes to service," Chef Clarke calls out.

The intensity ratchets up. Mebel's mind is silent. She moves around like an automaton, squirting sauce in a circular pattern on the plates. When every plate is painted with her homemade sauce, she places two crepe rolls in an X, then carefully puts some garnish on top of it. She's chosen to go with a sprig of scallions and red chilies, both of which she has sliced into thin hairlike strands and steeped in ice water to make them curl up.

"Time's up!" Chef Clarke says just as Mebel finishes putting the garnish on the last dish.

The tension in the room breaks, and everyone cheers. People hug one another. Mebel smiles and claps along, feeling slightly lonely, but then Adam and Bella come over and they both embrace her.

"Oh, I am so proud of you kids," Mebel says.

"We've been jerks," Bella says, squeezing Mebel.

"Yes," Mebel agrees, "but is okay. Is very stressful situation."

"Yeah, thank god we made it," Adam says.

"Technically, we haven't yet made it," Bruce says, walking toward them. "The guests still have to taste the dishes."

"Oh, Bruce, stop being such grouch," Mebel says.

Bruce smiles and wraps an arm around Mebel. "You're a pain in the ass, Mebs," he says.

"But you love me."

"I do."

They all serve one dish to Chef Clarke and Alain, then the servers come into the kitchen to pick up their dishes to deliver to the dinner guests. Mebel watches her Peking duck rolls being loaded up onto trays. It's like watching her child go off to college, she thinks. She utters a small prayer that the dish goes over well and that the guests love it as much as she and Gemma do.

"That was delicious," a soft, low voice says from behind Mebel.

She turns to see Alain there, gazing down at her affectionately. The old anger, which has so far been mollified by the hustle and bustle of the day, ignites again. She could imagine herself reaching up and slapping him across the face, a smack so hard that it would leave her own palm smarting. Somehow, Mebel manages to stop herself from doing so. Somehow, she even manages to wrestle her face into a smile. "Thank you."

"The layer of crunchy duck skin crumbles was inspired," Alain says. "The perfect topping for the dish. And the spices you used to age the duck meat, that was a flawless blend. I love how you've poured so much of your own culture into the dish. Well done, Mebel."

Mebel bites her tongue. She is this close to blurting out that the entire idea had come from Gemma and not her. When Alain leans down to give her a kiss on the cheek, she holds her breath to keep from smelling his cologne. She catches sight of the other students looking on with sour expressions, no doubt wondering if her relationship with Alain is going to bias him toward her. If Alain notices the other students' discomfort, he does not seem to care, lingering near Mebel for another minute before sauntering away.

What a prick, Mebel thinks. He doesn't care about how this would affect me. He is too high up, beyond the realm of reproach, and nothing he does here will affect him.

She comforts herself with the knowledge that she is about to show Alain that he is, in fact, fallible. Well, that is, if her plan works. If it doesn't, then . . . well, who knows? Then she will probably be expelled from the culinary school and be blacklisted from every restaurant, just as Gemma was, and she will have no choice but to return to Jakarta with her tail between her legs. Wouldn't that just be so typical Mebel?

For the next hour or so, as the dinner goes on, the students chat among themselves and nibble one another's leftovers. Everyone who manages to get a bite of Mebel's duck with crumbled skin tells her how delicious it is. Mebel goes around tasting the other dishes. She's probably biased, but she thinks Adam and Bella's dish is the best of the bunch, the meat cooked to a tender medium rare and well flavored. She is pleased to see that Kate and Matt's fish dish hasn't quite worked out as planned. The orange peel is overpowering, its fragrance an annoying distraction instead of a good accompaniment to the fish. She also catches Kate looking guiltily at her, which fills Mebel with a smug satisfaction. Still, she doesn't do anything about it. She was young before and filled with ambition. She doesn't fault them for doing what they did. Much.

"All right, folks," Chef Clarke calls out finally. "Let's all go out. The guests have cast their votes and we have a winner."

The Pemberton College banquet is a black-tie affair, and everyone has arrived dressed to the nines. For Mebel, it is an entirely new experience, because for once, instead of wearing a slinky, fancy, crystal-studded dress, she is wearing an understated chef's uniform. She files out of the kitchen alongside the other students, and they line up at the head of the dining hall. Conversations die out, and an expectant silence falls over the room. Every pair of eyes is now on them.

Alain strides out, waving at everyone as he does so, obviously used to the spotlight. "Good evening, ladies and gentlemen," he says. "I trust you have all enjoyed the meal tonight?"

There are enthusiastic applause and cheers.

"Some of you have had the pleasure of eating a seven-course meal prepared especially for you tonight. And here are the student chefs responsible." Alain sweeps his arm wide open, gesturing at Mebel and her cohorts.

More applause, along with a few whistles.

"They have done well, eh?" Alain says. "It's hard to believe that they are first-year students. I have tasted their dishes and found them to be excellent. Now, you have been asked to vote for your favorite dish of the night, and I believe we have a clear winner."

Mebel is barely breathing. Next to her, the other students are equally as tense. None of them even blinks as they watch

Alain remove a piece of folded paper from his suit pocket. In the few seconds it takes for him to unfold the paper and raise the mic to his lips, Mebel sees the last few months zipping by before her. Henk dropping a bombshell on her. Her moving in a huff halfway around the world. Her getting to know everyone here. Her tumbling in bed with Alain. She feels as though she is floating outside of her own body, looking down and watching herself standing there, with hands behind her back.

"Mebel Tanadi for her Peking duck confit dish!"

All at once, noise rushes back in. Mebel blinks. Bella is hugging her and shouting something. Chef Clarke is leaning over and shaking her hand. Alain is walking toward her. Now he is kissing her cheek, his lips moist. She reaches up and wipes the sensation off her cheek. She blinks again, and she thinks: *My god. What now?*

You know what now, her mind replies.

Chapter 20

MEBEL WALKS UP TO THE PODIUM IN A DAZE, BUT WITH every step she takes, she forces herself to take a deep breath. She squeezes her hands into fists, digging her fingernails into her palms to recenter herself in the moment. This is not a time where she can afford to be out of it, she hisses to herself mentally. And by the time she gets there, she feels far more grounded. Her mind is thinking with startling clearness. No more self-doubt or living in the past or worrying about the future. She is all here, every part of her.

Alain picks up a small glass trophy along with a thick piece of paper and hands it to her. Everyone cheers as Mebel receives the trophy and paper from him. It's Mebel's first time winning a trophy for anything, and she allows herself, just for one second, to revel in it. She feels its weight in her hand and takes in its triangular shape, its shiny surface glinting in the light. Then she leans over to the microphone and begins talking.

"Thank you, everyone." Mebel waits a few seconds for everyone to stop applauding, then says, "My name is Mebel Tanadi. I am Chinese-Indonesian and I am sixty-three years old. This is first time I win anything in life." She grins as everyone claps once again, nodding until the noise recedes. "I never know what is like to win a trophy, especially one as important as this. And so I am very sad to say that I cannot accept this."

The room goes quiet. Mebel glances at Alain and sees the confusion written on his face. Before he can say anything, she continues talking. "And I don't think anyone should accept the prize. I know the prize sound so good—wow, a job at Canard et Vin! But what Chef Alain fail to tell us is that the winner who accept the contract must work at Canard et Vin for at least five years, and anything they create while working there is belonging to the restaurant." She pauses to let her words sink in. "I read the contract myself. I don't know about you, but to me this is sounding very bad. And that is not the only reason I cannot accept this prize. You see, is not me who come up with the Peking duck confit dish."

Murmurs rise up among the crowd.

"I come up with the Peking duck idea—well, that's not a new idea, is it? Is just a piece of duck inside a crepe. But the one who come up with the flavors to dry-age the duck with, and also that crumbled crunchy duck skin topping? That one is all my partner, Gemma Stevenson. Gemma, where are you?" Mebel squints into the crowd, trying to make out the familiar face. It's hard because there is a spotlight shining right at her face, which makes the rest of the dining hall look dark, but she spots a figure waving at her. "Okay, I think she is there." She glances over again at Alain. He looks livid. She's not going to have much more time before he cuts her off.

"Gemma was a student at this school, but she recently quit, just like that. All of a sudden. She leave without telling anyone why," Mebel says. "It take me a long time to figure out what happened, but I know something must have happened because is just not like Gemma at all. She is a talented chef. You can tell because, like I say, the duck dish is all her creation. But you know why she quit the school?"

Alain is now next to her, his arm around her shoulders. He leans down over the microphone and says, "All right, thank you Mebel for that speech. Let's give her a round of applause." He straightens up and whispers in Mebel's ear, "Whatever you think you're doing, stop it now."

A smattering of applause rises from the dining hall, but it is weak and soon stops as people stare in open confusion. Alain is strong and he is ushering Mebel off the podium firmly, and she is unable to resist him without struggling. But no matter, because as Alain leads her off the stage, she catches sight of Agatha striding up to take her place. Alain nods at Agatha as they pass her, clearly expecting Agatha to defuse the situation.

"Hello, everyone," Agatha says into the microphone. "My name is Agatha Wells, and I work at Saint Honoré. As the receptionist, I am basically invisible. A human ornament, always seated behind the desk to serve anyone who needs assistance."

"You can forget about continuing your studies at the school," Alain is hissing in Mebel's ear. It's a good thing he's so busy whispering threats to Mebel, because his attention isn't on Agatha, but Mebel is focusing on Agatha's words.

"The thing about being a human ornament is that I see and hear everything," Agatha says. "And over the last few years, I have observed a curious pattern: young attractive female students would enroll at our school, and then after Alain visits the campus, these women would either suddenly drop out or become quiet and withdrawn."

Chef Clarke is rushing toward Mebel and Alain as though prepared to escort Mebel out of the dining hall, but at Agatha's words, he pauses. He looks up at the stage, his eyes wide, and when he turns back to Alain, a quiet coldness has settled over his face. "Is this true?" he says.

Alain waves a flippant hand. "Is what true? Nothing but gossip and hearsay."

"Here I have a statement," Agatha says, holding up her phone, "signed by over a dozen of our students, asserting that Chef Alain Moreau has been sexually harassing them and coercing them into doing inappropriate activities with him, and when they refused, he told them they would be blacklisted by every restaurant in Europe."

Gasps erupt from the dining hall. Chef Clarke's mouth curls up with disgust. "You've been doing what?" he says to Alain. His gaze drops to Alain's hand, which remains wrapped around Mebel's upper arm. "I think you should take your hand off her this very minute."

Mebel is released, and she nods her thanks to Chef Clarke before turning to face Alain. Alain wears a poisonous expression, and Mebel wonders how she could've ever found him attractive. His whole face has turned red, his forehead shiny with perspiration.

"This is an outrage," Alain hisses at Mebel. "Your little trick here is called slander, and I won't stand for it. You will be hearing from my lawyer."

"Maybe you will hear from police," Mebel retorts.

Alain opens his mouth to say something, but Chef Clarke says, "Please remove yourself from the premises, Alain, or I will have the porters remove you."

"This is a joke!" Alain snaps. Then he wheels around and storms out of the dining hall, every pair of eyes following him.

"My word," Chef Clarke murmurs, brushing his hair back. "I can't believe—so it's all true?" he says to Mebel.

She nods. "I talk to these young women myself. Agatha give them all my number, and they call me and tell me what happened. There are many of them, just from the branch here in Cowley. I imagine if you look into the branch in Paris, you will find even more women who go through the same thing."

"Good grief." For a moment, Chef Clarke looks so lost that Mebel feels slightly sorry for him. But this is no time for her to be standing around feeling bad for a man.

"Mebs," someone says.

Mebel turns around and is engulfed in a hug from Gemma.

"I can't believe you pulled that off," Gemma says. She is shaking.

Mebel pulls away so she can look at the young woman. "Not just me," she says. "You do it too. You and the other students who are brave enough to come forward."

Adam, Bruce, and Bella approach them. "Dude, that is some crazy shit," Adam says.

Bella has tears in her eyes as she reaches out and hugs Gemma. "Why didn't you tell me?"

"I'm sorry," Gemma says. "My head was just so messed up and—"

"No, you don't have to apologize," Bella says. "I'm sorry for not realizing something was off."

"No one should be sorry for anything," Mebel scolds. "The only person who should be sorry here is Alain."

"Hear! Hear!" Adam says.

"What a prick," Bruce says.

For a moment, they stand there looking dazed at one another. "What do you think's going to happen now?" Gemma says after a while.

"Well, I don't know how the law here work," Mebel says, "but I imagine Alain might be busy defending himself from lawsuits."

"I wonder if the school will get shut down," Bella says.

Mebel's mouth closes. She hasn't thought of how the school might be liable in this case.

"Yeah, if I were a victim, I would sue the school for a shit ton of money," Bruce says.

Bella rolls her eyes. "Bruce, can you stop being yourself just for once?"

"No, he's got a point," Gemma says. "I think the school should be liable."

That sounds so unlike the usual, mousy girl that Mebel has come to know and love that she stares at Gemma, pleasantly surprised.

"It failed to protect its students," Gemma says simply. "And Alain is a shareholder of the school. I think the business is directly liable for his actions." She sees everyone's startled expression and shrugs. "I mean, it just seems to make sense to me."

"Are you going to sue the school?" Adam says.

"I don't think I'd do it on my own," Gemma says slowly, "but if the others want to band together and do a joint suit, then . . . maybe. I don't know, I'm still kind of trying to process the whole thing."

Mebel pats Gemma on the shoulder. "You take your time. You can figure out slowly what is good for you. You work on your own timeline, not others'."

Funny, Mebel thinks to herself, *how it's easy to give advice to others without realizing how appropriate that same advice would be for yourself.*

Epilogue

The London School of Culinary Arts is much bigger than the Saint Honoré School of Culinary Arts. As an added bonus, it isn't located in Cowley, England, but in Ealing, which is to the west of London.

"I think is lying when it says, 'London,'" Mebel says as she and Gemma walk out of the tube station and make their way to the school. "This is very far away from actual London."

"Close enough," Gemma says cheerily.

"Very far," Mebel grumbles.

"I mean, this entire place is technically still London. What is it that constitutes London to you?"

"Harrods," Mebel says without hesitation.

Gemma grins. "Of course. Well, that's only a few tube rides away, so I think we can just about manage. It's far better than Cowley, at least."

And at this, Mebel has to agree. It's their second week of

class here, and Mebel has gotten used to the new place. The school has a lot more students enrolled, and because it is London, the student body here is a lot more varied, with people from all around the world. Most of them are in their early twenties like Gemma, but there is a handful of older people—people in their mid-thirties who decided they would like a career change. There is even a woman in her fifties who told Mebel that she had enrolled in the school because when her kids went off to university, she found herself at a loss for what to do. It warms Mebel's heart to meet others who, while not quite in a similar situation as hers, at the very least, are going through something adjacent.

It is the third week of January, and though it is one of London's bleakest seasons, even the gloomy English winter is unable to take away from Mebel's deep sense of joy. So many things have happened over the last couple of months, and Mebel feels like a whole new person.

After the Pemberton Ball debacle, Mebel flew back to Jakarta for a while to sort her life out. There, she sought out an attorney from a female-owned law firm and began the divorce proceedings. As expected, Henk chose to fight her all the way, refusing to agree to any of her proposed terms. It was expected, and Mebel did not care either way. She knew it was only a matter of time before Henk found a new Wendy to catch his interest, after which Mebel was sure he would agree to the divorce.

One good thing about Henk is that he is wealthy enough to not care about their joint accounts. There is more than enough money for Mebel to peacefully live off for a couple of years, provided she doesn't buy any more luxury goods. This would've been unthinkable just months ago; the idea of not being able to march into Dior or Gucci and buy everything she likes the look of would've been torture back then. But now, Mebel is done with shopping sprees. Well, she is done(ish) with them.

She even does a sort of spring cleaning with Hannah. They go inside Mebel's vast walk-in closet and sort through her items one by one. Hannah tells Mebel that she will open up an online shop and sell all of Mebel's unwanted items, which will provide Mebel with more income. What Hannah doesn't know is that Mebel plans to give all of the money that comes from selling her luxury bags and shoes to Hannah to start up her own business. It's Mebel's way of apologizing to her daughter-in-law for raising a son like Sammy.

Speaking of Sammy, Mebel only sees him once in Jakarta, when he comes over to drop Luciana off at Mebel's. He is obviously uncomfortable around her, his eyes only meeting hers for a split second before skittering away.

"How is everything going?" Mebel asks him, and he shrugs.

"Hannah's got lots of funny ideas now. Probably inspired by you," he adds, his voice dripping with resentment. "The other day, she said, 'How come children take their father's last names when it's the woman that gives birth to them?'"

Mebel laughs, and Sammy glares at her. "Oh, come off it, Sammy. You know she has a point. It's utter bullshit that children take their father's surnames."

Sammy stalks off, shaking his head and muttering to himself. Mebel is somewhat sad to see her son leave, but she is learning to let go of attachments to things she can't control. The only thing she can do now is hope that Sammy is a big enough man to open up his mind and heart to Hannah and the girls. She thinks he will, one day.

Surprisingly, while Mebel is in Jakarta, she receives quite a few invitations to dinners and lunches. Not as many as before, and no big formal events, but enough to keep her somewhat busy. The invites come from Meimei and Natalia and other women at the country club who, since hearing about her troubles with Henk, have opened up their lives to Mebel. Over several sumptuous meals, they come clean about their own marriage problems, and Mebel hears it all. Infidelity, sickness, toxic marriages. She listens while nodding with empathy, marveling at how they've all gotten so good at pretending that everything is perfect on the outside that they have come to believe that everyone has got it together and the only ones falling apart are themselves. But now she knows that this is far from the truth, that as it turns out, most people are just treading water, trying to get by.

After Christmas, Mebel flies back to England, where she stays at Gemma's tiny Cotswolds home for two weeks before their term starts. There, in Gemma's house, they shoot countless cooking videos, each one more creative than the last. They re-create the now iconic Peking duck confit, and the video goes viral, gaining over two million views in a matter of days. The comments are full of people exclaiming over how delicious the recipe looks and how they were geniuses for coming up with it. A few people who are in the know also pipe up about the controversy surrounding Alain.

"He's gone back to France," Gemma says, when they see the comments mentioning him.

"Good riddance," Mebel says. She has been trying her best to develop a British accent, but it sounds more Australian than anything.

"Wrong move for him," Gemma says, "because more women

than ever are coming forward in France. And not just from the school, but from the restaurants he owns. Like waitresses and receptionists and such."

Mebel wishes she could say that surprises her, but nothing about Alain can possibly surprise her now. She still struggles with some guilt at not figuring things out sooner, and disgust at herself for the relationship she had with him, but she knows that this, too, will pass with time. She's learning not to blame herself for everything, not to shape her purpose and existence around the men in her life. She's learning so much, and with every lesson she takes in, she is coming to the realization that at the age of sixty-three, there is still so much more to life, so many more things to discover, to humble herself with.

And so it is with a smile on her face that Mebel walks up the steps to the London School of Culinary Arts. She pushes the double doors open with enthusiasm, her face bright with eagerness. The world is at Mebel's feet, and she is ready to march right through and experience every wondrous, painful, messy moment of it.

Acknowledgments

WITHOUT VERA, MEBEL WOULD NOT EXIST, AND WITHout my editor, Cindy Hwang, neither would exist. I am so grateful to Cindy for encouraging me to write Vera years ago, and later on, for giving me space to write more stories of women in their sixties. Cindy is a dream of an editor, someone so supportive and so easy to work with that I hesitate to talk about her with my fellow author friends because it would come across as bragging. (And I am totally bragging, because my editor is definitely The Shit.)

The entire team at Berkley has gone above and beyond to bring my books to the hands of readers everywhere, and for that, I cannot thank them enough.

A huge thank-you to my agent, Katelyn Detweiler, for always putting up with my shenanigans and for relentlessly paving new paths for me to take. Most authors do not have the luxury of writing in multiple genres. It is because of Katelyn's brilliance that I am fortunate enough to be allowed to publish in so many genres.

I have this sneaking suspicion that no one reads the acknowledgments, so I'm going to put a test here to see if you do. If you're reading this, please say "Hi" to my sourdough starter, Carrie Breadshaw, on Instagram. Otherwise, *hah*, I knew it; I knew you didn't read the acknowledgments!

Photo by Donny Wu

JESSE SUTANTO is the award-winning, *USA Today* bestselling author of the Aunties and Vera Wong series along with several stand-alone thrillers. She grew up shuttling back and forth between Indonesia, Singapore, and Oxford, and considers all three places her home. She has a master's degree from Oxford University and a bachelor's from the University of California, Berkeley. Jesse currently lives in Jakarta with her husband and two young daughters.